SAVING
MISS
Everly

SAVING MISS *Everly*

A Regency Romance

Inglewood Book Three

SALLY BRITTON

ALSO BY SALLY BRITTON

The Inglewood Series:

Book #1, *Rescuing Lord Inglewood*

Book #2, *Discovering Grace*

Book #3, *Saving Miss Everly*

Book #4, *Engaging Sir Isaac*

The Branches of Love Series:

Prequel Novella, *Martha's Patience*

Book #1, *The Social Tutor*

Book #2, *The Gentleman Physician*

Book #3, *His Bluestocking Bride*

Book #4, *The Earl and His Lady*

Book #5, *Miss Devon's Choice*

Book #6, *Courting the Vicar's Daughter*

Forever After:

The Captain and Miss Winter

Timeless Romance:

An Evening at Almack's, Regency Collection 12

Entangled Inheritances:

His Unexpected Heiress

For my husband, with who I would happily be stranded on an island.

And for my friends, near and far, who encourage me every single day.

JUNE OF 1814, LONDON

The carriage slowed to a stop again, and outside its doors people shouted over the delay in their travels. Hope Everly peered out the glass window, tilting her head in an attempt to see ahead of them. "I think we are nearly there."

"The smell is getting stronger." Her friend, Miss Irene Carlbury, put her handkerchief to her wrinkled nose.

Mrs. Carlbury, Irene's mother, tutted. "Really, my dear, that is London in the summer, and it is hardly ladylike for you to call attention to it with such frequency."

Although Irene did not acknowledge the correction, she immediately changed the subject. "I'm not certain I made the right decision about the blue shawl."

Mother and daughter began discussing the merits and drawbacks of the wardrobe they had meticulously packed, unpacked, and repacked nearly every day for a fortnight. Hope had never seen two women more indecisive about shawls and ribbons in her life. Perhaps not everyone had her gift for making swift decisions when it came to fashion. But then, Hope worried less about what she wore and more about where she intended to go.

Her current destination, the London docks, occupied her entire being. Her heart thrummed with excitement, her head buzzed with anticipation, and every muscle in her body stayed taut as she leaned forward—as though that would somehow make the carriage move with greater speed. All of this not because the dock-yard held mystery or adventure, but because docked there was a ship where she held a berth.

A ship bound for the Caribbean.

"If you young ladies will converse quietly for a moment," Mrs. Carlbury said, "I would be most grateful. I have something of a headache. A few moments rest before we board ship would be most restorative." She closed her eyes and leaned into the corner of the coach, releasing a heavy sigh.

The two friends exchanged amused smiles, lips pressed tightly together. Mrs. Carlbury often begged moments of quiet only to fall into heavy napping. The sort of naps that included soft snores and strange nasal whistles.

Miss Irene Carlbury had invited Hope to accompany her on the Carlburys' voyage to the Caribbean as a companion, granting Hope her dearest wish and much longed-for dream of venturing out into the world.

That was before everything went horribly wrong at home. Hope tried to brush those thoughts away, however.

Irene laid her hand on Hope's arm, drawing Hope's anxious attention back to the conversation. "I hope you do not find your-self seasick as I did on my first voyage. It takes a great deal of the enjoyment out of the crossing."

"I am certain I will be well. I have always had a strong constitution." Hope kept her tone even, though she clutched her hands tightly in her lap. Every moment for the previous fortnight she had forced herself to remember to act staid, placid, and much more calm than she felt.

"One never knows until they are at sea." Irene tilted her head to the side, regarding Hope with wide eyes. "Did you send your sister the letter you wrote last evening? You were most intent upon writing her."

Hope's throat threatened to close, but she had come too far to betray herself. She refused to choke out an answer like a guilty child caught in falsehood. She had come too far to betray herself. Instead, she lowered her eyes to her lap and offered a tentative nod. "I gave it to the butler this morning. I could not go without offering up one last farewell. We have never been apart in this manner before."

"You poor dear." Irene's expression softened, and she covered Hope's hands with one of her own. "To be so close to your sister and have to leave her behind like this must be difficult." Irene leaned in closer, lowering her voice. "Especially given the circumstances."

The carriage slowed once more, but the noise of the docks, of sailors shouting to one another, grew steadily louder. Hope's heart fluttered in a manner that dismissed the guilt attempting to settle within.

"I have a marvelous idea." Irene withdrew her hands again, waving them before her excitedly. "What if we write a whole packet of letters to send to your sister when we arrive at port? We can both send her every thought in our heads and perhaps even include a small gift." Irene sat back against her seat, a wide smile on her pretty face. "Hope loves presents."

Hope gritted her teeth behind her smile for an instant before answering. "She certainly does." Speaking of one's self in such a way never grew easier.

Irene completely misinterpreted Hope's strained expression. "You need not worry so, Grace. I am certain your sister holds no ill will toward you."

Hope, pretending to be Grace due to her twin sister's plan, knew that statement to be true. Precious little of what she'd said since joining the Carlburys in London had been completely

3

honest, given the fact that she spent every moment lying about her identity.

Despite knowing Grace intimately, Hope had not attempted to take on her sister's disposition and character since their days in the nursery. Even back then, they had never switched places for more than a day.

The wheels of the carriage stopped, but when Hope glanced out the window she saw they still had not yet come to their destination. The coachman started shouting for someone to clear the way.

"Oh, I do detest the docks." Irene pressed a handkerchief to her nose, her thin eyebrows drawn sharply together.

Mindful of the sleeping Mrs. Carlbury, Hope whispered as consolingly as she imagined Grace would. "Things will improve as soon as we sail."

She had done nothing by halves. She wore Grace's favorite traveling gown, and kept her dark hair—the color shared with her sister though Grace's always appeared so much thicker—in the almost matronly manner preferred by the quieter twin.

Thankfully, Hope had proven herself a somewhat proficient actress. Irene had not seemed to think anything amiss in any of their conversations.

At first, when Hope had joined the Carlburys in their coach to London, she had entertained the idea of confiding her secret to her friend. However, if Irene let on that anything was out of the ordinary or treated Hope as she normally would, Mr. and Mrs. Carlbury might suspect something. They would be duty bound, of course, to return her home.

For two long and exhausting weeks, Hope had pretended to be Grace. Today, they would board a ship for the West Indies, and with England safely behind them, Hope would make a clean breast of things to her friend. Then perhaps Irene would advise her on how best to give the news to her parents.

The carriage moved forward again, most abruptly, waking Mrs. Carlbury.

"Gracious me," the matron said, putting a hand over her heart. "Have we arrived?"

"Nearly, Mama." Irene swiftly dropped her handkerchief to her side. "Look out the window; you can see the ship."

Hope turned back to the window, her excitement nearly escaping in a soft gasp. Yes, there were the sails Mr. Carlbury had shown the girls the day before. They had accompanied Mr. Carlbury on an errand to speak to the captain, and Hope had barely contained her true delight.

To think, one rash decision had nearly stolen these moments of rapture from Hope. If Grace hadn't suggested switching places, hadn't convinced Hope it could be done, she would be sitting in her room at home while Grace anxiously stared out at the ships. Both sisters avoided misery through this deception. Grace remained at home, where she was happy, and Hope evaded punishment and regret by setting sail.

Irene rarely mentioned it was Grace rather than Hope making the trip across the ocean with the Carlburys. She hardly ever spoke at all of the twin who had been left behind, but perhaps that was because she wished to avoid making "Grace" upset.

Hope only cared that Irene did not realize the Everlys had switched places until they were out to sea. Focusing on that goal, Hope thought of little else. A few hours more and she would count her sister's plan a success.

The previous night, unable to sleep for the exhilaration of setting sail on the morrow, Hope's thoughts had drifted back to Suffolk and her sister. Grace's acting, among the people who knew the Everlys best, must have proved superb. For days Hope had expected her father to arrive in a coach, thunderously angry, to drag her home and deny her the only adventure likely to ever come her way.

Hope's father loved her, but he did not understand her. He did not know what grief he had dealt, or how he had broken her heart, when he forbade her from sailing with Irene and the Carlburys. He had tried to punish Hope, but Grace had saved them both. Mr. Everly, when Hope's mistake in a pony and cart race led to the injury of a neighbor, had decreed that she did not deserve to go on a voyage and see the islands of the Caribbean. Instead, he had determined to send Grace.

Despite being twins, Grace had absolutely no desire to leave the familiarity of home. The details of the adventure which most delighted Hope would have only proven a torment to Grace, while the things Grace most loved about home struck Hope as dull and endlessly repetitive.

The day of departure, dawn came after hours of Hope imagining the adventure before her, yet every moment dreading the discovery of her secret.

"Eight weeks aboard a ship," she whispered to herself, peering outside as the carriage rolled to a full stop at last. "Eight weeks aboard a vessel bound for adventure in the Caribbean."

"We are part of a diplomatic party," Irene insisted at once, startling Hope from her thoughts. "Escorting a member of parliament to St. Kitt's and thereabouts is no place for an adventure. Everyone will be discussing plantations, and Mr. Wilberforce's reforms, and the price of sugar. It will be as completely colorless as politics usually are."

Perhaps Irene lacked an imagination from time to time.

The coach door swung open and interrupted Hope's attempt at a response.

The footman stood aside and Mr. Carlbury appeared, his expression open and cheery. "Ladies, here you are at last. I worried the tide might arrive before the lovely half of our party, making it necessary to leave you behind." He handed his wife out first.

"Oh, do not tease so, Papa." Irene huffed and held her hand out when her father turned to help her down next.

Mr. Carlbury chuckled. "Miss Everly, I would not dream of leaving any of you behind," he reassured her when it was Hope's turn to step down from the coach to the cobbled street. "Here now. What do you think, now that you are to board ship at last?"

Hope drew in a deep breath, the scents that Irene found distasteful invigorating her. "I think I cannot wait for the voyage to begin." Her eyes swept up the planks of the boat, the ramp Mrs. Carlbury walked up with the assistance of a man in uniform, all the way up to the top of the white sails.

Taking her father's arm, Irene covered her nose with her free hand. "Do hurry, Grace. Perhaps below deck we might escape the smell."

Then Albert Carlbury, tall, lank, and with his nose in the air, appeared at Hope's side. He offered her his arm. "Good morning, Miss Everly. Are you prepared to board? Might I assist you?"

Though she would rather attempt the ramp herself than touch the young gentleman's arm, Hope twisted her lips into a pleasant expression. "Thank you, sir. That is most kind." Though Grace disliked him as much as Hope did, she would never show it. Grace always exercised polite behavior.

The moment her feet touched the deck of the ship, Hope released his arm and hurried to Irene's side, where her friend prepared to go below deck.

"Come, let us get you out of the air," Irene said. "And we must do something for your hair."

Hope's hand flew up to her bonnet. "My hair?" She didn't have Grace's ability to keep her thick locks in place with a few pins. Hope's curls were forever limp, her coiffure often frizzed, and it took all manner of concoctions to keep it in place.

"A strong wind would be enough to bring the whole of it tumbling down, and I can testify that such winds are common out at sea." Irene shook her head in disapproval. "I can see it is already loose. A lady must always care for her hair, as my mother says, because it is her crowning glory."

Hope had never precisely understood why that would be so. Hair was hair. Everyone had it atop their heads, and it was most useless in vast quantities. She had begged her mother to allow her to cut it short a few years ago, when even the women of the *haute ton* were attempting to mimic Caesar and Brutus with shorn locks, but her begging and pleading had been firmly denied.

They descended into the dimness below deck, following a ship's boy who had likely been instructed to show them to their quarters.

"I am grateful you will be with me. When we made the crossing years ago, I only had Mama and the captain's wife for companionship, and they insisted I was too young and impressionable to be left alone on deck where any sailor might dare speak to me." Irene threw a skeptical glance over her shoulder, pursing her lips. "Having a friend accompany me will make the whole journey more enjoyable."

Though Hope wanted nothing more than to be on deck, she forced a calm response. "I am glad you do not mind my company." That is what Grace would say. "Thank you for seeking to reassure me as to the safety of the journey, too."

"I enjoy your company, Grace. In fact, though I was pleased that Hope decided to join us initially, I am somewhat relieved that it is you who is with me instead."

They stopped before a door the boy opened for them. "Here you are, misses." He bowed. "Are you needin' anythin' else?"

"That will be all for now, thank you." Irene dismissed the child with a flick of her hand.

How kind of Irene, to try to make the twin she thought was Grace feel like a desired companion. Hope examined their small room, cots stacked upon each other, with interest. "I am grateful to you for being so kind when you expected Hope to join you."

"No, I truly mean it. After thinking on it, I should much rather have you along than your sister." Irene stepped around Hope to pull her trunk from beneath the lower bed, thankfully missing Hope's startled frown. "Hope is a very dear friend, of course, but she is often too wild for my tastes. I love that she is bold and daring, but I cannot really enjoy that sort of behavior in large doses. For parties and picnics, for brief outings, Hope is the very best of company. But to be in close quarters with her for eight weeks, and then keeping up with her upon an island—"

Irene broke off suddenly. "Bother. I cannot find my needle and thread. I've only ever sewn hair up for balls and such, but if we cannot secure your hair it would do as well to wear it all down for the whole of the crossing." Irene hurried to the door. "I will return directly. I know where Mama packed hers." Then she disappeared.

Hope pulled in a trembling breath. Irene did not want Hope. She wanted Grace, and she had admitted it in such a way that made it difficult to imagine telling the truth. What would Hope say without causing embarrassment for both of them?

When Irene returned, Hope had not moved, and her friend took up the conversation as though it had never paused.

"It is good that I will have you with me, Grace. You will not get me into any scrapes, and I will not feel as though I have to watch you at all times to prevent any catastrophic events. Besides, Albert will be with us and I know he thinks Hope is somewhat unsophisticated. But he likes you."

It took a great deal of control for Hope to not shudder at the idea of Albert Carlbury liking anyone. The man was a tall, thin, ridiculous snob. He took great delight in explaining things to people as though everyone but he must be stupid. In fact, his attendance on the voyage had been the one negative aspect that Hope had attempted to overlook in order to remain excited.

"Mr. Albert Carlbury... likes me?" She hoped she did not sound as disgusted as she felt by the idea.

"Oh, yes. In fact, should the two of you get on, I would not be surprised if he proposed to you." Irene giggled and started working upon Hope's hair with a needle and thread, pulling braids and twists and curls together as one might attach lace to a hem.

For the first time since Hope had begun the deception, she considered admitting to the whole of it, so the Carlburys would send her home and she need never think of their eldest son again. Facing her father and staying at Everly Refuge would be preferable to receiving an offer of marriage from that rather pompous man.

But the ocean, a ship, and the unknown beauty of faraway islands had tempted her this far, and they still held an allure for Hope that she did not fully understand herself. Perhaps she could put him off with less-than-perfect manners, or make it most obvious she had no intention of allowing any romantic sort of pursuit.

Someday, Hope would marry, but it would not be to a man who thought it his duty in life to lecture her upon things which she had long since understood. When she married, whether it was in her present twenty-fourth year or when she was a white-haired woman of eighty, the man she chose as husband would be the other half of her soul.

Her sister would call Hope dramatic, but Grace had fallen in love with a man she had known since birth.

Oh, Hope had noticed the way Grace stared at their friend Jacob Barnes. It had frustrated and amused her that Grace would never have the courage to say anything about it to Jacob. Out of respect for them both, Hope never breathed a word of her deductions to either of them. But really, Grace's predicament proved to Hope that her romantic ambitions were best.

Hope wanted to fall deeply and passionately in love with a man who had no comparison. He and she would meet, perhaps in a crowded ballroom or on a ride through the countryside, and they would know with the surety of a thunderbolt they were meant to be together.

In the meantime, she would have her adventure on the sea and shores of the West Indies. Nothing, not Irene's lackluster view of adventure or her brother's presumptuous self, would stand in her way. Hope meant to enjoy every moment of the journey before her.

Even if she had to pretend to be Grace to do so.

❧ 2 ❧

SOMEWHERE IN THE CARIBBEAN SEA

Another wave crashed against the shore, pounding and dragging at the white sand as though determined to claim every single grain for the ocean bed. Alejandro ignored the sound, a constant thrumming that had once nearly driven him mad, too used to it now to pay it any attention. His focus lay elsewhere, on a herd of seals basking on a small outcrop of rocks near the shore.

Alejandro hadn't seen a seal in months. He'd been living off of fish, crabs, and the occasional turtle. The island provided several edible plants, yet he took from them sparingly. His diet had little variety, which made a *seal* a most desired delicacy.

They were beautiful animals, their smooth pelts glossy in the sun and their large eyes somehow reminding him of both a dog and a cow at the same time. Hunting them, eating them, would have filled him with guilt were it not a matter of his survival.

The seals did not stir, unaware of his approach. He was downwind, and the waves masked any sound his bare feet might have made on the sand. He gripped the spear he had fashioned out of a tree limb and a knife, certain of where to strike.

A little over a year ago, he never would have pictured himself in his current predicament. What would his father have thought, seeing his eldest son creep across an island half-naked, bare-footed, bronzed by the sun and with the physique of a malnour-ished laborer? Unshaven, washed only by the saltwater of the ocean when he went into the water to fish, his parents likely would not even recognize him.

Hours later, as he used deadfall from the trees to cook a portion of the meat, Alejandro leaned back against the trunk of a large tree—the tallest on the island—and tried to remember his life before the island. What would he give for a pair of shoes? Or a warm bath? A large portion of his father's wealth, easily.

"I am Alejandro Felipe de Córdoba y Verduzco," he said aloud, as he did every night. "Son of Felipe Abel de Córdoba y Castellano and Marie Josefina de Verduzco Loayza." He repeated his ancestry back four generations on each side, the Spanish names falling from his lips like a prayer. Then he actually prayed, every prayer he could remember, and he made up several of his own.

His mother, a gentle soul, had patiently helped him memorize his family history before he was ten years old. "It is important," she had admonished him in her lilting Castilian, "to remember where you came from. You might be a *criollo*, but your people are from Spain. Your ancestors love you and will guide you in all you do."

If his family, his father, had remained in Spain, Alejandro's life would look very different. As a *criollo*, a Spaniard born in Buenos Aires in the Principality of Río de la Plata, his life had been in constant upheaval. His mother nearly died of a disease no doctor knew the name of, and the same disease took his younger sister. Alejandro, along with his brother and his parents had made their way in the new world with their farm and cattle, hearts broken for her loss.

"Where were my ancestors when the fighting started?" he asked the fire, poking at it with a long stick meant to join the flames.

"When the British came? When the loyalists and the revolution-aries formed militias? Eh? Where were you, *mi familia?*"

He switched from English to Spanish, then from Spanish to French, and always prayed in Latin. The learning of languages had come easily to him and repeating himself in each of them kept his mind sharp.

He had read *Robinson Crusoe* as a boy when he had learned English. The story had fascinated him and he spent hours playing at being marooned upon an island. Living as a castaway had erased all pleasure he'd once had for that book. Whatever fool had written it barely understood what it was like to be alone for months, now a year, frightened that every storm would leave him without food.

The seal meat tasted incredible. It did not taste like fish, or any land mammal he had ever eaten, but it was magnificent. The fat on the animal would hopefully give his body some reserves. A great deal of the meat he intended to dry, and the pelt would be useful in strips. Every piece of the animal he would use in one manner or another.

In his former life, he had not thought himself wasteful. Yet how many times had he left meat on his plate, or seen a table laid with more food on its boards than those gathered could ever hope to eat?

Those parties he had attended, flirting with young women dressed in bright colors and fluttering their fans in his direction, dressed in the finest fashions from Spain, had faded in his memory so he could not even conjure up the face of any *señorita* from his past.

That night, even after his stomach was filled, Alejandro had work to do to preserve the seal's meat. Working by firelight, Alejandro wasn't bothered by the hours of toil. Nor did he fear remaining in the dark. He was the largest predator upon the island. The iguanas and geckos posed no threat to him. The birds were tiny, too, and bedded down at night. The most dangerous things on the island were the spiders, which were easily avoided if one knew where they preferred to hide. The poisonous trees were dangerous too, he supposed, but he had learned as a boy what that particular type of tree looked like.

The silence of the island continually tore at his mind.

Why had he allowed his father to send him away to the former British colonies? He had wasted years there, then boarded the cursed ship to come home at last, to be with his family. Would he ever see their faces again? Ever embrace them?

Alejandro did not sleep. He stayed awake, drying the meat over the fire and then the coals, carefully tending to it. The meat would last a while, if he could keep it dry. He'd learned this skill riding with the *vaqueros* as a boy when they went looking for stray cattle. Perhaps he could have discovered the technique on his own, but he uttered prayers for blessings on the heads of each man who had been there that night to explain the matter to him.

Birds started their song before he had finished his task. The sun rose in the east, and he turned to admire it from his spot on the tree-covered hill. The beauty of a gray sky turning yellow, then blue, had long since stopped giving him any measure of hope. Yet if the sun kept rising, so too would he.

"*Dios mío*, strengthen my faith. Give me hope." The day stretched before him as the horizon, empty and lonely.

3

AUGUST OF 1814, ST. KITT'S ISLAND

"I am not certain this is the best sort of entertainment for young ladies," Irene said for the fifth time. Hope had counted each of her friend's protests and soothed them away as gently as possible.

"It is an excellent educational experience," she countered this time. "Doctor Morgan will be with us, and Mrs. Morgan, too."

Wrinkling her nose, Irene peered up at the rising sun from beneath her wide-brimmed bonnet. "What if we are overexposed? You might not worry overmuch about freckling, Grace Everly, but I will turn red and speckled for certain."

Four months of being called by her sister's name had nearly made Hope forget her own. She had maintained the ruse after arriving on St. Kitts. The week previous, she finally received a letter from her sister letting her know of their father's reaction to their deception. Father's letter to the Carlburys had yet to arrive, but Hope expected it would be on the next boat from England. Then they would know her secret and likely devise some sort of consequence for her if they did not send her directly home.

When Doctor Morgan presented an opportunity for one last adventure, small as it was, Hope leapt upon on.

"You have your bonnet, your parasol, gloves, and a shawl," Hope pointed out to her friend. "And you may stay below deck while we sail to the island and beneath trees once we are there. Only think of your sketchbook and all the lovely plants and birds you might add to it."

After a moment of quiet, Irene's concerned frown disappeared. Placating her into doing the things Hope most wished to do, and seeing the things she had dreamed of all her life, took patience and creativity. Discovering Irene's weakness for sketching exotic creatures and plants had increased tenfold Hope's abilities to persuade the more demure young woman.

They stood on a dock with a small party preparing to board a sloop, which bore the name on its side in Latin, *Angelus Maris*. Hope eyed the tall white sail, nearly bouncing upon her toes in her excitement. When they'd disembarked on Saint Christopher's Island two months before, she had privately wished to never step foot aboard a ship again. Yet after walking about in the limited society of the island, and constantly refraining from acting as her true self, she needed some excitement.

Visiting a nearby island on a scientific expedition sounded like the perfect distraction. Doctor Morgan, as organizer of the event, had invited the entire Carlbury family to accompany him to study the flora and fauna of an uninhabited island.

"I do hope we are back before dinner," Albert muttered from behind Hope, veering her away from her pleasant thoughts. When she turned to see him, he was staring at a pocket watch in his hands. "Devoting the whole of a day to this sounds less appealing by the minute."

Hope forced a smile, though the gratitude she felt was real. "I am glad you agreed to accompany us. I do not think your parents would have allowed us this marvelous expedition had you not volunteered to come, too."

His narrow chest puffed up, and he tucked the watch away as he bowed to her. "As it pleases you, Miss Everly, I will endeavor to enjoy the outing."

Pretending she did not see the significant glance Irene gave her, Hope stepped closer to Mrs. Morgan. "Have you been out to the island with your husband before, Mrs. Morgan?"

"Yes, twice before." Mrs. Morgan tucked a light brown curl back behind her ear. "It is a charming little island. It is a joy to walk on a shore where few others have stepped before. Oh." She stretched her neck to peek around Hope. "It is time to board, I believe."

Hope turned to see the doctor gesturing for those waiting to join him on the boat, crossing the gangplank onto the small vessel. She did not return to Irene, but kept next to the doctor's wife instead. Irene was still standing directly next to her brother, and Hope had no wish to take his arm for assistance in boarding.

The doctor and his wife, Hope, Irene, and Albert, were joined by three sailors and two other gentlemen. The other men were strangers to Hope until that morning, which was surprising given the limited number of people upon the island with whom Mrs. Carlbury permitted them to socialize with.

One of the men was Mr. Phineas Thorne, a gentleman not much older than Hope. He was visiting his uncle's property and had barely spared Hope and Irene a glance. Then there was Mr. James Gibson, who was perhaps the oldest member of the party. He was a colleague of Doctor Morgan's and a professor at Oxford.

Once they were underway, Hope saw Irene make directly for belowdecks. Without Hope beside her, Albert was obliged to go down with her and act as chaperone so she would not find herself alone with any of the gentlemen or sailors. Hope pushed away the guilt by telling herself she would join them beneath the deck after a quarter of an hour.

Standing next to Mrs. Morgan, Hope lifted her face to the morning sun and closed her eyes. A spray of ocean water moistened her face and she laughed, opening her eyes to see the waves slapping against their boat.

"Two hours," a deep voice said from the other side of Mrs. Morgan. The doctor leaned against the rail and grinned at his wife. "Smooth sailing and good weather all the way, they think. We have a wonderful day ahead of us."

Though he was at least a dozen years older than the woman he'd married, the doctor exuded an energy that Hope could not help but admire. His enthusiasm for life and the world around him had been obvious to Hope from the moment she met him at a stuffy dinner party. Everyone else attempted to impress the Parliamentary party with how sophisticated island life could be, while the doctor expounded upon its wonders and oddities.

Hope had asked him dozens of questions at the dinner party, embarrassing Irene somewhat. But Doctor Morgan had answered all of them cheerfully.

When Hope thought enough time had passed, she left the railing with a sigh and went to sit with her friend. If Albert left them alone, she could content herself below deck. Thankfully, Albert had a small case of seasickness and much preferred to be in the fresh air. Irene had brought a deck of cards with her, so they passed the time playing games.

When they came to the island at last, a small dinghy was lowered with the members of their party. One sailor stayed aboard the anchored boat, the other two rowed the group the short distance to the shore.

"After a tour," Doctor Morgan announced once everyone was on dry land, "we will picnic just there, beneath that grove of trees. Then we will return back to St. Kitt's."

Shading her eyes, Hope looked from the island back out to the ocean, the wind whipping at her skirts. The world was vast and beautiful, and even this small part of it made her wish to be daring and bold.

"Are those clouds in the distance?" Irene asked, peering in the same direction Hope stared. She pointed with her lace-gloved hand to a small gray smudge near the horizon. "I do hope it does not rain."

"I am certain it will not." Hope linked arms with her friend, not willing to even entertain the idea of her latest adventure being rained upon. "Come, let us attend to Doctor Morgan. I am entirely fascinated by this island. We must keep an eye out to find the perfect specimen for your drawing."

Hope intended to enjoy every second of the day, even if stodgy Albert followed along behind her wherever she went.

THE STORM CAME UP WITH A SWIFTNESS WHICH BARELY GAVE Alejandro time to cross the island to his shelter. The thunder and lightning raged over the water all night long, and the wind left him in real worry of a hurricane. If the storm's violence swept up his food sources or frightened away the fish, starvation might finish him as it had attempted to only four months before.

The wind at last died down mere hours before sunrise, and the sky cleared in time for dawn's rosy light to fill the sky. Alejandro at last emerged from beneath the rock shelf he used as shelter. He walked through the trees to the western beach, taking in the damaged foliage. Fear had overcome him during the storm, making it hard to even breathe, but seeing the relatively unscathed trees gave him a measure of reassurance.

The birds called to one another, and the frogs chirped too, which finally allowed him to relax. If the wildlife had survived, chances were the fish would stay near as well. The birds had remained, thankfully. The doves were his favorites, and their gentle call to one another through the trees comforted him more than any other sign the island might give of its distress.

"All is well," he murmured to himself as he stepped from beneath the trees to look out over the ocean and the rising sun. It was a brilliant gold beneath the receding line of gray clouds. Though he knew well enough the havoc elements might cause on the mainland, such was nothing compared to how easily a storm or blight might kill him on the island.

The storm had begun midday, and the sun set late at this time of year. All night the rain had fallen, churning up the sea. Sometimes such storms brought him things. Driftwood, new wildlife, a confused pod of dolphins that played in his shallows for days until they recovered from the tossing. It had already grown light, so any gifts from the ocean left the night before would be easily found.

Alejandro tramped through the trees again, heading for the eastern beach. If he started on the east side of the island and followed the sun's morning light around the northern tip, he could well comb the beaches and pull ashore anything drifting in the surf before midday. Being inactive, hiding beneath shelter most of the previous evening, meant he had plenty of energy for the work.

For the next hour, he dragged ashore armfuls of seaweed that might prove edible. A few pieces of driftwood. The only sound accompanying his grunts and occasional snatches of song were the dull roars and slaps of the waves, and the frogs in the trees.

There was not much bounty this time. He reached the northwestern tip of the island with nothing but piles of green and a few pieces of driftwood for the trouble of the storm. The northwestern side of the island consisted of rocks and a black cliff face, which he had no wish to traverse. But most of the island was covered in smooth white sand, which made it easy to spot animals scuttling about that might not appreciate him stepping on them.

He noticed something in the distance. A large swath of white lay on the beach, at the point where the waves broke upon the shore, and appeared to glow in the morning light. He ran to it, his heart tripping with excitement. White cloth. From a ship, no doubt. Even were it riddled with holes or shredded, Alejandro had a dozen uses for it already in his mind. Shelter, clothing, twine, storage—linen sailcloth, even cotton sailcloth, had infinite worth in his new world, whereas in the old he had hardly given it a thought.

The sailcloth's length matched his height at least, and appeared to be attached to a wooden pole. The tide would pull it out if he did not get it far enough up onto the land. Spurred on by all his plans for both the beam and former sail, Alejandro took hold of the end pointing out of the water and toward the trees, both hands beneath the splintered wood, to drag it out. He made it several feet, the sailcloth coming along, when everything halted and he nearly dropped the wood in his abrupt backward stumble.

Something had caught the linen. Perhaps a rock on the shore, or another piece of wood wrapped in the material. Alejandro carefully lowered the beam to the ground and went to investigate, tugging at the linen instead. It was tightly wedged beneath the wood, but after he had fistfuls of the former sail in hand he gave a tremendous pull, freeing one end of it and stumbling back a step.

Alejandro regained his balance, then raised his eyes to see what had become caught in the folds of the mostly intact sailcloth.

He dropped to his knees.

Never, in his whole life, had he seen a creature more beautiful than the being laying in the folds of white. Mermaid, angel, goddess, all in one before him. She was on her side, facing him, eyes closed and hair wildly splayed across her shoulders. The breeze stirred the still-damp locks, and that finally spurred Alejandro into movement.

He crawled to her side, still too unnerved to try to stand. His eyes frantically searched for life before his hands landed against her throat and chest. His hand sought for the pulsing beat within her neck to ensure her blood still ran through her veins, while the other hand on her chest above her breastbone felt for her breath. At first, his own blood pounded too loudly in his ears for him to be aware of whether hers still ran in her veins.

She took in a shallow breath, the vein beneath his fingers throbbing sluggishly.

"You are alive," he whispered in his native Castilian tongue. He brushed her hair back over her shoulder, staring down at her.

Alejandro should not hesitate, should not indulge in the moment of his first sight of another living human in over a year, but his eyes ruled him as he desperately studied her features. The morning light coupled with her fair skin made her appear more like a marble statue than a living, breathing, warm woman of flesh and blood.

"I am sorry," he said, "but I must take some liberties if you are to survive." He worked one arm beneath her legs and the other took her shoulders, then he stood. Supporting her weight did not prove as difficult as he had feared, though he knew he had not had the benefit of healthful meals for some time. Although the sensation of carrying her to safety, further up the shore and nearly to the trees, gratified him somewhat, Alejandro did not have the luxury to be proud of himself.

Once she was safely away from the water he returned for the sailcloth and beam, and dragged it up beside her. If she survived, if she woke, he would have an even greater need of the bounty the storm washed up to the beach. Though he wanted to sit and stare, to discover some way to rouse her, Alejandro had to remain practical.

She needed him to keep his head.

"*Angela*," he said, stroking back her hair again. "I do not know if you can hear me, but I will help you." Before he moved her again, he needed to check her body for wounds or breaks. "Forgive me, but we must dispense with propriety for a time." He spoke as though she might answer, as though she could protest to the way his fingers started their inspection at her shoulders and moved down both her arms. No breaks. Then he started at her feet, smaller than his, bare, and he gently felt along them up to her knees.

Then he checked her ribcage but found her underpinnings still bound around her. He pressed gently upon her stomach, over her clothing, searching for bloat or wounds, and when he exerted that pressure she gasped.

Alejandro's gaze flew to her face, finding her eyes open and staring upward into the trees. Carefully, he removed his hands from her abdomen and sat back on his heels. Whatever she had been through, he doubted her first sight of him would prove as joyful as his had been of her.

4

The mast had fallen. Hope remembered that. It broke with a crash and snap that she felt through her bones. The doctor told everyone to go belowdecks, saying it was too dangerous to abandon the sloop for the smaller boat. Had she managed to take a step to shelter before being swept overboard? People yelled her name, but the waves and the wind made it hard to know who had called to her.

Then she remembered swimming. Kicking at the water, knowing how ineffective each movement was even as she struggled, fighting against her skirts. The last time she had swam, she had been eleven years old at Inglewood Estate. The boys—Silas, Jacob, and Isaac—had dared her to jump into the water with them.

Swimming across the deepest part of the stream was nothing like being tossed about in the waves of the Caribbean Sea.

Somehow, after an eternity of clinging to floating wood and kicking to keep her head above water, her feet had hit something solid. Darkness, wind, rain, all whipped at her as she forced herself to walk until she'd collapsed.

How long ago had she escaped the sea?

Hope sucked in deep breaths, eyes open and staring above into darkness. Bright light revealed shapes above her, blurred and moving. It took some time for her to make sense of her surroundings. Trees hung overhead. Sand below. Her hands closed over the grains, the gritty texture sifting through her fingers. Then she laid her palms flat on the ground and tried to push herself into a sitting position, but she hardly lifted her head before a fierce pounding overtook her.

Groaning, Hope dropped the few inches she had risen back to the ground.

"¿Vosotras en el dolor, ángel?" The voice, deep and with a slight rasp, spoke words she did not recognize. Yet hearing someone, knowing she was not alone, momentarily eased her fears.

"I do not understand," she whispered, her throat raw and aching worse than her head. She blinked again, turning to the side, trying to see the person she sensed beside her as her eyes adjusted to the light. "Where am I?"

"Ah, inglés," the voice said, sounding surprised. "You are secure. Safe. I have come to help." The accent he spoke with, his 's' sharper than hers, the lilt in his vowels, made the familiar words sound more like music to her tired ears than anything resembling conversation. "Tu nombre, señorita? Your name?"

For a moment, she did not remember how to answer. Grace? No. She was tired, so tired, of being her sister. "Miss Everly will do." She put one hand to her temple and used the other to push upward, propping her elbow beneath her to try and gain her bearings, to see the stranger who spoke to her.

A large hand, the roughened skin warm, grasped her forearm and steadied her. "You might not be ready to move yet, Miss Everly."

Opening her eyes again, Hope blinked several times until she made out the white crests of the waves, sunlight turning the sea cerulean and silver. She took in a deep breath and winced, the pounding in her head increasing in tempo. Then she turned, trying to see the man who had pulled her from the water. He was not a member of the crew, as she had heard their accents and they were not Spanish.

The shadows cast by the tree confounded her eyes. She saw only the outline of a man, though not as she was used to it. There was a shine to his skin, revealing he wore nothing on his shoulders. No coat. No waistcoat. No shirt. Like a dock laborer or the slaves she had glimpsed in the fields.

"Did the others make it?" she asked. Why was it a stranger, rather than her friends, by her side?

"How many were with you, *señorita*?" he asked, his hand still supporting her.

She tried to remember. "Two sailors? No. There were three. The doctor and his wife, Miss and Mr. Carlbury, and two other gentlemen."

His answer came almost hesitantly. "I have seen no one else upon the beach this day."

Her heart faltered and her stomach rolled. Hope's eyes filled with tears before she willed them back again. "Perhaps the boat held. Maybe they are looking for me, even now." Her voice wavered but she willed herself to move, to act, rather than sit and worry. Worrying never accomplished anything. "I should like to look for them myself."

"I am not certain you should rise yet, Miss Everly."

Why was everyone always telling her what she could and could not accomplish? Yet when she tried to push herself from the sand, her stomach imitated the waves in a harsh rolling motion. She stilled and lowered herself back to her elbows. "Perhaps you are right, sir." She looked up at him again, blinking rapidly. Her eyes had apparently adjusted while she stared at the sea.

He had moved closer when she attempted to stand, kneeling less than a foot away, and she peered up into his face again. The man had a great deal of hair, long and uncombed, with a beard in an equally unkempt state. Though his appearance ought to frighten her, Hope met his gaze and instantly knew, though she could not say how, that she was safe. His eyes were warm, calm, and curious. They were intelligent and dark, like rich earth.

"What is your name?" she asked quietly.

"You may call me Alejandro." He studied her, but not in a lewd manner.

"Thank you, Alejandro, for helping me." She wriggled her toes and realized her feet were bare. The waves had stripped away her shoes. Or had she kicked them off when she tried to swim?

When she stopped talking, her aching head attempting to make sense of her shoeless state, Alejandro had remained perfectly still next to her. He said nothing, though she knew he must have as many questions as she did. The man seemed to understand the need for quiet. For steadiness.

In possession of herself once more, Hope turned her gaze to the white sand, the empty beach. The sun, hanging bright above them, comforted her. The clouds had gone, at least.

Hope faced the man at her side, a thousand questions about him attempting to rush into her mind at once.

He was taller than she was if his long arms were anything to go by. His hair was long, brushing his shoulders. Had she come upon him in England, she might've thought him a beggar. But she had seen scroungy men during her time aboard a ship, and on the islands, and most had not addressed her with complete deference. As he did.

"Where are we, Alejandro?" His appearance did not give her much confidence that it was someplace civilized. Perhaps they were at the edge of a plantation, or near a fishing village.

"We are in the middle of the West Indies, *señorita*."

"Is there anyone else nearby?" she asked, though she already sensed his answer.

The man slowly shook his head, never breaking eye contact. "The island is empty, except for me and, now, you."

ALEJANDRO WATCHED THE YOUNG WOMAN, READY TO PUT HIS HAND out to steady her should she fall into a faint. Her labored breathing, the way she placed a hand against her temple even as she tried to sit up again, told him more than enough about her physical state. Of course, to touch her again, even if only in brief support, would be something out of his dreams.

A person, a woman, upon his island. His eyes drank her in, wondering if she was as beautiful as he found her or if his lack of human contact had skewed his sense of what was and was not attractive. Her long hair hanging in snarls down her back made her appear more like a water sprite than a being from a civilized world.

If there were others who had survived, perhaps with a boat of some kind—No. He didn't let his thoughts dwell there, easily snuffing out the momentary flicker of hope in his breast. Hope had no place on his island.

Señorita Everly's expression changed from a strained frown to a smile. "I must be grateful that you found me, Alejandro," she murmured. "You saved me from the waves, did you not?"

"It was not an act of great heroism, Miss Everly. You would have woken on your own soon enough." He wanted to return her smile, but he was somewhat out of practice. Instead he settled slowly onto the sand beside her, dragging his gaze away from her lovely features. The woman's eyes were a shade of blue he had only seen before in the sky.

Any moment, she would realize the grimness of the situation. She would collapse. Have hysterics.

"How long have you been here, Alejandro?" she asked. He saw her rubbing her temple from the corner of his eye.

"A very long time. Over a year." The saltwater had roughened her voice, yet he could not recall hearing anything so wonderful as another human's words to him.

She stilled and her arm touched his, her fingertips brushing against his wrist. "I am so sorry. A year. Have you been alone all this time?"

"*Sí.*" He stared at where she touched him, marveling at how soft her fingertips felt against his skin. He wouldn't tell her about the other man. Not yet. It would only frighten her.

Miss Everly withdrew her hand and put it upon the sand again. His gaze followed the movement, noting her ragged nails. She had clung to the mast for a long time through the storm. It was a miracle she had not been dragged from it and drowned. A miracle. Not precisely what he had expected in one so delicate, either.

Why would the heavens curse another soul to the lonely island? His heart ached for her, for what stretched before her. Her family would think her dead. Her friends would forget her. The island would claim her life.

Unaware of his morose thoughts, the woman smiled at him again with a gentleness that smote his heart. "I am sorry, Alejandro. I cannot imagine how difficult that would be for you. Please. Will you help me stand? I should like to look for the others."

A futile exercise. He had been over half the island already, and she could not traverse the other half in her state. If he took her back toward his shelter, and the well for water, that would likely exhaust her. He could check the rest of the island later.

"I will help you, *señorita.*" As much as he could. Alejandro rose first and brushed his hands off on his tattered trousers before reaching for hers. She laid both hands upon his, palms down, and lightning shot through his veins at the contact. The woman sucked in a deep breath, almost as though she had felt it, too.

Alejandro dismissed the wild idea. That was what came from being alone for so long. Nonsensical thoughts and feelings at the first sign of human companionship.

Assisting Miss Everly to her feet, Alejandro offered his arm to her. She took it, more like they were about to stroll through a ballroom than across an empty beach. The breeze blew a disheveled curl into her face, and she brushed it back.

"Come, this way. You need water before anything else," he said.

The woman did not argue. Instead, she leaned against him, the top of her head barely reaching above his shoulder. "And here I thought I had already had more than my share of water." Her eyes sparkled, her pale pink lips turned up at the corners.

How did she do it? How did she make a jest at all, given her situation?

His heart warmed to her a little more. The woman had courage. That, or madness. But when her lovely eyes sought his gaze, peace settled upon his heart. Courage and hope. That was what made her smile.

If only he had the ability to hope again, he might have smiled, too.

"Is there a source of fresh water on the island?" she asked with cheerful interest, and when he glanced at her he saw her pretty eyes grow brighter.

"Not any natural sources that are easy to come by." He pointed down at the beach. "I have dug two wells in my time here, and I have learned where rainwater pools."

"Dug wells?" Her forehead wrinkled. "How did you know where to dig?"

"A sailor told me of an old trick, when I first left my home. Do you see the hill there, above the water?" He pointed again, tracing the line of the hill with his finger. "On the side where the beach is, the land slopes directly into the waves. On that side of the hill, the ground is protected from the saltwater. If you dig a hole deep enough, below sea level, there is fresh water."

Her head tilted to the side and she started to nod. "I suppose it is seawater, too, but the earth it passes through strains the water and keeps back the salt. Like cheesecloth."

Impressed by her quick understanding, Alejandro studied her profile again. "Somewhat like that, yes." He said nothing more until they reached the base of the hill they would climb to the well. She was content to remain silent.

At first, the well had been no more than a five-foot-deep hole in the ground, but he'd soon lined the hole with rocks so it would keep its shape. Then he wove together thin branches to create a cover, to keep animals from falling inside when they came looking for freshwater. Though it was hardly a great feat of engineering, Alejandro still regarded his work with pride.

"You built this?" Miss Everly released his arm to put her hands on the side of the well, where stones came up two feet from the ground. Alejandro removed the rocks holding the cover down, then the cover itself.

"*Sí*. I had to." He picked up the rope he'd tied to a stick laying across the four-foot opening. He lifted the bucket already attached to the rope from his morning ablutions and dropped it inside. "I want to make it easier to lower and raise the bucket, with a handle, but the well is not deep, and there are other things that take my attention."

She bent to look into the hole, nodding as she listened to him. "I am very glad you have a well, Alejandro. I certainly would not have known where to go looking for water."

The comment struck him as painful, though he was sure it was meant to be grateful. His time on the island, lonely and without hope, had forced him to focus on his survival every single day. Forced him to recognize the agonizing truths that he would live out his life without his family, without another soul at all. He'd rather be anywhere in the world with people than stuck on the island. But his misfortune, his work to stay alive, gifted the woman at his side with drinkable water.

She would survive because he had lived on the island for fourteen months, learned its ways, and dug a well.

Emotion clawed at his throat, but Alejandro refused to give in to it. He had dug a well, this woman would drink his water and live, but for what? To end her days as he would?

Perhaps it had not been a miracle that brought her to his side after all.

　　　　🦜　5　🦜

Many gentlemen had taken Hope's hands over the years. They had helped her in and out of carriages, escorted her, clasped hands while dancing, but nothing strange had ever happened to make her take notice of the first moment her hand touched theirs.

Yet when Alejandro clasped her hands with his larger, work-roughened hands, his dark eyes upon her, it was as though thunder cracked overhead. Her heart pounded against her chest, her breath caught, and the world shifted to make room for something she instinctively knew would change her.

Hope knew she ought to be frightened. Terrified, most likely. Doubtful of what she felt. Yet calmness had overcome her almost immediately, a sureness enveloping her in warmth that had nothing to do with the sun overhead. She averted her eyes and made a quip about the water, her thoughts racing along ahead of her.

He explained the water might not agree with her, but only a few small sips were necessary at present.

After drinking the water directly from the bucket, supported by Alejandro as her arms seemed unwilling to hold the heavy thing aloft, Hope's attention turned to the trees. "Is that a path?" She pointed at a track of dirt leading up the hill, disappearing beneath the shade of the branches.

"It leads to my shelter." Alejandro's deep voice had a soothing quality to it. He spoke to her as if she was in need of gentleness, lest she break with a too-harsh word. While the effort must be appreciated, Hope did not precisely wish for it to continue. "I come down that path several times a day."

She peeked at him from the corner of her eye, taking in the way his eyebrows drew together when he frowned. What unpleasant thoughts was he thinking? Perhaps he did not like that she had landed upon his beach for him to worry over.

"We need to search for the rest of my party," she said, and he slowly turned to face her. "If I survived, falling into that horrid sea, they must have made it. They were in a boat. Though it was caught on something. Shoals, I think."

That careful look came into his eyes again. "You are not strong enough to walk the whole island, *señorita.*"

The pounding in her head had not lessened by much, but surely she was capable of walking along a beach. Hope opened her mouth to argue with him.

He spoke before she could. "Rest for a few hours, and then we will go look. Together." There was a sureness to him that made her hesitate. Hope's friends knew her to be stubborn. To rush about when she ought to remain still. Yet this man, when he met her gaze squarely with his own, stilled that desire. "Trust me. Please."

A twist of her heart made her study him more carefully. There was nothing demanding in his words. Instinctively she knew if she insisted, he would accompany her. "Very well." His shoulders relaxed, he held one hand out to her and she took it, bracing herself for another moment like before. Instead, a different sensation settled calmly within her. She did not have a name for it, but it felt familiar, somehow. He gently squeezed her hand and tugged, pulling her toward the shade of the trees.

"Here, *señorita*. Rest." Alejandro gestured to the ground covered in some sort of grass and ivy. He kept hold of her as she lowered herself to sit against the tree, then released her. "Are you hungry?"

"I do not think so." It was still difficult to tell what her stomach would and would not tolerate. The water had felt wonderful on her parched lips and injured throat, but her stomach still twisted and turned. Hope tilted her head back against the trunk of the tree, closing her eyes.

He sat as well, an arm's length away. "You have but to tell me what you need. I will do all I can to help you. I promise." His words held a weight to them that reassured her.

With her eyes still closed, Hope asked, "Where are you from, Alejandro?"

"The Viceroyalty of Ria de la Plata," he answered, the R's rolling from his tongue like a purr. "South America."

"England," she said. "By way of St. Kitt's." Hope peeked at him with one eye, only to find him watching her, a sorrow in his eyes she had not noticed before. He must miss his home. Did he have a family longing for his return? That turned her thoughts to her own family, across an ocean, without any knowledge of the hardship she faced. What would they think, when she told them of this particular adventure?

They spoke, voices as soft as the breeze, for what must have been an hour. He told her of his home, the beginnings of the revolution which turned his father fearful of Alejandro's safety, of his being sent to the United States to learn more of creating a new government. His voice flowed over her, settling what remained of her worries. He was well educated. Cultured. Lonely. When he fell silent after speaking of his younger brother, wondering if the boy had gone to war, Hope told him of Sir Isaac. This naturally lead her to speaking of her home.

"I have a twin sister, then a younger brother, and two more

sisters." Her thoughts drifted to Grace. More than ever, she knew they had done the right thing when switching places. Grace would not have reacted this calmly to going overboard in a storm, washing up on a beach with only a stranger for company. Mostly because Grace would not have the immediate connection to this man Hope had felt.

Her name. She could tell him her name. Hope fell silent, debating the wisdom of such a thing. The others were out there, she knew. Revealing her name to Alejandro, then coming upon a group of people who thought her someone else, might cause more confusion and awkwardness than necessary.

And what would he think of the lie she had told?

"I wish you were not here," he said, murmuring his words as though they were thoughts which had escaped him. He winced and lowered his head. His hands scooped up some of the ivy and began twisting it.

Her stomach fell. "Why?" And how much less would he want her near if he learned she was a liar?

He looked up at her through a curtain of black hair. "Because you will always be here, Miss Everly. Just as I will always be here. I wish it were not so. No one deserves such a fate."

Though pretending to be her sister had often caused her frustration, in that moment Hope acted as kindly as Grace ever had, and quite naturally. She moved closer to Alejandro and placed her fingertips against his cheek. She had never dared touch a man in such a way. "Neither should anyone be alone as you have been."

For a long moment they stared at each other, his eyes studying her, measuring something. His hand slowly covered hers, holding it gently against his cheek. Alejandro closed his eyes. "I thought you were an angel when I first saw you. A miracle."

Heat rose in her cheeks, a stray breeze rustled the leaves above and cooled her skin. "I cannot say that I am either."

His eyes opened again, warmth within them. "You are the most beautiful woman I have ever seen." His eyes lowered and he pulled away just enough that she no longer touched him. *"Perdón.* I do not wish to frighten you."

The words fell from her lips without thought. "I am not afraid." Not of him. Instead of fear, she felt a pull toward him, a rightness about being near him she could not explain. "How can I be? I was washed ashore here for a reason. Perhaps that reason is you."

Their conversation flowed easily, as comfortably as if they sat in a drawing room rather than beneath a tropical tree for which she had no name. It was as though she had always known him. She could not feel any safer with Alejandro than she did with Silas, Isaac, or Jacob. Yet the stirring in her breast had never occurred near any of her lifelong friends.

Hope knew the truth in her very soul. Whatever came next, she was precisely where she ought to be. The sudden understanding in Alejandro's eyes gave her leave to believe he felt it, too. Peace wrapped around her heart, and she took his hand in hers, twining her fingers with his.

Somehow, everything would turn out as it should.

WHAT DID A MAN SAY TO SUCH A PROCLAMATION? THE Englishwoman spoke with such surety, a conviction burning in her eyes, that he could not refute her words. They had stirred his heart as nothing before. Not even the desire to defend his country had moved him in such a manner.

Alejandro kept her hand in his, grateful for the contact.

But they could not sit beneath the tree all day. He needed to get her up the hill, if possible, and fed.

A lizard darted from beneath the ivy near Miss Everly's feet, startling a small yelp from her. The tiny green and brown beast hesitated a moment before darting away into the trees. Miss Everly put her free hand to her head and loosed a nervous laugh.

"Come. You have sat long enough, I think. You need to eat."

Alejandro kept her hand and stood, tugging her up to her feet. She came up easier than the last time, giving him a measure of reassurance. Her strength would return to her. He pointed to the path with his free hand. "Can you make it up the path?"

She pursed her lips and narrowed her eyes at him. "I am not a weakling, sir, though I admit I have had better moments." She exhaled sharply and stared at the hill. "I can make it to the top."

Alejandro started their climb, mindful of her bare feet and the branches in their path. He guided her carefully around stones and roots he normally did not notice, all the while keeping hold of her hand. What would his mother say about such a familiarity taken with a perfect stranger? Without a chaperone? The rules of courtship were strict.

Not that he thought of courting the woman at his side. The impossibility of such a thing nearly made him snort aloud. What a thing to think. They were stranded on an island. Her cheerful outlook would change before long.

The sound of her breathing grew louder as they went higher. Alejandro shortened his steps, giving her more time to catch her breath. The climb up would be difficult for anyone unused to the exercise, but her situation made it more so.

"Tell me," she said between pants, "what is that around your neck?"

Alejandro's free hand reflexively took hold of his mother's ring. "It belonged to my mother. She gave it to me when I left home, so I would have her with me." Did that make him sound foolish, to cling to his mother's memory in such a way?

"She must miss you," Miss Everly said, voice raspy once more. He ought to have carried the bucket of water up with them. It would be an easy thing for him to return for it, once she was settled and eating. The berries he had gathered the day before, and some of the dried seal meat, would have to do for her meal.

He said nothing more about his mother, letting silence hang between them. Birdsong in the trees, the distant roar of the ocean, was all the sound they heard until they entered the clearing.

Alejandro let her sink to the ground again, beneath the trees. When he released her hand at last, stepping away, something twisted in his gut. Then the lovely woman smiled up at him, almost encouragingly. He was supposed to be the one taking care of her, yet the irrational fear that she would disappear when he turned his back kept his eyes trained on her. He took several backward steps before forcing himself to turn around to enter the shelter. Still, he looked over his shoulder before passing through the entry.

Miss Everly remained sitting beneath the trees, arms wrapped around her knees and blue eyes upon him.

He gathered the food quickly and returned, using the lid of one of his baskets as a platter to present his meager offering to her. Two strips of seal meat, several berries, and a few nut-like pods. She took the woven lid from him almost daintily, examined the food, and then ate. She did not ask questions, nor turn up her nose at the strange food.

The woman had a practicality about her he could not help but admire. Could it be possible she would not be a burden, but a help? How often had he longed for a companion, for someone to converse with?

But why did it have to be someone so beautiful it made his heart ache to look at her?

"I will get you more water," he said hastily, then turned away with purpose. His thoughts were inappropriate. His feelings without purpose. Even though Miss Everly expressed no fear of him, no fear of her situation, it was wrong to entertain any thoughts outside of his duty to keep her safe.

Alone as they were, he could do nothing to make her uncomfortable. He had already acted like an oaf, holding her hand, staring at her. Calling her beautiful.

Alejandro muttered to himself about his behavior all the way down the steep hill, rehearing for good measure everything his mother had ever told him about women. She deserved respect, protection, and he had to act with honor on her behalf. It was the duty of every gentleman. No matter the situation.

Even alone on an island in the middle of nowhere, Alejandro had a responsibility toward Miss Everly.

He fetched the water, then made the climb back up the hill. He had nearly convinced himself that he could be more indifferent toward her charms, that he could carry himself with greater formality, when he stepped into the clearing again. The moment his gaze fell upon her, his heart beat with greater force against his chest.

She had finished eating and sat where he had left her, examining the woven basket lid with a most serious expression, her fingertips tracing its edge. She looked up, sensing his return, and a smile lit her face, and the entire clearing, to welcome his return.

Alejandro swallowed back an emotion he would not name and carried the water to her.

❧ 6 ❧

Though Alejandro wanted Miss Everly to remain beneath the trees, recovering from her ordeal, she refused to rest any longer. Somehow, it did not surprise him. There was a liveliness to her he could not help but admire.

They made their way back to the beach shortly after the sun began its descent. She walked with more certainty in her step, and without taking his hand, which disappointed him despite the way he had lectured himself before.

The cool breeze coming from the ocean kept them from growing overly warm, but Alejandro tried to direct their path beneath the trees to protect Miss Everly from the sun. Which was ridiculous. She would eventually be exposed to its rays, living on the island. Would the light freckles already upon her cheeks spread, or would her skin bronze as she spent more time in the sun?

He shouldn't be thinking about it at all.

"It is a beautiful island," she said, pulling him from his thoughts.

"A beautiful prison," he said. "I am grateful I am alive. But I hate that I am here."

She bit her bottom lip and nodded, her eyes sweeping from the beach before them out to the horizon. The woman still held hope that she would find the people she had been with before. Most likely, they had either drowned or left her behind when they could not find her after the storm. They would think her lost, if they survived, and would not come looking for her. As no one had come looking for him.

Measuring his steps to hers, Alejandro did not rush her. Instead, he kept looking for more debris brought up by the storm. There wasn't much. Just seaweed. Shells. Nothing useful.

They passed the place where he had pulled her out of the waves. The mast and sail waited for him beneath the trees, likely with small creatures attempting to turn the cloth into new homes. Maybe there would be a few crabs for their supper.

They came to where the beach jutted out—the tail of the albatross-shaped island. They rounded the narrow neck of sand between the sea and the trees. Alejandro looked out to sea, a leaping dolphin catching his eye.

"There they are," Hope said, her voice a joyful shout. "Alejandro! They're all right." She briefly turned, grabbing his arm and grinning up into his face.

He stared at her cheerful expression, uncomprehending a moment, then Alejandro tore his gaze from her to look over her wild head of curls, only to see a group of people standing near the same rock where he had found the seals two days before.

For his eyes, unused to people for more than a year, they appeared to swarm up the beach toward the sound of Señorita Everly's voice. His muscles nearly froze, his heart rising into his throat, and he had the sudden wish to disappear. There were too many of them, all at once—and yet, he had never thought to see another man or woman again. He needed them. Needed to be near, to touch hands, to speak and be heard, before he woke and discovered the whole of it to be a dream.

"Grace," a woman shouted.

"Miss Everly," came the relieved calls of several other voices, those of men.

Why had he not known her Christian name was Grace? Why had he not asked?

Gathering up her skirts to avoid stumbling, the señorita at his side ran forward, all signs of her weakness gone. He loped along behind her, trying to count the people. How many had she said accompanied her? Nine?

A woman, near in size to his discovered angel, ran before the rest and threw herself into Señorita Everly's arms, sobbing.

"Irene," Miss Everly murmured, holding her friend tightly. "Irene, it's all right. I am unharmed. We are safe."

A man arrived next, his eyes on Alejandro rather than the scene of the women greeting one another. "Who is this?" he asked, his tone sharp and suspicious.

It took Alejandro a moment to recall why someone would look at him with such distrust. A woman alone might be wary of him, of course, but another man? He debated a moment if he should announce himself as a land-owner's son, but Miss Everly spoke before he decided on his course.

"This is Alejandro. He saved me from the sea." She kept both arms around her friend, who still shuddered with sobs. "He pulled me ashore this morning. Alejandro, this is Mr. Albert Carlbury, a friend. This is his sister, Miss Irene Carlbury."

Miss Everly gave Carlbury a beauteous smile, and Alejandro's insides tightened. The jealousy overtaking his heart surprised him. He had not thought to find anyone. He ought to rejoice with her. Yet the magic between them, the strange feelings stirred by her arrival, must cease amid her friends.

Alejandro tried to ignore a pain he had no right to, focusing instead on what he must always think of first: survival. "Have you a boat?" he asked, taking a step closer to Carlbury. "Did you make it ashore in a boat?" That his heart still dared to dream of escaping the awful place surprised him, though his practical mind immediately mocked him. He would never leave the island. He had accepted that.

One of the other men answered, his accent thick with the mixed tongues of the Caribbean. "It smashed against the rocks, the hull is destroyed. We barely made it ashore."

No boat. More mouths to feed. Alejandro looked up at the sun, descending from the highest point in the sky and ushering night upon them. He touched the chain about his neck, finding his mother's ring.

Another man approached, older, limping. "Who is this?"

Before anyone else introduced him, Alejandro executed a formal bow. "Alejandro Felipe de Córdoba y Verduzco, at your service, Señor."

"A pleasure, sir. Though I wish we met under different circumstances. I am Doctor James Morgan, lately of Saint Kitt's." He turned to the young women, their arms still wrapped about each other. "Mr. Carlbury, would you escort these girls back to my wife? I believe she has need of their assistance."

Carlbury's stance changed from superior to reluctant, his shoulders dropping. The expression on his face one of unwillingness. "As you wish, Doctor."

The doctor watched the man and both women retreat, Miss Everly still comforting the other, and once they were far enough away not to be overheard, he turned back to Alejandro. "Señor Córdoba, I am somewhat familiar with the islands in this part of the Caribbean, but we were blown far off course during the storm, and I am disoriented more than I should like. We are not on a colonized piece of land, are we?"

Appreciating the man's ability to come to the point, Alejandro answered without softening his response as he had for Miss Everly. "There is no one here but me, and I have been stuck here for fourteen months. In that time I have seen no ships. You are trapped here, Doctor."

"Castaways." The doctor folded his arms and tilted his head

back, as though looking to the heavens for guidance. "Let us hope people come looking for us."

Alejandro did not scoff at the doctor's words, but he did not let them touch his heart, either. "Have you any wounded among you?" he asked, glancing where the small crowd of people had come together on the beach, near the trees.

"My wife, and one of the other men. Otherwise, we are well. I wonder, *Señor*, if you might have any shelter you could offer? Though the day appears clear, I cannot like my injured wife exposed to the elements. If not, then perhaps you have a water source on the island?"

"I have a safe place to stay. It is not far. It will not hold everyone comfortably, but your women will be as comfortable as we can make them. Water will be a different matter." Alejandro scratched above his right ear, measuring time by the moon and the lapping waves. "There are several hours yet until dawn. Gather your people, Doctor. I will give them a place to rest."

The doctor bowed his thanks, then he and the sailor rejoined their group. Alejandro stayed where he was, his bare feet planted firmly in the sand. His whole way of life, every routine, every rule he had made for himself, would be dismantled by these people. If he did not make them understand, if he could not persuade them to follow his rules, their ignorance might cause the death of them all. But he was one man, and they were many. The sooner they saw him as an ally, the better.

Carlbury was the first to approach Alejandro again, though the others came along behind, the doctor and another man supporting a woman, the weeping girl still clinging to the lovely Miss Everly, and the rest following behind.

The tall Englishman did not stop at a respectable distance, but came to stand directly in front of Alejandro. Staring down his nose, the man spoke in a low, aggressive manner. "If you try to do harm to any of these people, I swear you will regret it."

"Do harm to them?" Alejandro asked, not bothering to hide his

45

displeasure. "It is very well all of you who will get me killed." Then he walked away, smirking despite the dark truth in his words.

Whoever Carlbury might be in England, or even on the settled islands, the man was no one here. He knew nothing. Contributed nothing. The frailty of mortality on an island might well humble the Englishman as it had Alejandro. Until then, he had no reason to show any more respect than he felt. Which was none.

Yet a very real worry took hold of his thoughts. It was up to him to keep all these people alive. Not just Miss Everly, whose hand he dared not hold again, but all of them.

ope tried not to trip over the dips and rises in the ground when they left the beach to climb the hill, but it grew increasingly difficult as Irene had started crying again and gave almost no attention to where she stepped. They nearly fell twice, and Irene's reaction each time had involved increasingly louder sobs. Mrs. Morgan, injured and on her husband's arm, hadn't even made a sound of distress or pain.

Though Hope recognized the seriousness of their situation, she did not understand how Irene could be so overcome. Disasters could hardly be mended by losing control of one's emotions. Mrs. Morgan's reaction reassured her in her own. Yet her impatience with Irene grew with every step.

The third time Irene caused them to stumble, Hope stopped walking completely and pulled away from her friend's clinging grip.

"That is quite enough, Irene," she said firmly, her voice loud enough that it carried ahead of her and everyone stopped walking. The gentlemen behind stopped as well. "You are going to do yourself harm if you carry on like this, and you have nearly caused us both a fall."

Irene's sobs cut off, but before Hope could feel any satisfaction in the other woman's silence her friend started bawling like a calf. "I'm going to die. We are all going to die. We're lost. I want Mama, and Papa."

One would think, given Irene's previous experience living in the Caribbean, she would be made of stronger metal.

"Stuff and nonsense." Hope pointed up the hill, in the direction the whole group had been walking until she'd stopped them. "That is where we are traveling. Up. We will not discuss our fears at present. We are all tired, we are all afraid, but it is only you who are carrying on like a child. You must be brave and walk up this hill with me, without causing us to stumble. There is shelter and rest ahead."

The shaking of brush alerted her to the arrival of someone from the front of the line, and Hope turned to address Mr. Carlbury in some relief. He had come to take his sister in hand at last, it would seem.

But it was Alejandro. Señor Córdoba. She had to think of him more formally now, with others present.

"Señoritas," he greeted them. Irene whimpered and drew herself behind Hope. "Is there a problem?"

"I am afraid my friend is overtired and distraught." Hope rubbed her hands up and down her arms. "But we are nearly there, aren't we?" She gave Alejandro an encouraging smile, silently asking for him to treat Irene gently.

"*Sí.* Almost there." He glanced behind her. "Perhaps Miss Carlbury would prefer to be carried?"

Irene crowded against Hope's back.

"That will not be necessary, though I thank you for the suggestion." Hope cleared her throat. "We may carry on, if you wish."

Alejandro hesitated a moment, his eyes seeming to say to her,

"*We have our hands full with this lot.*" Then left without another word, tromping back to the front of their line.

Irene kept sniffling, but she started walking when Hope did. "I cannot believe you would say such things to me," she mumbled through her tears.

Somewhat surprised, Hope did not immediately respond. While it had been relatively easy to assume her sister's identity before, she had forgotten herself in the frustration of the moment. Being herself with Alejandro for the time they had alone had also blurred the lines between who she was and who she must pretend to be.

When the doctor had told their group they were on an uninhabited island, save for the gentleman who had rescued Hope, her ruse had fallen from its position as the most important thing upon her mind.

What would Grace say to Irene? Although Hope knew her twin lacked an adventurous spirit, Grace had always kept her composure and knew how to be exceedingly practical. Hope could do that.

"I am sorry for speaking harshly," she said, keeping her voice low in an attempt to soothe her friend's pride. "My own worries quite overcame me. However, I do believe we must be sensible in this ordeal. I do not want you to sprain your ankle or any such thing because you are too distraught to walk carefully. We must take care of Mrs. Morgan, after all."

Irene said nothing in return, but her sniffling stopped.

Where was Mr. Carlbury? Still at the front of the line? How rude of him, and inconsiderate, to leave his sister alone. Doubtless he could better calm Irene than Hope. Wouldn't it be a brother's duty to at least assist his sister in walking up the hill?

They emerged from the trees into the grassy clearing, and when Hope turned to look back the way they had come she gasped aloud. She had not paid attention to the view before, too caught up in her thoughts of Alejandro and determination to find the group.

Now she marveled at what lay before her. It appeared as though they were at the top of the island, with nothing but trees, a thin line of white sand, and the ocean stretching on behind them.

The group kept moving, the grass beneath her feet softer than the uneven ground of the hill. There were rocks ahead, thrusting out of the ground as though they had been pushed outward from the earth, three times the height of a man. That was Alejandro's shelter, where he had kept the food he gave her.

Alejandro's accented explanation drifted back to her. "There is a fire inside the shelter, and another banked for the rest of us outside."

Irene picked up her pace, and Hope smiled despite herself. The hours of the storm had been fraught with terror, every moment seeming to be their last. But here they were on solid land; they were not alone and uncertain, either. Alejandro had come before and could care for them in a manner they could not care for themselves.

Alejandro went inside the shelter first, and the doctor held his hand up to stop anyone from entering after. In a few moments, a light appeared inside the combination of cave and hut, flickering orange and yellow.

Alejandro came out again with a bundle of things beneath his arm. He went and spoke in low tones to the doctor and Mrs. Morgan. The sailor assisting the doctor stepped aside.

"Miss Everly," Doctor Morgan called, and she hurried forward to him. "Please, will you be so kind as to go ahead of us and help Mrs. Morgan."

"Yes, of course." Hope went into the hut, her eyes adjusting in moments to the dancing shadows and light. The fire had been built at the back of the shelter, against the rocks, where there was a natural gap between two giant stones to allow the smoke an escape. There wasn't a great deal of room, but she found a pile of fronds and leaves against the right wall of braided branches.

As a child, she'd set up house many times beneath the trees of

Inglewood's estate. She'd used pine needles and old leaves to create a bed, laying out her cloak in fall and winter as a bedspread. This was far different, of course. She recognized none of the leaves of this resting place, and she had not come to play at sleeping under the familiar branches of silver beechwood trees.

Hope kneeled by the bedding and fluffed the leaves as one might a down pillow, then smoothed it over, searching for any uncomfortable twig or curious insect that might disturb Mrs. Morgan's rest. Then she backed away as the doctor came in, allowing him to help his wife. As she had not been with the group when they came ashore, Hope had yet to learn what injury Mrs. Morgan had sustained from the accident. As she began to withdraw, thinking it best to give them privacy, Doctor Morgan called her back.

"Miss Everly, I am in need of some assistance. Please, invite Miss Carlbury inside as well."

With a quick nod, Hope ventured to put her head outside the shelter's door. "Irene? Come inside. The doctor needs us." She did not wait to see her friend's reaction to the summons, but came back to the doctor's side and kneeled upon the ground. The doctor had bent low when he walked inside, supporting his wife, but Hope had no trouble standing at her full height once she had entered. Irene had to stoop slightly to avoid the top of her head brushing the ceiling of the structure.

"What can I do for you, Doctor?" Hope asked.

The doctor had removed his wife's shoes and set them aside. "Mrs. Morgan requires assistance taking off her wet clothing. Her injury must be tended to as well. Señor Córdoba went to get water."

He unknotted his wife's shawl, which had been tied tightly around her waist. Irene moved around behind the older woman and started untying the laces of her gown, then moved on to the stays beneath.

"You expect us to do what, exactly?" Irene asked, her voice high-pitched, nearly shrill. "Assist in tending to her wounds?"

Doctor Morgan stilled a moment, and Hope saw over his wife's shoulder that his brow wrinkled.

"I will help the doctor," Hope said before he spoke. "You watch for Alejan—Señor Córdoba. He need not come inside with the water." The doctor met Hope's eyes and acknowledged her assistance with a grateful nod.

"I am sorry, Richard," Mrs. Morgan whispered to the doctor.

"It is hardly your fault, my love." The doctor's voice changed when he spoke to his wife, growing gentler. "If it weren't for me, we would not have been caught in the storm."

He helped her out of one sleeve while Hope assisted with the other. "No one could have predicted that we would find ourselves on the edge of a hurricane," Mrs. Morgan said.

Hope pretended not to hear their conversation, or the intimate tones they used for one another, instead helping her new friend strip down to the waist. As she had no familiarity with nakedness outside her own, and her younger siblings' from the years she had assisted them with bathing and dressing, she flushed with embarrassment to be near another woman so exposed.

Yet it could not be helped. They were in the middle of an ocean, with no one to assist the doctor, no medical tools at his side, and less than ideal lighting for an examination.

The doctor examined his wife's midsection. "Miss Everly, is there any discoloring or abrasions upon Mrs. Morgan's back?"

Hope moved her eyes to the pale skin, not able to make out much. "It is difficult to tell, sir, but—" She peered closely. "Perhaps here, on the left side."

The doctor touched his wife's left ribs and Mrs. Morgan cried out, but stopped the sound with a gasp. The doctor folded the shawl and wrapped it around her waist, tightly, eliciting another yelp from her. "Your ribs might be broken. Let us hope not. I cannot make a full examination in this poor light. You must lay down, darling, on your good side."

"You must lay on my lap," Hope said, shifting her position.

"Thank you, Miss Everly." The doctor eased his wife back, while Mrs. Morgan breathed shallowly, her chest hardly moving. "That is good, darling. Don't breathe too deeply, as your lungs will shift the ribs."

With Mrs. Morgan's head upon her lap, Hope could do little else to help. The doctor maneuvered his wife's clothing to cover her, then took off his coat and laid it atop her. His coat was not as damp as his wife's dress.

"I will withdraw after I've put these near the fire." He took his wife's outer dress and laid it out on the stone near the small blaze, which had dimmed somewhat. "Tend the fire, rest as much as you are able." He gave Hope a look, curiosity shining in his eyes as though he had a question he wished to ask. Apparently, he changed his mind and left the next instant.

The three women said nothing. Irene leaned against the rock and cried softly until she slept. Mrs. Morgan drifted off as well, exhausted by her injury and ordeal.

Hope wondered what Grace would have done in the unique situation but could think of nothing with surety.

———

THE SUN CREPT OUT OF THE SEA WITH ALEJANDRO THE ONLY PERSON on the island watching for it. He had climbed atop the stones making up his shelter, determined to keep an eye on the horizon as well as on his guests. Outside of the hut, the men slept around the fire he'd brought to life with the banked coals from inside, where the women slept. After he brought up fresh water in his bucket, allowing everyone a drink while he learned their names, he'd withdrawn. For a short time, the men below him had discussed what might be done about their situation. But, as Alejandro suspected, they fell asleep without deciding upon much. The women had been awake longer, judging by the sniffles and low murmur of voices he heard drifting up with the smoke. They slept through the late afternoon, into the night.

He did not see Miss Everly again that night. Somehow, he already missed her.

With his eyes first on the stars, and then the sky turning from black, to gray, to yellow and blue, Alejandro formed a plan on his own. After more than a year on the island, he understood the necessary things for survival, the subjects he must discuss with them, the lessons he must teach the English and their three sailors.

He worried least about the seamen. They were obviously familiar with the islands, given their accents and coloring. Even if they had never lived alone on an island before, they would recognize the dangers and respect the delicate balance of living close to nature. But the Englishmen posed a potential difficulty.

Rising with the sun, Alejandro pulled his worn, tattered shirt over his head. He couldn't remember exactly when he'd given up wearing it, but given the mixed company he now kept, it would be wise to attempt to appear more civilized.

Alejandro climbed down from his perch and went in search of his bucket. Everyone would doubtless wish for fresh water when they rose again. He would need to boil it. Though his body had long since accepted the water of the island, the newcomers weren't prepared for it.

Alejandro took the empty bucket, which someone had thoughtfully put beside the fire, and started down the hill toward the beach and his well.

He hadn't gone far, however, when he noticed someone ahead of him on his well-worn path to the beach. Miss Everly. He checked to make certain he'd tucked in his shirt correctly, though there was nothing he could do about the long tear in one of his sleeves.

How strange, to actually concern himself over dress when she had been with him all the day before when he was half-naked.

Holding her dress up with one hand, her bare feet picking the smoothest portions of ground to step upon, her concentration on the path was such that she did not hear him approaching behind her.

"*Buenos días*, Miss Everly," he said at no more than five paces behind her.

She jumped and twirled around, releasing her skirt in the process. "Alejandro." Her face flushed, and she clasped her hands before her. "Good morning." She smiled up at him, almost expectantly, as though they were the oldest of friends.

He could not let that continue.

"You should not wander from the others." He took in the tangle of her hair, hanging loosely over her shoulders, the dirt and sand clinging to the fabric of her dress. How did she appear so beautiful to him still? "It is not safe."

"I know." She shifted, lowering her blue-eyed gaze to the ground between them. "But no one was awake, and I had—I had to step into the trees a moment." He caught her blush darkening before she turned away, gesturing in the direction of the beach. "And then I thought I might go down to the water and wash. I feel dreadfully dirty."

Alejandro looked from the smudges on her gown up to the streak of soot on her face. "Did you tend the fire last night, *Señorita?*"

"Yes. I couldn't sleep." The dark circles beneath her eyes, the tense worry in her expression, made it all too easy for him to recall his first hours on the island. "Mrs. Morgan hardly slept either until a short time ago. Irene, my friend, cried through most of her dreams."

He ought to send her back up the hill and tell her to wash later, with her friend. But she had already passed a long night of worry, and if the others slept on she likely could do no more than sit in silence with her thoughts. "Very well. Come. But remain close to me."

"Oh, thank you." The relief in those two words gentled his thoughts toward her still more. She fell in step with him, her feet on the well-trodden dirt and grass, while he walked just off to one side. "Why are you up so early? Looking after all of us must have exhausted you."

It struck him as strange that it was so easy to speak with her. The evening before, he had struggled with the conversation. Hadn't wanted to speak to the others. It had been so long since he'd talked to anyone besides himself and God. Before his unfortunate fate brought him to the island, he'd spent any number of hours charming beautiful women. The American women in particular had found his accent charming.

"Everyone will be thirsty again. Your ordeal took a great deal of strength, as you know, and the only way to get it back is to eat and drink."

"Yes, of course." Miss Everly pushed her hair over her shoulder and lifted her face to the cool morning breeze. "I am grateful you helped me yesterday. As I said, there is a reason we met." They had come to the well.

"You should go wash," he told her, his tone gruffer than he meant for it to sound. "I will wait here in case you have need of help." Then he turned away from her, pulling the full bucket up again.

The woman took a step back, and he caught her confusion from the corner of his eye. "Of course. Thank you." She walked away, her feet barely making a sound in the sandy dirt as she went over the hill toward the beach.

Alejandro thought through his plan again, or tried to. The strict list of rules he had prepared for the new castaways marched through his mind, but the blue eyes of the woman he'd found on the beach continued to encroach upon his thoughts. Miss Everly's beauty was impossible for him to deny, the connection he had felt the day before even more so. He still felt it, was pulled to her by it.

Regardless of whatever attraction she held, Miss Everly was not for him. If the newcomers were trapped on the island with him, then his attention must necessarily fall elsewhere. When Miss Everly crested the hill again, her step somewhat lighter, Alejandro hardened his expression and acknowledged her with nothing more than a nod before beginning the climb back up to his shelter.

The young woman remained unaffected by his manner. Indeed, she kept a one-sided conversation going quite effortlessly.

"I cannot imagine what it has been like for you, all alone in this place for so long. I hope we will not be a great burden for you. But you must be happy to have company at last, and I doubt it will take long for people to come looking for us, and then you will be rescued, too. Saved from this place." She barely paused for breath, and though he wanted to ignore her, she made it quite difficult to do so.

He'd been in the silence too long, he well knew. Having someone else fill it, and with a voice that lilted and swayed so the words were like a song, gave ease to his heart.

"Nearly all my life I've wanted to be part of an adventure. I never imagined it would be Robinson Crusoe's story that I fell into. Though I will be grateful to have this over and done, I am nearly as grateful it happened at all. How else would anyone have found you here? But now there are several of us and things will turn out all right."

It pained him to know how wrong she was. Miss Everly would learn, soon enough, and without much help from him, that the island was not lovely nor something out of a novel. He didn't stop her prattle, though. He took in every word, storing them up in his memory for later, for when she stopped being so hopeful and recognized the harsh reality of their situation. For when she forgot the connection they had shared, and the way her hand fit perfectly within his.

They were castaways upon an empty island, with only well water for drink and what the island provided for food. No amount of conversation or hope changed those facts. The island had claimed them all in life, and the island would keep their bones long after they had turned to dust.

❧ 8 ❧

When Hope left the canopy of trees walking at Alejandro's side, she saw that the others had at last begun to awaken. Albert stood near the fire, speaking with Irene, who appeared rather angry. The sailors were at the edge of the clearing, the two who were uninjured, gathering wood and brush. The doctor was missing, most likely sitting with his wife.

"The water?" Hope asked Alejandro, glancing at his bucket.

He answered with a brusque tone. "It must be boiled first, to make certain it is clean." He glanced at her from the corner of his eye, bent his head slightly, then walked with greater speed to the fire, leaving her behind.

Hope watched him go, studying the way he moved with interest. She'd never seen a man walk like that before. At home, everyone carried themselves stiffly, as though a rod ran from the base of their necks straight down their spine, holding them upright and unbending. The sailors she'd watched when they came across the ocean moved rapidly, almost jerkily, as though perpetually in a hurry to get from one task to the next.

Alejandro's movements reminded her of a cat. His shoulders rolled slightly as he walked, his head tilted down as though he listened to the world around him rather than trust his eyes alone, and his feet fell lightly on the ground. Yes, where the gentry she knew strutted and posed like well-feathered birds, and sailors ambled about on land as though they were still at sea, Alejandro moved like a stalking feline.

Despite the warmth of the morning, Hope shivered and wrapped her arms around herself.

Irene caught sight of her and pointed, drawing Albert's attention, too. With a little wave, Hope called out, "Good morning." Everyone glanced her direction, even the sailors gathering wood. She approached the crackling fire, where Alejandro had placed the metal pail upon a rock amidst the flames, and walked around to properly greet Irene.

No sooner had Hope parted her lips to speak, however, than Albert took hold of her arm and pulled her toward the shelter's entrance.

"What do you think you are doing?" he asked, his words spoken through gritted teeth. "You cannot go wandering off. It isn't safe."

"I was so worried," Irene added, her voice tremulous. "What if you were hurt?"

"I was with Señor Córdoba." Hope tugged her arm away from Albert, then pushed her loose hair away from her cheek as an excuse for the movement. "I'm certain he wouldn't let any harm befall me."

Albert's eyes narrowed. "We know nothing about him, Grace. You cannot trust that man, and you cannot behave indecently by traipsing about without an escort. How long were you alone with him yesterday?"

Although a protest formed in her thoughts, Hope kept it back. Her sister's Christian name served as reminder enough that she played a part. Grace would be the first to make peace in a difficult situation, rather than stir up disagreements. What would she say, though? How did Grace smooth rough patches in conversation and conflict?

Usually by paying compliments to the enemy.

"Not long at all, and Señor Córdoba was a perfect gentleman. How kind of you to worry for me." Yes, that was the right tact. Hope lowered her chin and forced herself to smile. "I did not mean to cause any alarm. I will be more careful in the future." Though she could not like them questioning the honor of the man they must all depend upon for help, Hope changed the subject. "How is Mrs. Morgan today?"

"Poorly, one would imagine," Irene said, glancing at the shelter. "Sleeping on leaves and stone, with her injury, I cannot think any of this is good for her."

Mr. Thorne approached from the trees, joining their small party. "Good morning." He glanced at each of them, a commiserating sort of grimace appearing on his face. "I see Miss Everly returned to us. What do you suppose we are to do next?"

Irene simpered up at the gentleman, though he had made it more than clear the day before he held no interest in flirting with her. Really, Hope found it indecent of her friend to try again when the gentleman had been forced to proclaim himself attached to another through expectation if not yet by matrimony. He'd made the pronouncement while walking on the island they had toured with the doctor.

"We will have to organize a method of attracting rescue, for certain." Albert adjusted the cuffs of the coat he still wore, though how he managed to keep the still-damp coat on in the morning heat, Hope could not imagine. "Perhaps a fire. A large one."

"Surely the sailors will have ideas on that count." Hope contradicted him without thinking. "I imagine they have lots of stories of what search parties might look for, or what might prove most effective."

Mr. Thorne nodded but Albert looked down his nose at her.

"Really, Grace. The sailors are not very well educated. I cannot think they would have any better ideas than the most obvious."

His continued use of the Christian name he supposed to be hers made Hope's neck prickle with irritation. Yet she kept her tone civil in her response. "If education is what is most wanted, we must appeal to Doctor Morgan. He is familiar with the area, and a naturalist. He will know what is best."

"Most likely," Mr. Thorne agreed, reaching up to tug at the knot of his cravat. He'd tied it himself, obviously, and with haste. Though he'd seemingly lost his coat, the rest of his attire had been tucked and tied properly. Like Hope, Mr. Thorne was without shoes. His bare feet were nearly as pale as her own.

Movement made Hope turn to see Doctor Morgan emerge from the stick and stone structure. His forehead puckered in concern, he caught Hope's eye and heaved a sigh before joining them. "Miss Everly. It is good to have you among us again."

Hope's cheeks warmed, but she lifted her chin rather than apologize again. She had only been gone from their sight a quarter of an hour, perhaps a few minutes more, but as they had all been sleeping when she left they could not know it had even been that long. Though Grace would admonish Hope to consider the feelings of others, Hope rather wished they would stop worrying over a grown woman perfectly capable of walking to and from the beach without incident.

"How is your wife, Doctor?" Mr. Thorne asked, all politeness.

"Tolerably well, considering her situation." Doctor Morgan rubbed at his cheeks, which were coarse with black and gray stubble. "With rest and time to heal, I believe she will recover. There do not seem to be any internal injuries. The ribs are merely bruised. Not broken."

Mr. Gibson, the professor from Oxford, had kept his seat near the fire until Doctor Morgan appeared. The older gentleman came to stand next to the doctor, putting his hand on his friend's shoulder. Hope looked about, at each member of their party, and the last of her temper cooled. Not a single person standing with her appeared confident in their situation. No one smiled. The surrounding air hung heavily, each man with drooping shoulders and dark circles under everyone's eyes.

"It is time we decide our course of action," the doctor said after the measured silence. "Come, we must gather the other men and speak with Señor Córdoba." Hope turned, prepared to join the men in their plans, when Albert touched her elbow again.

"Perhaps the ladies would do better to join your wife, Doctor?"

Irene started to nod, but Hope had no wish to be left out of any discussion involving their rescue. Appealing to Albert would not help, as he seemed determined to put her out of the way. She addressed Doctor Morgan instead.

"I cannot think I will be at peace until I know that there are firm plans, Doctor. I did not sleep last night, worrying over these dreadful circumstances. If you will allow me to listen, I am certain it will help me to recover my serenity." It wasn't exactly what Grace would say, or do, but Grace had never been stranded on an island with a group of men intent on leaving her out of important decisions.

Mr. Thorne surprised her by adding to her request. "If they wish to hear it, Mr. Carlbury, I think we must allow it. The ladies are less likely to have hysterics if they understand the situation in full."

"I agree," the professor said, somewhat impatiently. "Come, come. Enough dithering."

"Miss Everly, how old are you?" the doctor asked, tucking his hands behind his back and regarding her with narrowed eyes.

"Four and twenty, sir," she answered, tilting her chin upward.

A tired smile appeared, though it did not quite lighten the doctor's expression. "Ah. You see, Mr. Carlbury, Miss Everly has reached her majority. I think it best we allow her to make her own decisions, given the circumstances."

The victory, small as it was, gave Hope a feeling of accomplishment, but she refrained from casting a smug look in Albert's direction. The bossy gentleman had no say, and she must be gracious in her triumph. With her hand on the doctor's arm, she walked with him to the fire.

Alejandro had been tending to the ashes and coals, banking the fire carefully while keeping watch over the pail of water. When he saw the group shift in his direction he came to his feet. The sailors returned, too, with arms full of sticks and dead foliage. They put their burdens down and then stood, arms crossed, everyone waiting for decisions and plans.

"Señor Córdoba, I must again offer our sincerest thanks for all of your assistance. The shelter you provided for the ladies, and your hospitality extended to all of us, has been a tremendous blessing."

The way Señor Córdoba regarded them, completely relaxed, the confident tilt of his head, intrigued Hope. Had the man stood before Parliament, she imagined he would hold himself with the same self-assured posture. Had he always stood that way, or had his time on the island influenced his character? The day before, with her, he had been all gentle solicitude.

"Given the circumstances, we must appeal to you for an even greater service. We must wait for rescue, as you have done, and it is our God-given duty to make the best of things. To survive, of course, and to maintain ourselves in an appropriate manner until help comes."

Hope watched Alejandro so intently she did not fail to see the emotions flickering in his eyes, though his expression remained hard and unyielding. Did he mistrust the others in her party?

When he spoke, his words were flat, without inflection. "You believe you will be saved, even though I have been here for fourteen months without sighting a ship even once?"

Albert spoke, his voice sharp, startling Hope enough that she leaned away from him. "As it so happens, several members of our party have important enough connections that there will be an outcry if we are not found with speed."

"Oh?" The castaway's eyes flitted briefly from the doctor to Albert. "You are that important, that they will search every island until they find you? They will comb every reef in search of your boat's wreckage? Even though there are hundreds of islands capable of supporting life, and thousands of rocky shoals suited to destroying boats and the men aboard them? What faith you have in your connections." He shook his shaggy head, as though amused rather than put out.

Could rescue truly be that difficult? Hope turned her eyes to the trees, and the sea beyond them, stretching out in a vast blanket of blue and green. There were dozens of people who knew their party's route when they had set out. Albert had a point, too; the doctor was a famous naturalist, the Carlburys' family hosted a member of the House of Lords, and those things mattered. Someone would come looking, surely.

"We must have hope, Señor," Doctor Morgan countered. "Hope —and faith—that we will come away from this experience as better men. In the meantime, we must behave ourselves in an appropriate manner, conducting ourselves as gentlemen."

Alejandro met Hope's eyes. "This is not an adventure sent to test your abilities." Though the men present would think Alejandro addressed the doctor, Hope felt the rebuke keenly. Her heart gave a harrowing squeeze. He was angry. At her? But what had she done? The day before, the way he held her hand, looked at her—had she imagined their connection?

He turned his gaze back to the leader, folding his arms across his chest. "As to maintaining 'an appropriate manner,' as you say, I am not certain what you mean by these words."

"Only that we should conduct ourselves as gentlemen, as I said." The doctor rocked back on his heels, a crease wrinkling his brow. "The ladies' sensibilities must be considered."

If her position had granted her the right to speak up at that moment, Hope would have informed everyone she knew perfectly well the difference between Hyde Park and the island, and the behavior at the former most certainly would not prove useful at the latter. Surely the doctor did not expect her to walk about with a parasol and comment politely upon the weather.

She gritted her teeth and turned her attention back to Alejandro, who gazed briefly to her before going back to the doctor.

"And if rescue does not come, as you hope it will? If you are here as long as I have been, for fourteen months, for twenty, for a hundred?" Alejandro gestured to his chest, to the worn shirt he had donned. "My fine coat and neckcloth did not last long. I pulled them apart for other uses, such as bandages for the only other person to survive the wreck of my ship. After he died, I stripped him of his clothes."

Her blood went cold, despite the perspiration she felt building at her lower back. Irene's hand clutched at Hope's wrist. Alejandro hadn't told her this the day before.

"Sir," Albert blurted, stepping in front of Hope and his sister. "There are women present."

"And should these women not know of the hardships they may soon face?" Alejandro's retort was cold and without sympathy. Not at all how he had spoken to Hope when they were alone. "Each item of clothing I had to use, as rope, as net, as twine, in order to survive. My shoes I lost before coming ashore."

Hope curled her toes in the dirt and put her arm around Irene's shoulders.

"My companion I buried, down on that same beach where you pulled yourselves ashore." Alejandro took one step closer to them, his hands falling to his side, balling into fists. "For two weeks, I nursed him, treated his wounds, fed us both on what edible plants I found. Then he died in the night, far from home, and I alone present to weep for him. Weeks afterward, I wondered if I would do better to join him than to fight every day for a life of forced solitude."

Doctor Morgan raised both his arms, as though that might placate the sudden indignant response of their host. "Señor, I am dreadfully sorry for all that you have been through. Truly, no man should be made to suffer as you have."

Falling back a step, hands relaxing though he appeared as tense as before, Alejandro returned his attention to the doctor. "Yet here there are ten more of you, unready to live as I have lived, for as long as we are trapped here."

Irene whimpered. "Oh, Grace. I don't want to die here."

Although Hope wanted to hush her friend, she forced herself to respond gently, squeezing Irene's shoulders and answering with as much care as Grace might have used. "We must do as the doctor said. We mustn't lose hope." As she spoke the virtue after which she had been named, Hope tried to find it in her heart. That morning, walking to the beach, she'd told herself that all would be well, and that rescue would come. Hearing Alejandro speak of death, of a grim survival, altered her view of the situation most unpleasantly.

"You must prepare yourselves for the worst," Alejandro continued when their party remained quiet except for Irene's weeping. "There is nothing more important now. You must learn how to live on this island. The manners that served you well in a drawing room are worthless in this place."

Albert shifted in the sand, his chin jutting out. "You speak as though you expect to have some authority over us."

"Mr. Carlbury." The doctor spoke the younger man's name sharply, glaring at him. "Though I might understand something of the flora and fauna of the islands, I have no practical experience living among them. Have you?"

Albert's jaw tightened, and he sank his gaze to the ground.

The doctor next turned to the three men that might be of the most help. "What of our sailors? Madden? Hitchens? Smith?"

The broadest of them, a man with large arms and dark skin lined with scars, answered for all three. "We might know some things. But not so much as this man. I grew up working with the cane until I ran to the sea. Hitchens worked the docks his whole life. Smith—he was with tobacco farmers."

After a brief nod of acknowledgment, Doctor Morgan turned to the rest of the party. "Thorne? Gibson?" The gentlemen shook their heads. "As you see Mr. Carlbury, while we might collectively learn what is necessary to live in this place, it would take time. Some of us might die, or starve, or grow sick, or mad, in the interim."

Irene's fingernails dug deeper into Hope's arms.

With an air of entreaty, the doctor turned again to the bearded and bedraggled man on the other side of the fire. "Señor Córdoba. Will you teach us what we need to know to live here?"

For a long moment, the man only stared at them, his gaze moving from one face to another. His eyes lingered for an extra second upon Albert, then fell to Hope's. She forced herself to smile, to prove herself ready and willing to do what she must. Strangely, he frowned in return.

Perhaps she had imagined what had passed between them in their hours alone together. He may have only been relieved to see another person, while her whole heart had reacted with wonder at his touch.

"I will teach all of you. What choice do I have? It is that, or risk you destroying what I have built." He did not relax, did not appear in the least pleased by the agreement. "The first thing to worry over is food. You are all hungry?"

"Starving, more like," Irene muttered. Alejandro heard. His eyes darted to hers.

"You know nothing of starvation, Señorita. But you will before long." A chill went down Hope's spine hearing Alejandro speak with such surety, but seeing the haunted, dark look come into his eyes stilled her protests. He spoke from experience.

Albert stepped in front of his sister, putting a hand on her shoulder. But whether the gesture was meant to comfort her or shield her from Alejandro's words, or something else entirely, Hope couldn't be sure.

"If I might enter the house." Alejandro nodded to the structure of twigs, mud, and rock. "There is dried seal meat. It is not much, but it will help."

The doctor stepped aside and went in first, Alejandro behind him.

"This is wretched," Irene whispered, closing her eyes against more tears. "Dried seal meat? What can he mean, asking us to eat such a thing? Oh, I would rather starve."

Rather than say something of sense to his sister, Albert murmured to Hope and Irene both. "He is doing this on purpose, though I cannot guess why."

A retort rose to her lips, in a hasty defense of the single man present with the qualifications to keep them alive for however long it took rescue to come. Yet Hope took her tongue sharply between her teeth and said nothing. Grace would say nothing, and she must remain as Grace for the time being. How did her sister always maintain calm composure in the face of such stupidity? If only Hope could end the ruse.

With everyone's heightened fear, and the Carlburys behaving somewhat irrationally, throwing any more confusion into the situation by declaring her true identity to them struck her as unwise. The truth would divide the Carlburys and Hope further, and as she knew no one so well as they, she must keep their trust and friendship.

Even if Albert acted like a strutting peacock.

9

Ten people to feed, care for, and instruct on the dangers of living on an island smaller than the plot of land his father owned outside of Buenos Aires. As Alejandro doled out the seal meat, he paid close attention to each person's reaction. First, he saw that the women had what they needed, including the doctor's injured wife. She took the food with a grateful nod of her head and whispered thanks. Miss Carlbury winced and accepted the food he offered, saying nothing but expressing her disgust clearly enough with the wrinkle of her nose and the dainty way she held the dried meat between two fingers.

Miss Everly did as she had the day before, accepting the strips of meat from the dry leather wrappings with a wide smile. "Thank you, Señor Córdoba."

He almost responded to her. Almost told her it might be even drier than the day before. Instead, he stepped away, saying nothing. Their familiarity had come to an end almost as soon as it had begun. He took the meat to the sailors next.

"Wait a moment," the idiotic Carlbury said. "You would feed the common laborers before the gentlemen?" He stepped closer to Alejandro, his posture rigid.

Why did that protest not surprise him? It was time for the Englishman to learn his first lesson of survival.

"While there is enough for all," Alejandro said, not bothering to even look in the direction of the whining dog, "and I will always see to the women first, our survival depends on hard work. One look at these men"—he nodded to the sailors—"tells me all I need know about who is accustomed to such labor. I doubt you have ever lifted anything heavier than a book. You have likely never fished without a rod, either."

Carlbury spluttered for a moment, then his hand came down on Alejandro's shoulder. "Now see here—"

"Albert." The soft, lilting way Miss Everly spoke that absurd man's name made Alejandro's stomach twist unpleasantly. What was their relationship, that they spoke so familiarly with each other? The man had been protective of Miss Everly, too. Alejandro wondered if there was an understanding between them. "Please," she continued, appearing at Alejandro's side. "Will you help take the pail from the fire? It's boiled, and it needs to cool before we can take some to Mrs. Morgan. The meat is so dry—she needs something to drink."

Luckily for Carlbury, the Englishman removed his hand and moved away to do as the woman asked, leaving Alejandro to finish his task.

Food that would have lasted him two weeks if he rationed it carefully was soon gone completely. Aside from the cooling water, he had nothing else to offer the shipwrecked group. He found food as he needed it most of the time.

The Carlbury woman had gone back inside the shelter, but Miss Everly remained, arms wrapped about herself. The doctor spoke to her, somewhat earnestly, and she frowned up at him.

Alejandro clapped his hands, loudly, to gain attention once more.

"We have two objectives this morning. The first is to ensure we do not go hungry. The second is to take stock of supplies and how we might use them. I have two spears, for fishing." He turned to the sailors, meeting Madden's intense gaze. "Do you think you can manage them?"

Without hesitation, the large dark-skinned man made his answer. "Not me. But Smith and Hitchens know how to fish."

"Good. There are rock pools near the western bank." Alejandro kneeled and drew an outline of the island in the dirt.

Enough of his education and his over-familiarity with the land mass made it easy enough to make the outline of a bird in flight, the albatross, with a heavy midsection and wings curved outward and down, creating the space for the two coves. The narrowest parts of the island were from the inside of each cove across to the northwestern bank.

He pointed to the southern tip of the island. "We are here. If you walk through the trees, northeast, and then go west when the ground levels out, you will find the pools. I usually have good luck there."

"We go together," the one identified as Smith said, his accent heavier than Madden's. "We will bring back fish and wood." The sailors left without another word, disappearing beneath the trees. They were men used to hard work, and likely the only people in the group of shipwrecked newcomers with sense enough to survive whether or not Alejandro assisted them.

Alejandro would need to keep everyone else busy or risk their desperate ignorance harming everyone's ability to make the best of things.

"We ought to gather enough greenery to burn a signal fire," Mr. Carlbury muttered.

As long as he had been out of society, Alejandro had no concern for maintaining a polite veneer. Not with a fool. "And you think people are already looking for you? Here, when you were blown off course in a storm that lasted hours?" he asked, not even looking at the Englishman. "You would risk burning plants that we may eat or use for survival, too?"

"I had rather make an effort toward rescue than sit and do nothing," the man retorted hotly.

Alejandro whirled around. "I have no use for fools on this island, Señor Carlbury. We have known each other less than a day, but every word out of your mouth tells me exactly the sort of burden you will be. You have never soiled your hands. You are of no use here. I would rather have you sit and do nothing than even attempt assistance."

"How dare you—"

The doctor stepped forward, his face pale. "There is no need for this. I am certain Mr. Carlbury is as anxious as the rest of us to do what he can—"

Carlbury snarled. "I am not going to take orders from a man living like a savage."

"Savage?" Alejandro laughed without any true mirth. Had this man known him even two years ago, what would he have thought of Alejandro? "I do what I must to survive. If you refuse to see this, perhaps we need not suffer your company long."

Carlbury lunged forward at the same moment his sister cried out and fell against her friend, nearly knocking the shorter Miss Everly to the ground. The doctor and the other gentleman, Thorne, grabbed hold of Carlbury.

"Is this necessary?" Thorne asked, glaring at Alejandro.

"It is natural to be distraught, Carlbury," the doctor said. "But you must keep your head."

Alejandro dismissed the struggling men with a hand. "The sooner he accepts what must be, the better. It is the same for all of you." Without his meaning to, he looked directly at the lovely Miss Everly, who held her distraught friend with both arms. Her dark brows were drawn down sharply, but she did not glare at him as the others did. Her expression was different. Thoughtful. Intense.

He sensed something in her. A conflict. He didn't expect her to speak.

"Albert," Miss Everly said, her tone sharp. "Your sister needs your attention." The Englishman did not respond, though he stopped straining against the two men that held him.

Señorita Carlbury moaned, then released yet another sob. The girl would make herself sick if she kept on in that manner. The way she had wilted into her friend's arms gave him little hope of finding a use for her. At last her brother jerked his arms away from the other men and turned, taking his sister by the arm. "Come inside the shelter, Irene. Rest with Mrs. Morgan." Miss Everly bit her lip and watched them go, that strange indecision on her face again.

Alejandro had no time for these people and their fits. "Doctor, you say you are a naturalist." He tried for a less hostile tone, but heard the anger in his voice well enough. "Perhaps you might educate the others on what animals are dangerous to them."

The doctor sighed and his shoulders fell. "Of course, Señor."

Alejandro nodded and left. Without another word. Without glancing at Miss Everly to see if she followed her friends back into the shelter. It wasn't his concern, how she decided to behave.

He told himself she would likely be no better, no more apt than the rest of them, to be useful on the island. Once the novelty of being on an adventure, whatever that meant, wore away, she would be as prone to fainting spells as Señorita Carlbury.

The possessive manner in which Carlbury stood over her, touched her, and spoke to her, had not escaped Alejandro at all. The man attempted to claim her with every gesture, but she did not appear entirely accepting of that. Perhaps things would change when her faith in rescue dimmed.

His heart ached at the thought, though it had no right in its attachment to her.

He walked beneath the trees on a path he'd worn down with nearly as many steps as he'd made to and from the beach for water.

This time, he went in search of what he'd once had in abundance and abhorred—silence and solitude.

Instinctively, he kept his gaze sweeping the trees. He watched for the tiny, poisonous frogs, the venomous spiders, just as he kept aware for any animal or plant that might give him a greater advantage over the hardships of the island.

He went down the hill at a quick pace, putting distance between himself and the British, his thoughts tumbling all over themselves. Carlbury was a fool, of that Alejandro had little doubt, but he understood that the man's rash attitude stemmed from fear. For perhaps the first time in the privileged gentleman's life he had no control, no authority, and his lack of practical skills endangered him and those he cared about.

Pitying Carlbury would be easier than disliking him, but Alejandro had only to remember the way the Englishman turned his nose up, snide and arrogant, and he brushed the pity aside.

His awareness to the shuffling behind him brought Alejandro spinning around, digging his feet into the incline and raising his hands to ward off an attack.

Miss Everly gasped and pulled back, losing her balance. She overcorrected then, leaning forward, causing her to stumble and slide down the slope and into him. His hands already held upward, it was instinctual to open his arms and catch her, leaning into her to keep from falling backward himself.

Her hands caught his shoulders, and her eyes had turned round as the full moon. She stared up at him, her lips parted and face pale.

Alejandro had held beautiful women in his arms before. He'd danced with them at home, and during his time abroad. He'd even stolen a kiss or two when certain ladies had seemed amenable to the idea. But it had been a long time since he'd stood this close, so close he could see the flecks of green in her blue eyes, to someone who stirred more intense feelings within him.

If only they had met in a crowded ballroom far from the island. He would have asked her to dance.

"Are you steady?" he asked, dispelling the quiet.

Color rushed into her cheeks, blooming like the roses his mother had tried desperately to grow in her new homeland. "Yes." The word was a squeak, reminding him of a mouse sighting a predator.

He'd frightened her, and that sickened him. He released her and stepped back, certain she would not fall again. "What are you doing, Señorita?"

She pushed her loose hair back over her shoulder. "Miss Everly, if you please." She took in a shaky breath. "I wanted to make certain we did not overly insult you, Mr. Córdoba."

Did she? Her eyes told him she had another reason entirely for following after him. "I cannot think of anything you must apologize for, *Miss* Everly." He considered her for a moment, taking in the disheveled hair and a smudge of dirt across her cheek. "You said nothing wrong. But you had best return to your people."

She narrowed her eyes at him. "My people?"

"They were not happy with you for wandering off earlier. I doubt anyone will be pleased you are out of their sight again." Especially her Mr. Carlbury. That man would want to keep her safely within his reach.

"Mr. Córdoba—"

"*Señor* Córdoba," he corrected, amused to insist on the title in his native language.

Her chest rose and fell with a dramatic sigh. "Very well. Señor Córdoba. Surely you understand—everyone is frightened. For you to storm off as you did, without word of where you were going or when you might return, will leave *my people* to worry. I know we have not made a positive impression upon you."

"A positive impression," he repeated, the words strange on his tongue. For so long, he'd only uttered prayers and recited favorite snatches of poems, plays, and psalms. "The words of English drawing rooms have no place here, Miss Everly. There is no one here to impress." He took a step back. "I will return soon. You are welcome to tell the others that, if it eases their thoughts."

She took a step forward. "Where are you going?" Her eyes asked what she did not voice. *May I come, too?* She did not understand that the presence of the others changed everything.

"To think. I am going to think."

A puzzled frown turned her lips downward. "But—aren't you lonely? Do you not wish to—to have a conversation? To be with people? To be with—with me."

Yes. He wanted to tell her yes. He had yearned for company, for conversation, for companionship, for months. And it had been so easy with her, the day before.

Yet to go from silence to nearly a dozen people staring at him, speaking to him, depending on him, and at least one person expressing hostility toward him, had drained Alejandro of whatever desire he had possessed. His longing for company had been sated with a speed he had not anticipated.

Something of his thoughts seemed to have leaked through his mind and into the air. She fixed him with a sudden gentle expression, a softness in her eyes that nearly drew him forward. "I suppose we have overwhelmed you."

Perceptive. Inquisitive. Adventurous. Not at all what Alejandro expected of a gently bred woman, no matter where she might be from. She stood beneath the shade of the island's trees, her bare feet in the dirt not far from his, her expression earnest. What was he to do with a woman who stared at him in such a way, in a more than hopeless situation? A woman who had stirred feelings he did not know himself capable of experiencing.

"Go back, Miss Everly," he said, cutting through his own thoughts and his sudden desire to invite her along with him. Even if rescue never came, he did not think anyone of the people with her would tolerate their being alone for so long. "I am not your concern."

She stiffened and her chin came up as though she'd been startled. Hesitantly, she took a step back, then she marched back up the hill. Her bare feet skipped from one patch of dirt to another, avoiding roots and rocks. He watched until she crested the hill, and then he turned away and kept on his path through the trees.

He had to get his thoughts in order. Make plans.

A crowd of people on his island changed everything. How long would they last? Had anyone brought disease with them? Illness that would spread? What of the doctor's wife? How trustworthy were these people? If madness set in, even one unstable person might do enough damage to the others, to the island itself, to bring several others down with them.

As lonely as he had been, at least Alejandro had known exactly what must be done. How to survive. How to stay sane. He walked to the beach, not certain what to say, what to do, to instill enough fear in the people who had come that they would listen to him.

And women. Why did there have to be women involved? An injured woman, requiring constant care and in a fragile state. A second woman—no, Miss Carlbury was more like a girl, too young and inexperienced, too wrapped up in herself, to count as a mature member of her sex. She would prove as useless as if she'd been injured, more of a liability than a help. Unless she grew up quickly and accepted the situation in which she found herself. Given her brother's reactionary nature, Alejandro doubted that would be an easy change for her to make, if it wasn't discouraged outright.

Oh, and *Miss* Everly. Wandering around, asking intrusive questions. Yet try as he might, he couldn't find it in himself to think of her unkindly.

Alejandro pushed through the brush as gently as possible. He had no wish to run afoul of any insects or birds nesting in the smaller trees and bushes. He'd been stung and bitten enough to know how little the animals here feared man.

The beach waited for him, strewn with things washed up by the storm. That sail was especially needful. There would be many uses for it. What he'd viewed as abundance in the dim light of the moon he recognized now as a necessity. Bandages, wrappings, and all manner of things might be made from a single sail. But the idea of using it to signal for help, in case anyone did come looking for the new inhabitants of the island, was also a worthy need.

Ten people relied on him to be clever with each and every resource on the island. Though more had depended upon him in his former life, the task ahead felt more daunting than anything he'd faced before.

❦ 10 ❦

When Hope entered the shelter, she grimaced at the stale air inside. There wasn't a great deal of natural light coming in, except from the doorway and the hole for the smoke to rise out of. Though the fire had died down, the shelter was unbearably warm. Surely the stifling atmosphere would not meet with the doctor's approval.

Yet there the doctor was, kneeling next to his wife. Across the small room, Irene sat with her head resting against Albert's shoulder and both her hands clasping her brother's. Albert had his head tilted back, but she could not see his expression in the dimness.

"Oh, Miss Everly." The doctor's voice called to her and she came further in, grateful she did not have to stoop as everyone else did to walk beneath the thatched roof.

"Yes, Doctor Morgan?" She lowered herself to the ground, tucking her skirts back in as ladylike a manner as possible. "Can I help you, sir?"

"Yes, I think so." Doctor Morgan's voice, heavy with worry, perplexed her. "We are in a unique situation, Miss Everly."

Mrs. Morgan shifted and Hope realized the woman was awake. "Most unique, dear." Mrs. Morgan put her hand on her husband's knee. "And so we must have a conversation." She nearly whispered her words, her chest barely moving as she spoke. The bruising likely made it painful for her to inhale any more deeply than she must while talking. "You are not attached to anyone here, Miss Everly, beyond friendship. Is that so?"

It took some restraint to not look over her shoulder. Albert had hinted, more than once, that he would pay court to her if given the slightest nod of approval. Though why he had focused his pursuit in such a way she did not understand. She did nothing to encourage him.

"That is true, Mrs. Morgan." She matched the other woman's low tone, having no wish to involve the Carlburys in this conversation.

The doctor shifted on his knees, briefly glancing at his wife before meeting Hope's. "This is concerning. Your reputation is at stake, Miss Everly."

Was that all they were worried about? Had they no common sense? "I hardly think anyone can hold being shipwrecked against me."

"Of course not. But the fact remains that you are on an island with several unmarried men, and only two women to keep you company. You were also alone, for quite some time, with a man unknown to any of us." Mrs. Morgan's shallow breathing did not sound pained so much as patient. "I must rest and heal. I cannot watch over you unless you remain by my side."

Hope's insides prickled. "But Miss Carlbury—"

The doctor waved a hand to cut off her response. He kept his voice low enough it would not carry across the small room. "I think we both know your friend's nature will keep her inclined to remain near her brother or here, with Mrs. Morgan."

"From our brief interactions, I do not think you will be so willing to sit still," Mrs. Morgan added, a tight smile on her face. "I understand that desire completely. It is how I should feel, were I not in such a wretched state."

Guilt settled deeply in Hope's heart. She liked Mrs. Morgan, and to think of no one but herself when the woman had been injured was not at all how Grace would have behaved. Grace never failed to put the needs of others before her, whereas Hope knew well enough that she rarely spared a thought on such matters when she was in the midst of something that mattered to her.

After the silence continued too long, Mrs. Morgan spoke, even gentler than before. "We feel we ought to warn you to take care of your reputation. Guard it. Do not put yourself in a compromising situation."

Doctor Morgan spoke firmly, his voice louder as he made his declaration. "I am willing to take you under my protection until we are rescued. The presence of my wife, and her agreement, ought to help. But we need you to promise you will take care, Miss Everly, of your reputation and your health."

"This is not a holiday. We are in very real danger." Mrs. Morgan closed her eyes, her grim smile in place again. "A stumble and fall could injure you, there are things on this island that might harm you. Exercise caution, Miss Everly."

All Hope could do was agree with them. Even if she was of an age that meant she no longer required the approval of a guardian in manners of conduct, the situation proved a risky one. "Thank you, both of you, for your concern and kindness. I will take what you have said to heart."

"Good. I did worry." Mrs. Morgan sighed and reached for her husband again, touching the sleeve of his coat. How he could bear to wear it in such heat, Hope did not know. "My husband told me you wandered off alone this morning. With Mr. Córdoba."

Ah. That made their concern more pointed. Their mistrust of Alejandro. "Señor Córdoba showed me where to fetch water and escorted me to the beach. There was nothing inappropriate about his conduct, I assure you."

"We know nothing of him, Miss Everly," the doctor said. "While open-air walks might be acceptable in London parks, I am not in favor of embarking on them here. Please, do not leave this shelter or clearing without an escort, or without your friend."

Dragging Irene around the island would be nearly impossible. The Morgans were perfectly correct when they assumed the other young lady would have no interest in doing things that might lead to uncomfortable situations. Perhaps Hope might convince her to go down to the beach, but other excursions might be difficult.

Yet what could she do? Here she had an opportunity to live out something only written of in novels. Shipwrecked on a tropical island, and she was not even permitted to go exploring.

Of course, she needn't heed anyone if she did not wish to. But stirring up trouble by casting aside their practical advice would not end well. Sensing her discussion with the Morgans was at an end, Hope excused herself to allow them privacy and went across the hovel to her friends. They had not moved. Albert appeared to be asleep, but Irene blinked through the dim light and up at Hope.

"You should tidy your hair, Grace. Wearing it loose and down will only cause you a great deal of trouble as it snarls."

Hope's hands went up to her hair. She had been brushing it back all morning, but she hadn't any idea what else she might do with it. She sat down on Irene's free side and started combing through the mass of brown waves with her fingers.

"What did the Morgans want?" Irene asked, her voice soft in the darkness. "Do they think we have a chance of rescue?"

Hope shrugged, her fingers finding a snag that required more careful attention. "They did not speak about that. They were telling me to guard my reputation. To be careful and not wander far."

Strangely enough, that made Irene giggle. "Oh. I suppose that is kind of them, but we both know it is most unnecessary. Were you your sister, I should have cause to be concerned, but you are far too intelligent to see this as anything other than the tragedy it is.

It's something out of Shakespeare, isn't it? What is the play where everyone is shipwrecked on that magical island?"

It was actually one of Hope's favorites, though the oddness of living out even a portion of the play made her shiver. "*The Tempest.*"

"Yes." Irene lifted her head from her brother's shoulder. "You know, Albert might safeguard your reputation. It cannot be a surprise to you to know how much he admires you. I am certain, if you wished it, he would make an offer. Then once we are rescued you could marry. We would be sisters."

Would Irene be so willing for such an event if she knew she spoke to Hope rather than Grace? Albert certainly would not wish to attach himself to the sister he viewed as flighty and trouble-some. He'd hurled those insults directly at Hope, more than a year ago, when she had involved Irene in one of her less successful ventures. His open hostility toward her was yet another point in favor of remaining as Grace for the time being. Albert had already proven himself to have a temper, after all, nearly attacking Alejandro.

Hope stared down at her lap, her fingers finally untangling the last knot. "I am glad you find me an acceptable candidate for sister-in-law, but you know how I feel. I will marry when I fall in love, to a man I love." Alejandro's dark eyes appeared in her mind, their intensity making her throat close. She came to her feet less than gracefully. "Excuse me. I am going to fetch Mrs. Morgan more water."

What if Albert had been awake for that conversation? Hope shuddered even as she stepped into the morning sunlight. Then she took herself to the trees, sitting beneath the shade of the first one she came across. Her long hair hung about her shoulders and down to the middle of her back. It would prove troublesome before long, with no combs or brushes, no maid with deft hands and curling papers or hot tongs.

Leaning against the tree trunk, Hope let her eyes wander the clearing. The sailors were still gone. The professor was beneath another tree, sleeping. Mr. Thorne was nowhere in sight, either. Why should everyone else be permitted to do as they pleased and she was confined to this place?

Reputation did not matter so much as survival. No one could argue that. Hope could contribute. Finding edible berries, hauling water, collecting firewood, were all tasks she could easily perform. The water should be a good place to start, too.

She looked down at her bare feet, dusty again from walking about, and almost smiled. It had not been too long ago that she had walked barefoot along the shore of the North Sea, on her friend Isaac's property. Even Grace never hesitated to remove shoes and stockings to walk in the sand as they had when they were children.

Grace. Dear, wonderful, practical Grace. What would she advise Hope to do? Not sit still, certainly. But to exercise some caution while she went about doing as she pleased. That thought did make Hope's lips curve upward, and warmth stirred in her heart. Grace understood that Hope thrived on action, movement, and the desire to explore. Of everyone Hope knew, Grace was the only one who never expected Hope to be other than she was. The advice her twin gave her, time and again, was only to take care of herself when she went blowing about like a hurricane.

With her sister's countless admonishments running through her thoughts, Hope rose and fetched the pail from beside the fire. She would fetch water. A useful task. And it would allow her a few moments to herself to enjoy the island.

―――――――――

ALEJANDRO RETURNED AT MIDDAY WITH THE SAIL BUNDLED TIGHTLY and tied to his back, his arms laden with scraps of wood. The three men had not returned from their fishing expedition yet, as he expected. In fact, the only people present were the doctor and the somewhat hysterical Señorita Carlbury. They accosted him as soon as he stepped out from beneath the trees.

"There you are," the doctor said, his shoulders falling. The man's insistence in maintaining proper dress had his brow covered in sweat. "Miss Everly—"

"She isn't with you," the girl wailed, cutting off the doctor's question. "Wherever could she have gone? She's been missing for far too long."

As Alejandro himself had only been gone for a little over an hour, he doubted that was the case at all. "Was she in the clearing after I left?" he asked, carefully lowering his burdens exactly where he stood. Did anyone know Miss Everly had followed him for a time, before he sent her back?

The doctor cast an impatient glance at the young woman, then nodded. "We spoke for a time, and then Miss Everly said she would bring water to my wife. That is what she told Miss Carlbury."

"I think I upset her." The abrupt confession from the girl startled the doctor, if his sudden stiffness indicated this was new information. "I told her—well. It does not matter. But I know she did not like what I said. Oh, where could she be?"

"Thorne and Gibson went down the path where you said the well was located," the doctor added. "They returned perhaps a quarter of an hour ago and said they found no sign of Miss Everly or the pail. I did not think it possible for her to get lost. Gibson said the path was quite clearly marked."

Alejandro untied the rope at his midsection, releasing the bundled sail to the ground. He doubted her ability to get lost if she had stuck to her errand. The woman likely decided on another course of action. She did not strike him as the troublesome sort. In fact, Alejandro had confidence in her abilities, though there was no logical reason for such a thing.

"I will go in search of her. The island is not very large. She cannot have gone too far. If she finds the shore, she can find her way back here again."

"Thank you, Señor Córdoba." The doctor wiped at his brow with the back of his coat sleeve. "I have faith you will find her quickly."

With a brief bow, Alejandro took his leave. He went in the direction of the path he took every day to fetch water. While the other searchers may have gone down to the well, perhaps even to the shore in their search, he had a feeling Miss Everly's attention had wandered at a specific location.

The woman's thirst for adventure likely meant she would keep her eyes open for anything out of the ordinary or outside of her experience.

Along the downhill path to the sea, there was a smaller trail he took far less often. In fact, he had not walked that way in a few weeks. He took the small branch, his eyes on the ground searching carefully for signs of disturbance.

Ah. There, in the soft dirt, the clear, half-circle imprint of a heel pressing into the ground. The print was far smaller than anyone else on the island might make, perhaps with the exception of the doctor's wife. The fact that someone so small could cause such a large amount of trouble in a short time almost amused him.

Alejandro had been something of a troublemaker as a child, and perhaps his mischief would've followed him into adulthood were it not for the years of war and the people of Río de la Plata chafing beneath Spain's rule.

A massive stone forced Alejandro to walk along it, where the hill grew steeper. But once on the other side of the big black rock, the trees thinned. He drew closer to the bright blue of the sky and the crashing sound of waves.

Standing with an arm wrapped tightly around one tree, and her hand gripping the handle of the bucket, Miss Everly gazed out over the cliff and toward the churning sky and ocean. She'd found a sheer drop-off that fell into the water below, facing southward.

Storm clouds rumbled far in the distance, the gray and blue framing her prettily. The wind tugged at her dress and made her long hair wave like ribbons on a kite.

He drew nearer, as entranced by the sight of her as she was by the faraway storm.

"Señorita?"

She did not appear startled when she turned to look over her shoulder at him, her blue eyes full of an emotion he could not name. "Will the storm come this direction?" The question was nearly too quietly asked for him to hear.

Coming slowly closer, Alejandro directed his eyes away from her and to the clouds. After a moment's study, he shook his head. "We are not in its path. The wind will take it east, and it will stay away from here."

Her eyes remained on him. He could feel her gaze without having to look at her.

"Good. I do not think anyone wishes to face another storm so soon." She shuddered and hugged the tree at her side tighter. "I saw the path here at the same time I thought I heard thunder."

The explanation did not surprise him. "You must have excellent ears." He watched her from the corner of his eye. Despite her wandering off, there was fear in her expression. In her eyes.

"We live near the sea," she said, the heaviness lifting long enough for her to smile. "My family, my friends, we grew up watching the weather change and storms roll in. I think that gave me an ear for things like this, just as music lessons gave me an ear for song."

He ought to respond. Ought to speak to her about the worry she caused her companions, the dangers of wandering off in a strange place, but instead he let the silence settle between them. Missing the company of people had not meant he wanted a whole boat full of them to be dropped directly onto his island. Especially people desperate and frightened, and more ready to make trouble than to try and exercise practicality.

They were not the sort of people he had been accustomed to, even before he washed ashore on the island.

Hope did not seem to fit with the rest of them at all.

"Did I imagine what happened between us when you found me, Alejandro?" she asked, the question unexpected.

He looked down at the water crashing into the rocks. "What do you think happened, Miss Everly?" He knew what he had felt. Knew why he must put such things away. They would not be rescued. Even if they were, what then? He could not court her. He had nothing. Knew nothing of his family, of his homeland.

She took in a shaky breath. "I do not know how to explain it. Not precisely. But while we spoke, I felt as though we were tied together. That there is a purpose, a wonderful purpose, in us meeting." She turned wide, pleading eyes to him.

Alejandro considered the woman at his side. He sensed a strength to her, something that she kept hidden from the others, that kept her from falling to pieces. And then there was the attraction she spoke of, pulling them together, making his heart race when he stood this near to her. He could not answer her question. She had faith in a future she would never have again.

"What will you do when rescue does not come?" he asked, turning away to watch the white tips of waves appear and vanish only to reappear again, as far as the eye could see.

A bird sang above them and the thunder in the distance boomed a warning across the water. Miss Everly shifted, relaxing her hold on the tree. "I cannot think like that, Señor Córdoba. Not yet."

Expecting anything else would do a disservice to her. To all of them. Yet allowing her to continue under the delusion that anyone out in the world cared enough to search until they found her, that they might be saved from the hardship of living like primitives upon a rocky island, did not strike him as kind.

"There is no place for hope on this island," he said, turning to fully face her. She had to understand. Had to at least begin to grasp

89

the seriousness of the situation. "You are better off to bury hope and give your energies only to what you can control. Your survival."

She met his level stare with a fascinated glint in her eye. Tilting her head to one side, she studied him. She did not take in his beard, did not gawk or blush at his open shirt as the other young lady had. No, Miss Everly sought to look into his thoughts.

"I think you are quite wrong, Señor Córdoba. Hope is very much alive here." She withdrew a step and gestured to the path. "Should we return? I am afraid I have not even filled the pail yet." She would let the matter between them drop. He could be grateful for that.

The woman had to be on the verge of hysterics to smile at him like that when he had tried to present the grimness of their situation to her, though her attitude was preferable over her friend's whining and wailing. Alejandro stepped around her and led the way back to the path for fetching water.

He still wondered what the secret hiding behind her eyes could be.

❧ 11 ❧

If the lecture on proper conduct had been friendly, the rebukes Hope suffered after the return from the well were severe. Irene fell upon Hope the moment she stepped into the clearing, and with such a dramatic lunge that Hope nearly toppled. It was a good thing Alejandro had carried the full pail of water back up the hill. All her hard work would have amounted in nothing more than a puddle after Irene finished with her exuberant greeting.

"Where have you been? Oh, I have been so worried. You've been gone ages and ages. What if you were lost? Or hurt?"

"Lost?" Hope asked, slowly putting her arms around her friend to return the embrace. "I cannot think it possible to be lost. It is a very small island, after all." Her attempt at humor was met with a glare.

"It is not at all something to jest about, Grace Everly." Irene stepped back, holding Hope's shoulders tightly in her hands. "You cannot pretend all is well. Wandering off like that is dangerous."

"We were worried," the doctor added. He had appeared a

moment earlier, coming out of the shelter. "Everyone is out searching for you even now."

Everyone? Why had they sent out search parties with such speed? Hope winced, looking from the doctor to Irene. "I only meant to be helpful and fetch water. I was a little distracted, but I was in no danger."

"It is not like you to wander off. I am surprised at your thoughtless behavior." Irene shuddered and wrapped her arms about herself, though the sun shone down harshly upon them both.

Her actions had been precisely like Hope, but not at all like Grace. Biting her lip, Hope tilted her face downward and thought quickly. "You are right, Irene. I apologize for causing such trouble. I meant to help. I will not leave like that again, nor stay away so long."

"I expected better from you, Miss Everly." The doctor's grave voice delivered the chastisement almost as well as her father might have, had he been present. "Especially after our conversation earlier."

Hope did not think it possible to hang her head any lower. She had apologized. What more might she do? No one would have worried over one of the men disappearing for such a short length of time. Perhaps the Carlburys would not have worried over her had they known she was the more adventurous Everly sister. But as she had decided her course, she had to maintain it.

"Forgive me, Doctor." She caught a glimpse of Alejandro standing from the fire, where he had set the pail to boil again. He looked in her direction, his deep brown gaze catching hers. "I am overcome, I think." Overcome with disappointment in Alejandro. In herself. She had imagined what happened between them. Imagined that he had felt as she did. At least she had not mentioned that she thought, perhaps, she was falling in love with him.

Everyone was right about her. She raced into everything without thought, following her feelings. Hope blinked and directed her stare at the ground again. "I only wish to be useful, but it has been such a shock. I think the quiet helped me to settle my mind." It was almost the truth.

"You poor darling. You always were one to be contemplative." Irene patted her on the arm. "I am certain you are as distraught as I am, but you are putting on a brave face."

Agreeing would be the easiest thing to do, especially with the doctor still glaring at her in disapproval. "Yes. I am." She added a shudder for effect and leaned into Irene. "I think I had better rest for a time. I am most sorry to have caused anyone worry."

Irene wrapped an arm about her waist. "I am certain you are. Oh, but I was beside myself, and Albert went charging into the forest to look for you."

Hope thought she heard Alejandro snort from his place near the fire. She did not look, though she knew she could hardly blame a burning log for the derisive noise. When he turned without word to march into the trees again, the doctor called after him.

"Mr. Córdoba, where are you bound?"

He turned to answer but kept walking backward. "To search out your search party, doctor. Miss Everly may not have been lost, but it would not surprise me if some of the gentlemen were." He disappeared into the shadows beneath the trees.

"Insufferable man," Irene muttered. "Come, Grace. Let us attend Mrs. Morgan."

Attend her how? Hope had no skills with nursing. The doctor had done all he could. Did Irene mean to play at sitting in a parlor and visiting? Hope allowed herself to be guided into the hovel, though the rising sun had made the inside monstrously hot. Poor Mrs. Morgan, trapped in the heat. She shouldn't be left alone to suffer.

Irene soon filled the air with talk of rescue and how soon she expected it would come. Mrs. Morgan said little, and Hope did no more than respond when Irene required it of her.

The deep voices of men outside the small structure indicated many of them had returned, but no one came through the hovel door. It seemed everyone come back from searching for her. When next Hope stepped out, she anticipated she would she be greeted by angry glares and accusing comments. She truly hadn't meant to cause trouble, but it seemed she excelled at doing so.

The doctor came in at last, after what seemed like hours of sitting in the hot shelter, to tell them there was food prepared. He held a large leaf the way one might hold a plate, with a large piece of white meat upon it. "You young ladies step outside and get something to eat. I will sit with my wife for a time."

Hope needed no encouragement. At the same moment she burst out of the hovel, a cool breeze came up and wrapped about her bare ankles, then cooled her perspiring forehead. Her hair would be a mess again. Snarled and sticking to her. It did not bear thinking about, though, when she could smell something absolutely delightful.

Nothing had entered her stomach since the seal meat that morning. Nothing but water. The cooked and charring fish at the fire took up all of her attention. Two of the sailors were turning sticks with fish in the flames, quite low. Another was pushing what looked like a bundle of leaves into the ashes.

Albert rested in the shade, away from the fire, seated next to the professor. Mr. Thorne and Señor Córdoba were sliding fish from sticks using leaves to grip the cooked meat.

Would Hope be expected to cook her own food? She eyed the long sticks and studied the simple method of cooking. It reminded her of using toasting forks with cheese and bread during winter holidays. It didn't look all that difficult. Yes. She certainly could manage to cook a fish.

Mr. Thorne saw the ladies lingering near the door of the hovel before anyone else. He bowed in their direction. "Miss Everly, Miss Carlbury. We have your dinner."

Oh. Well. Perhaps another day she would try her hand at roasting fish over a fire.

Mr. Thorne gestured for the ladies to sit on rocks near the hovel, then he gave Miss Carlbury the fish he had wrapped in leaves. "It will be a tricky process to eat it," he said to them both. Mr. Córdoba appeared and handed Hope his own leafy offering.

"You have had fish for dinner before, Miss Everly."

She pursed her lips as she accepted the food. "Of course. Usually it is served with wine, but this will do."

Irene sniffed. "Wine and sauces, delicious roasted carrots."

Hope had meant to tease, not to complain, but Irene obviously did not understand her comment that way. "It is a picnic, Irene." Hope kept her voice lighter this time. She unfolded her leaves and looked down at the fish, sliced open down its middle, but still with eyes in its head and a few scales along its spine. It had a bright yellow stripe along its silver body and had likely been a very pretty thing in the water where it belonged.

Alejandro still stood near, arms crossed over his dirty, worn shirt, watching her with both eyebrows raised. What was he waiting for? Her opinion on the food?

She looked down again at the fish and picked it up with one hand. Even though she had sat on a beach before, with her friends, their picnics had still been far more civilized than this. There was no cutlery, no servants, not even a cloth to wipe her hands clean when she finished.

Yet, she knew what she had to do. She reached inside the already made slit, where the fish had mercifully been cleaned before being cooked, and used her fingers to pull out the white, fleshy meat. She popped it into her mouth and closed her eyes, the food more delicious than she imagined any fish could ever be. As fish had never been a great favorite before, she very well knew the delightful taste was more the result of her hunger than flavor.

She ought to give thought to decorum. Once she started eating, however, she stopped caring at appearing poised. Hope devoured her fish as swiftly as possible.

Irene, at her side, daintily picked at each little bite, her nose wrinkled all the while.

Alejandro chuckled and went back to the fire, where Mr. Thorne already cooked another fish.

"Detestable," Irene muttered. Hope ignored her this time. She wanted to enjoy her meal rather than soothe her friend's wounded sensibilities.

ASSURED THAT EVERYONE HAD EATEN, ALEJANDRO WENT ON WATER fetching duty. He reflected again on what must be done to help the newcomers adapt to the island. Miss Everly had withdrawn to the shelter when her friend did, casting him a look which clearly communicated her frustration.

That left the burden of caring for the group to himself, the three sailors, and Thorne. It would not take long for resentment to build, should more than half the group not take part in necessary chores. The first day, they might be excused from working toward survival, given that Alejandro's presence assured its possibility. But the next day, Alejandro would need to force them into action.

He saw no more of the ladies that night, except when the three of them slipped quietly out of the hovel to attend to personal needs nearby. They did not come out again. It had to be hotter than a galley kitchen in the shelter. He rarely used it himself, except in cases of storms or after the sun had gone down.

The men gathered around the fire again, after banking the coals. The sailors talked amongst themselves in a language that was a mix of several tongues. The doctor settled with his back against the hovel itself. He likely took up that position to be near if his wife or the other ladies had any need of him. Thorne settled himself near Alejandro, at the edge of the clearing. The irksome Carlbury stayed near the fire.

"What was your life like, before this?" Thorne asked as the sky darkened.

"Before the island, or before all of you turned up on its shores?" Alejandro asked, picking up a long twig to twist in his hands. He tried to always keep busy. It was the surest way to keep his mind his own, to give it tasks and stay occupied. He had baskets he'd woven from long grasses and twigs inside his shelter. The roof was in good repair. There were snares around the island to catch unsuspecting birds and lizards. He fished. He used fibers from the trees to weave into thin ropes for nets.

Every day, he worked for survival. To liven things up, sometimes he slept during the day and worked all night.

"Before the island," Thorne clarified. "How did you end up here? Where were you before? Obviously you have some education."

Was this an attempt to place Alejandro somewhere along the rungs of society? The very thought made his spine stiffen. It hardly mattered whether he had been a prince or a poor sailor. Yet while he studied Thorne, who waited patiently for an answer, Alejandro sensed no ill will. Only curiosity. He gripped his mother's ring where it dangled from the chain about his neck.

"I am the only son of a Spanish Don. My father left Spain to colonize in Río De La Plata. My life was..." He shrugged and twisted the twig back over on itself. "I think the word is privileged."

"Your English is exceptional." Thorne settled back on the ground, putting an arm behind his head. "Why did you leave the Spanish colonies? For education?"

"Something like that." Alejandro tossed the stick away. He had never wanted to leave. Only his father's commands, his mother's pleas, had made him board a ship bound for the northern continent and what he might learn in the former British colonies. That journey had been about his political education. But he supposed it had taught him more than he might have known of the world otherwise.

The stars came out before darkness had completely fallen. They flickered to life in the sky like far distant candles lit in a cathedral, each one a prayer or a dream in the night.

Did his mother still light candles for him, or had she given up praying for a son the ocean had swallowed?

"Foraging." Hope looked up from her place near the fire when Alejandro spoke the single word with a tone bordering on hostile. "Today, I will teach you what you can and cannot eat. Fish will not be enough to sustain you."

He wasn't speaking to her, but to all gathered at the fire. When the opening of the shelter finally framed the gray light of dawn, Hope had crawled off her bed of leaves and into the morning air. Though surprised at first by the coolness of the day, and the dew beneath her feet, as soon as the sun crested the horizon she warmed considerably. Sitting on a rock, her toes in the dirt, Hope had been combing her fingers through her hair again. Trying to ignore the desire to seek Alejandro out. He had made it clear he had no wish to be near her.

"I hardly think it necessary to go traipsing about the island looking for fruit and nuts." Albert's surly response surprised Hope not a whit. Why the man had persisted in being something of a mannerless layabout, she couldn't say. Perhaps he did not enjoy the fact that someone could claim more experience and cleverness than himself at something.

"You do not think it necessary?" Alejandro repeated dryly.

Mr. Thorne jerked up to his feet. He had fetched the water that morning and had appeared rather determined to keep busy, even if that meant nothing more than shoving rocks and logs about to provide better seating around the fire. "I should like to join you, Córdoba."

Had those two become friendly? That put both gentlemen up higher in Hope's estimation. She stood too, tucking her hair back behind her ears. "As would I."

Irene, who had come to sit near the fire, shook her head without looking up at Hope. "It is not an occupation for a lady, Grace."

Then whose job is it? Hope knew well enough that ladies gathered flowers from gardens and fruit from their orchards from time to time. Women sowed seeds alongside farmer-husbands, too. If Irene meant to be waited upon hand and foot, she must expect someone to do the waiting.

"I am thinking only of helping the group as much as possible," Hope assured her, patting Irene on the shoulder as she had seen Grace do in the past to soothe agitated people. "It will be like gathering flowers or herbs. Then you may have more than fish to eat."

"The doctor will not like it," Albert said hotly.

"I will not like what?" Doctor Morgan emerged from the shelter where he had asked for privacy to examine his wife's injuries again. He came out with his coat over his arm this time. Perhaps he had finally realized that maintaining proper dress was the very least of their problems.

Hope looked down at her own gown. It had once been such a lovely shade of blue. Now it was dingy, with strips of brown and gray from her time sitting and sleeping on the ground, not to mention her soiled hem from walking about. Everything about her person had become brown except for her face. The tightness of the skin across her cheeks informed her well enough that she had sunburned.

"I am taking a party in search of food." Alejandro stood in his confident manner, on the balls of his feet, arms crossed over his nearly threadbare shirt. "Mr. Thorne and Miss Everly have volunteered."

"We can come," the largest sailor, Madden, said from where he and the other two dark-skinned men had sat to whittle at long sticks. They appeared to be making more spears, perhaps for fishing.

Alejandro nodded at them, accepting their presence in his party with ease.

"There. You need no more people than that." Albert remained lounging indolently on the ground, leaned back against a log Thorne had exerted himself to pull from the trees into the clearing. He cast a glance at his sister. "The ladies would do better to attend to Mrs. Morgan."

Another hot day spent in the shelter was the very last thing Hope desired. She shook her head and opened her mouth to remind Albert he had no say in what she did or did not do, but the doctor spoke before she could.

"I think it a fine idea for Miss Everly to go, and I shall accompany them. It is my hope to find some of the plants I know to be medicinal. Mrs. Morgan could use some relief from her pain." He pulled his coat on again. "Will you need the baskets from the shelter?"

"Of course we will." Hope did not wait for anyone to say another word about her. She hurried into the shelter, ready to make herself useful. The baskets inside were not what one would find in an English market, but she had examined them the day before and found them to be tightly woven. It seemed Alejandro had done what he could to use his resources wisely.

Mrs. Morgan rolled over when Hope entered, her eyes glittering slightly. "Miss Everly. I hear everyone talking out there. What is going on?"

Hope briefly explained the food-gathering expedition as she

gathered up the four baskets available to her. All of them had covers, like lids, affixed to the top with clever bits of fiber forming hinges. "The doctor hopes to find you medicinal herbs," she said at the last.

"One can only hope he will be successful." Mrs. Morgan winced and turned onto her back again. "I do ache so."

"We will do all we can to help." Hope offered an encouraging smile. "I will see you soon, and I will bring you something delicious to eat."

"Thank you, my dear." Mrs. Morgan closed her eyes, ending the conversation.

As Hope approached the door, Irene appeared. Her wrinkled forehead and pursed lips clearly communicated her state of mind, but when she spoke there was no word to describe her but peevish. "I cannot believe you would rather traipse about in the dirt, without shoes and stockings, no bonnet or parasol, to pick filthy plants and roots like a common peasant. You ought to let the men see to the situation."

Hope bit back her tart response. Irene's amiable nature had vanished the moment hardship came their way, and while some of her complaints might be excused, her comments had begun to nettle Hope. She pulled in a deep breath through her nose, slowly, and counted to five before answering. "Many hands make light work, and the more of us who are knowledgeable of the island will mean we are better prepared for any further hardships."

"Albert says we will be rescued in no more than a week." Irene's chin tipped upward. "Especially if we light a signal fire."

"Señor Córdoba advised against doing such a thing." Did Irene really need the reminder? "Depleting the green plants to make a smoky fire that no one might be looking for might only cause us harm."

Irene scoffed. "Why do you think that *man* has been stuck here for so long? He hasn't the intelligence to escape. Likely he is a common servant or sailor who wrecked as we did. Men of greater understanding ought to be in command."

"Miss Carlbury," the doctor's wife called from where she rested. "What has my husband to say on the matter? He is well educated in terms of the islands in the West Indies."

That question made Irene wince and lower her gaze to the ground. "Doctor Morgan is in favor of doing as that Spanish man says."

Relaxing somewhat, Hope gifted Mrs. Morgan a thankful smile. "Then we should do as Doctor Morgan says. I am certain if he thinks there is something Señor Córdoba ought to do differently, he will say so. Now. If you two will excuse me, I am certain the men are waiting on these baskets." Hope stepped around her friend, keeping a sunny smile upon her face.

"Ah, here you are, Miss Everly." Doctor Morgan bowed to her and held his hand out. "Might I take a basket from you?"

Madden came forward and held his hands out for another, bowing slightly to her with a "Thank you, miss." Then Mr. Thorne took a basket, leaving Hope with the smallest of them which she hugged to herself so no one would try to remove it from her grasp.

"*Bueno.*" Alejandro surveyed Hope, Mr. Thorne, the doctor, and the three sailors. Mr. Gibson, the professor, slept beneath the trees, snoring as though he were on holiday rather than in a dangerous situation which required his awareness. "Come with me. There are quite a few fruit trees nearby."

He gestured to the trees and took the path Hope had tried to follow him down the day before. Mr. Thorne followed, then the doctor gestured for Hope to go next, with him behind her and the sailors following at the end of the row.

Alejandro's voice rose to be heard over the sounds of their footsteps in the leaves and brush. "There are many plants I have found that are safe to eat. *Pero*, if any of you see something you recognize, I hope you will share. I discovered most of what was healthy through tests." He chuckled, the sound without humor somehow.

Thorne's tone was somewhat shocked. "How often did you poison yourself?"

"A handful of times." Because she was marching behind them down the hill, Hope saw the broad shrug of Alejandro's shoulders. "What else could I do?"

As his words settled in her mind, her heart squeezed in sympathy. The poor man. All alone and without knowledge of the plant life, he had eaten likely any number of things that did not agree with him. Could she have done the same? Eaten plants that she knew might very well kill her? She shuddered. It would take true desperation for her to take such a risk.

As they walked, Alejandro pointed to various trees and talked of whether or not he had found them useful for any reason at all. Some made his fires smell terrible, others were favored homes to birds. They were passing a tall tree bearing drooping, feathery leaves and long brown pods when the doctor cried out.

"Mimosa tree," he shouted, his eyes widening. "This is perfect."

Alejandro stopped, as did the others, and put his hands on his hips while he studied the tree. "I admit, I did not find this tree particularly helpful."

"The bark, the branches, are medicinal." The doctor left the path and went straight for the tree, his basket tucked under one arm while he reverently stroked the trunk. "It induces sleep and eases pain." His voice shook somewhat as his hand gripped a loose strip of the bark. He pulled it back, inspecting it carefully before opening his basket.

A branch hanging low over the path was near enough for Hope to touch. She reached her hand out, stroking the feathery leaves, and then gasped as the leaves folded together tightly.

"It is a sensitive plant," Alejandro said. He had stepped nearer, likely to watch the doctor. His rich brown eyes studied her before he turned his attention to the leaves, reaching up to touch them himself with one long finger. The leaves closed, as they had at her touch, as though shrinking away from the attention. "The reaction has always fascinated me."

"How strange," Hope whispered, staring at the greenery.

"In the spring and early summer, it is covered in *flores rosadas*." When she looked at him again, her eyebrows raised, he met her gaze and shrugged. "Pink flowers."

The doctor came back, tucking a thin branch into his basket and closing its lid. "I cannot believe this find. Mrs. Morgan will be grateful."

Alejandro nodded, then continued down the path. Rather than fall back in line, Hope lengthened her step to keep up with him. Thorne fell just behind her, speaking with the doctor about the tree. Of course, she remembered, he had claimed an interest in botany when they first proposed their outing to another island.

After a few moments, Alejandro glanced at Hope and shook his head somewhat, as though his private thoughts about her were not entirely pleasant.

Rather used to people looking askance at her, Hope was unprepared for Alejandro's disapproving expression and it smarted her feminine pride. He had called her beautiful. Now, she didn't know what he thought.

Hope forced a smile onto her face, trying to ignore her feelings. Despite the perspiration at her brow, and the roughness of the ground beneath her feet, she needed to find the joy and wonder in the moment. Had she not had a mind bent toward adventure and courageous exploits, she very well might have been as hysterical or irritable as Irene.

"Are you tired, Miss Everly?" Alejandro asked, facing forward again.

"Not at all. I enjoy the exercise." She meant her words, too. Though even if she had been tired, Hope would not have said so. Her bravado had seen her through too many scrapes to let it go in the midst of the greatest calamity to ever befall her.

"I think Miss Everly must be distantly related to Magellan," Mr. Thorne said from behind, reminding her nothing she said was private during this march. "Not many young ladies of my acquaintance would sound as delighted by this romp as they would be by taking a turn in a park."

Hope sniffed and glanced over her shoulder at him. "Perhaps they would, sir. I cannot think many young ladies of your acquaintance have had the opportunity to prove themselves equal to the task."

Mr. Thorne chuckled and a genuinely pleasant expression appeared on his face. Yes, Hope saw why Irene found the gentleman appealing. He was a pleasant sort, and handsome. Yet he had said he was as good as engaged, and that ought to have been enough to keep Irene from staring after him.

Hope faced forward again, in time to see Alejandro holding a branch out of her way. As a true gentleman would. How Albert and Irene could doubt that about him she did not know. Surely anyone forced to endure what he had would appear more than a little rough around the edges. But he had kept his sanity and treated those now encroaching upon him with respect. Except Albert, which made sense as the man had been wretched to Alejandro.

"Ah, here we are." Alejandro stopped them near a large flowering shrub. "I knew this one was safe."

One of the sailors whistled a cheerful note. "Firebush."

The tall, thinly branched shrub was covered in leaves of green and gold, with purple fruit that appeared rather like grapes hanging from the smaller branches. The sailors fell to gathering them with haste and wide grins. They must be delicious given the excitement with which the men reacted.

"Have you never had them?" Alejandro asked. "They grow near my home, too." He plucked a purple berry where it nestled among several that were red. "Try it."

Hope studied the fruit before taking it slowly from his palm, the tips of her fingers brushing his warm hand. "Is it like a grape?" She turned it about, studying the shining peel.

Alejandro raised his eyebrows, a mischievous glint appearing in his eyes. What must he look like without his beard and long hair? Likely quite handsome, given how he managed to be charming even while attempting to act surly. "Are you afraid of it?"

His words were as good as a dare. Hope popped the fruit into her mouth and bit down. The fruit burst in her mouth, at first sweet and tart. Hope couldn't help but hum in appreciation and reached for another, the juice in her mouth immediately making her grateful for something other than dried meat and fish.

When she pressed the next berry to her lips, however, she winced. "Oh." The fruit had deceived her—bitter followed the sweetness on her tongue.

Doctor Morgan walked by her, too excited to stop, though he was muttering to himself. "What a find. Prevents sunstroke, heals burns. Absolutely marvelous."

Hope turned a glare onto Alejandro, whose dark eyes glittered with amusement. "That was an underhanded trick, *señor.*"

"*Sí.* Perhaps." He plucked a handful of the grape-like objects and held them out to her. "Not everyone tastes the bitterness. My father told me it was good luck if you did. I think he tried to make me feel better when I could not enjoy them as my brother did. But if you cook the berries, the bitterness is gone. Here." He gestured for her to open her basket, which she did somewhat distrustfully. "It is good for you, too."

"Of course it is," Hope said darkly. The way his eyes lightened made her wonder if he smiled beneath his beard. "Are there many more such helpful fruits on the island?"

Alejandro gestured to the path. "Many. But I will not surprise you like that again. Do you see that tree, over there? They call it *jaboncillo.* In English, soapberry. The berries are red when they are ripe, but if you peel them, you could use them as you would any soap."

"Fascinating, and likely useful, but I would prefer something that tastes like fruit." A breeze caused Hope's hair to lift and stir before her face. She pushed it back somewhat impatiently.

"They taste like lemonade." He studied the tree a moment. "But I do not see any ripe just yet. *Qué lástima*. A shame." He turned his attention back to her, and Hope cocked her head to one side. He snapped his fingers. "I think I have something." Alejandro whistled for the attention of the others. "Miss Everly wishes to sample a different fruit. Come, to the beach."

Hope followed, her basket tucked against her hip, and as they traveled down to the shore, the path opened enough for her to walk next to Alejandro. "How many of the wrong sorts of fruit *did* you eat?"

"More than you will, Miss Everly." He lifted a branch above their heads and gestured for her to go first. From behind, she could hear the doctor and Mr. Thorne speaking about the bark, roots, and fruit they had already gathered.

Alejandro came under the branch with her, leaving the gentlemen behind to clear their own path. "Next you will have sea grapes. They are very good. Then we will find edible roots. Many of them are edible, there is a particular kind which reminds me of potatoes, but they are richer. There is tamarind, or something like it. Wild onions."

He almost sounded cheerful as he listed off the fruits and seeds he had found during his time on the island. Considering how miserable he had seemed from the moment the others had come ashore, Hope hadn't expected to see any sign of good humor in him.

Anyone in his circumstances was entitled to feel grumpy. Had he experienced even one moment of actual happiness while alone on this island? It had been presumptuous of her, of course, to think he felt anything toward her other than gratitude for no longer being alone. The sooner she accepted that, the better.

Near the shore, with the waves crashing against the sand, he showed the group his sea grapes. Hope gathered plenty before she started looking back, out over the water. There were no storm clouds on the horizon today. It would be perhaps the first time anyone might brave the ocean to come looking for their party. By now the people of St. Kitt's had to realize something horrible had happened. Would her eyes catch the sight of a sail above the waves?

Without meaning to, Hope started walking to the water's edge. She stopped at the line in the sand where the waves had ceased their approach and shaded her eyes. The loud shushing of wind and water filled her ears, the waves collapsing against each other in heavy crashes. Water danced up, nearly to her toes.

She saw nothing but water, and birds flying overhead. Nothing in any direction she looked.

When Alejandro joined her, she did not glance at him. The vast water before her took up too much of her attention, too much of her hope. Somewhere out there, people were looking for her. They had to be. How else would she ever make it home again? Grace was on the other side of the ocean. And the rest of her family. Silas, Esther, Isaac, Jacob. They were all there, not even aware of her predicament. What would they say when they learned she had washed up on a tropical island where a real Robinson Crusoe lived? They would hardly believe it.

The salty breeze stung her eyes. Hope did not realize how it had irritated her until a tear slipped down her cheek.

"Miss Everly?" Alejandro's voice was nearly too soft to hear over the waves.

She looked at him, brushing at the tear. "Yes, Señor Córdoba?" He regarded her beneath his shaggy hair, as mussed by the wind as her own, with a most solemn expression.

"I will not let anything bad happen to you," he said quietly. "I promise."

A dry laugh that choked off like a sob escaped her. "Thank you." His sincerity made the promise no less ridiculous. What could befall her that would be worse than being stranded on an island, not knowing when rescue would come?

It would come. Hope knew it must. It was only a matter of time.

They rejoined the others and Alejandro took them back into the trees in search of edible food growing beneath the ground. He even climbed a tree to show them where they might find eggs, but admonished the other sailors—the only ones capable of that same physical feat—to always leave more eggs than they took. He added the small brown-shelled eggs to her basket.

After what seemed like hours poking through bushes and digging between the roots of trees, all the baskets were full. The doctor had even taken off his coat and made a rudimentary bag of sorts from it to carry more barks and leaves he said had medicinal properties that might help all those shipwrecked avoid dysentery. As unpleasant as that thought was, Hope appreciated his practicality.

When they arrived back at the clearing, Alejandro gathered the firebush berries into his pail, with very little water, and took up a clean stone. He apparently meant to make some sort of mashed concoction from the fruit.

Irene emerged from the hut when she heard their voices and met Hope's gaze but did not return her cheerful wave.

"It is nearly midday," Irene said, arms pressed tightly against her sides. "Did you find food?"

Forcing herself to sound cheery, as though she had not noticed Irene's chilly reception, Hope answered with vivacity. "Yes, a great deal of it." Hope opened her basket and took out a handful of the sea grapes. "Here. Try these. A lot of it needs to be prepared first. But there are these things like potatoes, and Mr. Thorne caught two crabs. There will be enough to eat."

Irene's bottom lip trembled. "I dare say that is a relief." She looked to the door of the hut as the doctor entered and stiffened.

"Mrs. Morgan has slept nearly the whole of the morning. I have been dreadfully bored."

Though she might still be frightened, Irene obviously coped with the feeling much differently than Hope ever would. The irritation in her voice, acting as though the entire experience was an inconvenience rather than an opportunity, made no sense at all.

Hope placed her basket on the ground. "Would you like to come to the beach with me?" Hope asked, holding out her hands. "I am afraid food gathering was quite a chore. I am covered in soil and sand."

"Then going to the beach will hardly help," Irene bit out. "No, thank you. Perhaps my brother will escort you." She pointed to where the professor sat beneath the trees and Hope shaded her eyes to peer in that direction.

"I do not see him."

Irene's hand dropped and she sucked in a harsh breath. "He was there a moment ago."

With a careless and somewhat relieved smile, Hope gestured to the beach's path again. "He is likely off exploring. Please come, Irene. Perhaps the water will help cheer you. Sea bathing is all the rage among the *ton*, after all."

"I have no intention of getting so much as a drop of water upon my person." Irene fisted some of her skirt in one hand. "Go on. Lead the way. I suppose I had better learn where this well is that produces our putrid water."

Hope looped her arm through Irene's, pleased with herself for acting as magnanimously as her sister would have. "It is not all terrible. The walk is lovely. We can discuss how we will share our story when we go home, impressing all the gentlemen with our level heads and capabilities."

"As well as our brown skin, chapped hands and feet, and horrid thinness." Irene issued the most ladylike snort Hope had ever heard. They left the clearing and started down the narrow path to the shore. "No gentleman will be impressed by this nightmare."

"It cannot last long." Reassuring Irene came more easily than reassuring herself had. "It is an adventure. You may fill your entire diary with this singular experience and speak of it to your grandchildren someday."

Though Irene continued to stubbornly disagree with any positive point Hope attempted, Hope's mood lightened considerably. Grace would be so proud of her when she heard the whole story.

✿ 13 ✿

T he third day, Alejandro organized the men into teams for fishing and tending the fire. Everyone but the belligerent *idiota* Carlsbury took up their tasks without complaint. Doctor Morgan stayed close to his wife, who was brought out to lay in the shade to rest. Based on the way the man looked after her, there was more to her ailment than bruised ribs. The woman herself spoke to Alejandro with great comportment, thanking him for all his help.

Alejandro gave himself the task of seeing to the things he had pulled up from the storm. He dried out the seaweed by laying it out on the rocks of his shelter. Most of the grasses the storm pulled up were edible. He tore some of the sail into strips, too, despite the sharp glares Carlsbury gave him.

The cloth was beyond saving, if the man had hoped to create a sailed raft. He had started speaking of the possibility of building a small boat shortly after dawn.

Once, Alejandro had considered the same. But he did not know how far from course he had blown, and he was not a man of the sea. While he might follow the Northern Star or the Southern

Cross as well as any boy versed in basic astronomy, he knew not which direction land and help might lie.

The sailors had listened to Carlbury's idea for a time, but as none of them were quick to agree with him, they likely faced the same trouble as Alejandro. That, or they were reluctant to risk themselves when help might still come for them.

He wound a long strip of cloth around his hand, contemplating the best use for it. Given the number of people under his care, it might be best to reserve the cloth for bandages and repairs to important tools. The largest section would hang off the rocks behind the shelter, over a steep wall of black rock. The sail would stand out to any boats that might come looking for the stranded English.

From where he sat on the rocks, Alejandro easily saw the clearing below. Carlbury had disappeared when Madden and Hitchens left to fish. They would be gone until near sundown, free to lay upon the beach away from the English gentleman's prattle.

A shrill voice caught his attention and he narrowed his eyes, watching as Carlbury's sister came storming up the path to the beach. She was shaking out her hands and screeching, punctuating her words with violent trembles of her body. "Disgusting, primitive, cursed island," she yelled.

Doctor Morgan stood beside his wife, still beneath the tree.

Miss Everly came into view, her eyes larger than normal. She spoke soothingly, too softly for Alejandro to hear. He looked down at his work and made a decision, scooping up a thin piece of sailcloth before pinning the rest into place with a rock and climbing down from his perch.

He approached the women where they stood, the Carlbury girl spinning about, inspecting her skirts.

"I am certain there are no more," Miss Everly said, holding her hands out in a placating gesture.

"*Qué les pasó, señoritas?* What did you see?" Alejandro asked, stepping up next to the calmer of the two females.

"A spider," Miss Everly said quietly, her lips twitching.

"A monster," shrieked Miss Carlbury. "A beastly, hairy, awful thing the size of a rat." She shuddered again and recommenced shaking out her arms.

Alejandro relaxed. "The larger spiders do less harm than the smaller."

The irate woman stopped flicking her skirts and glared at him, as though holding him responsible for the wildlife of the island and its treachery. "Where is my brother?"

"*No sé*, señorita. Perhaps he went on a walk." Alejandro didn't care where the man went if it meant hearing less of his complaints and superior attitude.

The woman stomped her foot, growled, and stormed toward the hut. She spent more time inside the stifling little shelter than could possibly be healthy. She paused in the makeshift doorway, turning to glare over her shoulder. "Are you coming, Grace?"

Raising his eyebrow, Alejandro turned to take in the disappointed frown on Miss Everly's lovely face. Even sunburnt, her fine features made his heart ache. Had a woman ever been as beautiful as she, or had she put him under some sort of spell when he saw her upon the beach for the first time?

She shuffled sideways rather than step forward, her indecision written across her face.

"Are you her maid?" Alejandro asked quietly. "Must you go where she wishes at all times?" He knew this was not the case. Knew from the way Miss Everly acted that she and the other lady were equals in station even if Miss Carlbury pretended to be superior.

Her gaze cut to his, and she shook her head. "No."

"Well?" the other woman called, impatience making her already acidic tone more distasteful.

Miss Everly tipped her chin up, turning to face her friend. "I cannot retire just yet. I am much too warm from our walk to endure the shelter. I will join you once I have cooled." One would think she spoke of entering a fine house after a walk in the garden rather than a climb uphill in the humidity.

"Please yourself, then." With that tart response, the unpleasant young woman disappeared into the darkness of the shelter.

Alejandro glanced from her point of departure back to Miss Everly, who appeared to rethink her decision. Each time he spoke to her alone, her good cheer and bold smile had fed his curiosity about her, made his heart stir in an alarming manner. But as soon as she was near the Carlburys she shrunk inside herself, becoming coaxing rather than confident.

"Should I tell her I have found spiders in the hut before?" he asked on a whim, voice lowered.

Her eyebrows flew up and she turned, her mouth dropping open. "You have?"

He chuckled. "Once or twice, in the beginning. We are on their island, Miss Everly. They go where they please."

She covered her mouth with one hand and looked again to where her friend had gone. "Dear me. Irene does hate spiders. But you have seen none inside the shelter of late?" she asked, tilting her head to the side as she regarded him.

Alejandro pretended to think on it, but when he caught her lips curving upward he relaxed his stance and shook his head. "She is safe enough. I promise." Another promise to her. What was it about this woman that inspired that word to slip from his lips with such ease?

Brushing aside the uncomfortable thought, Alejandro held out the bit of cloth he had brought down from the rocks. "Here. It is not a satin ribbon, but it is the best I could do."

Her already pink cheeks reddened as she looked at his pitiful offering. He felt his cheeks warming, too. At home, gifting ribbon to a young lady was a flirtatious thing to do, a way to indicate interest if they were not yet courting. Here, it could only be practical. He had watched Miss Everly continually struggle to comb through her long hair with her fingers, watched her attempt plaits that only undid themselves after a few moments of movement.

"It is not pretty," he said, studying the limp, ivory-colored cloth. "But it will solve your problem." If she did not wish to accept the ribbon, such as it was, he could understand.

She put a hand to her hair and raised her eyes to his. "It is rather dreadful, isn't it?"

His eyes skimmed her hair from the smooth plane of her forehead down to where it curled about her ear, then cascaded down to her shoulders in rich brown waves. She had braided it, knotted it about itself, pushed it out of the way, and even tucked it into her dress that morning. Still her hair rioted about her, blown by the breeze and teased by twigs and leaves when she passed beneath trees.

"No. Your hair, it is *cabello hermoso. Muy bonita.* I only think you wish not to catch it in the trees so often, yes?" He held out his makeshift ribbon again. "Try it. *Por favor.*"

"Even at home my hair does not do as I wish." She forced a smile and held her hand out, accepting the ribbon from him. Alejandro was careful not to brush her skin as he pooled the ribbon in her palm. "My sister, however, has absolutely perfect hair. If she wished it to curl into rosebuds, I think it would."

"Which sister?" he asked, watching as she started twisting the dark strands before realizing a gentleman would not stare at a woman dressing her hair. He averted his eyes, then winced. A few hours in the presence of others and he acted as if society's rules had a place in his life. What was next? Dressing for dinner? Starched cravats and shining leather shoes? He ran his hand through his hair, more wild than Miss Everly's, and considered the futility of assisting her to keep herself put in order.

"My twin sister. She and I look rather like a matched set of gloves. Except her hair behaves better." She pushed her now neatened plait of hair over her shoulder. "Thank you for your gift,

Señor Córdoba." She did not speak her thanks shyly, but strongly, with a bold grin and sparkle in her blue eyes.

Alejandro brushed his hand through his beard. "*De nada*, Miss Everly." He rapped his knuckles against his thigh, glancing about the clearing. "Is there anything else I might do for you?"

She hesitated to answer, darting a glance over her shoulder at the hut. "Perhaps. If you do not think it too forward to ask. Would you mind escorting me to the well? There are so many of us, the water disappears dreadfully fast, with only the one pail."

"Of course, if that is what you wish." He went to fetch the pail, a piece of equipment he had once never paused to consider in his life before the island, and now it was an important part of his existence. He hauled water, boiled in it, cooked food inside it. Something others took for granted had become a treasure to him, washed ashore by the sea.

He arrived back at her side, bucket in hand, and gestured to the path they had traversed together two days previous. Miss Everly went ahead of him on the narrow path, her hands swinging at her side like a child rather than a lady taught proper decorum.

Her bare feet skirted tree roots and larger stones. How had she adapted to that aspect of the island with such speed? He never heard her complain, whereas her friend never spoke unless it was to vent her spleen.

What had her life been like before she came here? Not a single woman of his former acquaintance would have accepted their fate upon this island as she had.

"Where did you say you were from, Alejandro?" she asked, as though she had read his mind and found herself as curious as he. She peered over her shoulder at him. "Río de le Plata?"

"Part of a viceroyalty," he answered. "There is a governor, tied directly to the politics of the courts in *España*, who oversees everything from the laws to tax collection." The path widened enough for him to lengthen his stride, coming to walk next to her. "My father, he is a *peninsular*, one who was born in *España* and came to the colonies to seek his wealth. He is from an old family that ran out of estates to give to younger sons."

The young woman nodded, her lips pursed as she considered what he said. "Were you born in Spain?"

"No, Miss Everly. I am *un criollo*. Of a sort. I was born in Buenos Aires and educated by monks at our only university."

"Yes. So you could learn how to properly run a country after a revolution." At that her expression changed from one of curiosity to amusement, her lips twitching upward. Every time she did that, he wondered how easily he might make her laugh. "I should not say as much to the others, señor. There are some among my party who doubtless still hold out hope the former colonies will beg for English rule once more. I have heard as much from many gentlemen, especially since the revolution in France has proven such a debacle."

"People will always fight for their freedom, Miss Everly, even if it takes several tries to get it right." Alejandro moved a branch out of their way, letting her slip beneath it before ducking under himself. "My father was loyal to the courts for many years. Until the British attacked our lands and Ferdinand's government proved weak." He stared up at the cloudless sky, his father's severe frown coming to mind. *"Papá,* he called Ferdinand *un león sin dientes.* A lion—"

"—Without teeth," she finished for him, her eyes sparkling. "That is an apt description for a king imprisoned."

"*Sí.* You speak *español*, Miss Everly?"

"I have some knowledge of Latin and French, Señor Córdoba." She stepped over a large rock as gracefully as she could with her long tattered skirts. "It is not difficult to understand what you say, even if I am not entirely capable of speaking the language myself."

That made sense. Alejandro stepped out of the trees and into the small ditch, his eyes on the well. The dune beyond it hid the shoreline from sight but the crash of waves were easily heard.

"I am grateful for that sound," Miss Everly murmured, pausing at the edge of the stone well. "If I close my eyes, I can pretend I am home." She did just that, her dark eyelashes resting against her sunburned cheeks. Alejandro let himself enjoy the moment, watching the beautiful woman experience a moment of peace in their uncertain situation. Her pink lips, somewhat chapped, even turned upward in a wistful smile.

Such a shame that she would not hear the waves of her home-land again.

That thought shot through him, bitter to his mind as cardamom to his tongue, and he turned to his task at the well. He tied the rope to the pail and dropped it into the water, glaring into the shaded pool below.

"Is something wrong?" Miss Everly's voice had such an inter-esting quality to it. He would not describe her manner of speaking as soft, though he sensed kindness in her nature. No, she demanded answers, even if she did so politely.

"I am sorry that you are here," he answered, granting her truth rather than a perpetuation of the lie that rescue would come. "You have a family who will miss you. This is no place for a woman such as you, Miss Everly."

"It isn't really a place for anyone," she said, tone light. "I am terribly sorry that you have been here alone all this time. I cannot think it has been easy for you. Yet it must feel as though we have invaded whatever peace it is you have found in your time here."

Surprised by that observation, he looked directly at her. How had she stumbled upon that thought? It was one he had turned about in his own mind without having found a satisfactory way to explain himself. "I cannot be happy there are more people trapped here," he said. "And it is true, I am troubled by what it means to have people to care for who might not wish for my help. But—" He broke off and frowned into the water, then started hauling the bucket up again.

"But it must be somewhat of a relief to know you are not all alone." Miss Everly took a step closer to him, though they were still easily an arm's distance away. "I think I can understand that, señor. Where I am from, I have a wonderful family and friends I love and treasure. To be without them is difficult. There is no one like my sister. I tell her everything."

"You have Miss Carlbury," he reminded her, wondering if that was any sort of balm to the loneliness she expressed. "She at least knows you."

"Yes. Irene knows me." She turned away from him, toward the dune and the waves beyond. "But I would not say she understands. Not the way my sister does. You know, it was nearly my sister who came on the voyage with the Carlburys instead of me."

He clasped the handle of the pail and lowered it to the ground beside him, covering the well again. "Does it give you relief to know you are here instead of her?" he asked. "I cannot imagine wishing another in my place."

"I would never wish that for her," she admitted easily. "My sister is not the sort who likes to be far from home. I do not think she would have had quite Miss Carlbury's reaction to this disaster, but I imagine she would be more likely to sit quietly and wait for instruction than I have been." Her eyes gazed further than the skyline, likely reaching into memory as she considered her sister. "It is a good thing I came in her place."

That was a strange way to phrase it. Alejandro picked up the bucket and stepped onto the path. "We have your water, Miss Everly."

"Oh. I suppose that means we must go back." Her stare sank to the ground, then she clasped her hands behind her back. "I hoped it would take longer." She started up the path again.

Why would she say that? Did she wish for more time with him, or less time sitting idle? He considered how he might ask without being too forward, but immediately chastised himself. He had already made it clear through his actions that nothing could pass between them.

It did not matter if he longed to spend more time in her

company. They were not in the fine parlors of Virginia, where he had paid court to the daughters of prominent lawyers and merchants, nor were they taking refreshment on his mother's veranda in Río de La Plata. They were not in England, where he had heard customs were just as strict in terms of the relations between men and women. They were walking in the dirt and sand, barefoot, without the rules of any society to enforce consequences upon them.

Yet he wanted to hear, perhaps once more, what she felt when she came near him.

"Why do you wish to be away from the others?" he asked from behind her.

She hesitated and he nearly bumped into her, but instead pulled the bucket closer with both hands to avoid losing any water.

"It isn't that I wish to be away." She turned, the slight elevation of the hill bringing her nearly eye level with Alejandro. "I enjoy speaking to you. And moving about. When I am with the others, they expect me to behave myself as I would at home. Sit quietly, make conversation, and wait for others to tell me what to do." Her eyes took on a somewhat sly look which he caught just before she turned again. "Of course, I do not exactly do those things, even in England." A bittersweet smile graced her lips. "With you, I feel happier."

Then she started up the hill again, leaving him to wonder what sort of young lady she was at home and if they would have liked each other had they met under the watchful eyes of England's propriety.

He made her happy. If only he could free her from the island. If only Carlbury did not hover about her with such an air of possession. If only Alejandro knew, with a surety, that his family remained safe and their wealth secure. Then things would be different.

But there were far too many "if onlys" for him to entertain.

❧ 14 ❧

"**M**iss Everly?"

Hope raised her gaze from the berry and root broth she had made in the bottom of their water pail, trying not to make a face as bitter as the taste. The concoction wasn't precisely tea, nor was it really soup, but the doctor had assured her it would prove a restorative drink for his wife. With an earnest desire to prove herself helpful, Hope had volunteered to create the potion for Mrs. Morgan.

Albert Carlbury stood over her, shifting from one foot to the other with hands hanging limply at his side. "Would you, perhaps, wish to join me on a short walk? After you are finished here, of course."

Kneeling by the fire, perspiration upon her forehead and dirt beneath her fingernails, Hope had never felt less like a gently-bred young lady in her life. Yet Albert conducted himself in the exact manner he would have in any English drawing room. The incongruity puzzled her for a moment.

"A walk?" Hope came to her feet and brushed the soil and bits of grass from her dress. "I suppose a respite from the clearing would be welcome." She used the corner of her gown to take the handle of the pail. "Let me make certain Doctor Morgan finds this acceptable." She did not clarify whether it was the contents of the bucket or Albert's company for which she sought the doctor's approval.

Though Albert had always conducted himself as a gentleman, she had no desire to do anything with him that could be even remotely construed as inappropriate.

The doctor and Mrs. Morgan were in the shade again, he leaning against a tree and she resting with her head in his lap. Hope approached with her steaming pail, admiring the picture they made together. Rarely had she seen married couples outside of her own parents display such affection in public. But Mrs. Morgan's injury and their predicament had apparently given the Morgans leave to relax some social customs. They stared at each other, conversing, with such gentle expressions. Neither smiled, yet one could immediately tell they were comfortable and happy with one another.

Their happy intimacy stirred a new sort of longing in Hope's breast. Courtship had not interested her so much as filling her days with activity and excitement. But as tired as she was, their peaceful companionship struck her as something secure even in the uncertain circumstances the whole group found themselves in.

"I have your medicinal tea, Mrs. Morgan," Hope said as she drew closer, not entirely certain they were aware enough of the world around them to see her approach.

Mrs. Morgan directed a pleased smile to Hope. "Thank you, dear. I am most grateful."

The doctor helped her sit up, keeping one arm about her until his wife leaned against the tree. "Here. Let me fill your cup, Lillian." The doctor produced a tall wooden cup, gifted to them by Alejandro only that morning. He had provided the sailors with more wood suitable for carving, as all three had knives about their person, and given Mrs. Morgan the only cup he'd made for himself before their coming. A most thoughtful gesture.

As the doctor tipped the contents of the pail into the cup, Hope glanced over her shoulder to see Irene and her brother on the opposite side of the clearing conversing.

Maybe he had invited his sister on their walk, too.

"Doctor? Mr. Carlbury has asked me to accompany him on a walk. Does that meet with your approval?"

He glanced up briefly, his eyebrows drawn together. "You did not inform me yesterday where you went when you fetched water with our island host."

No, she had not. "And you made certain I knew I ought to do so next time," she reminded him, forcing sweetness into her smile. "I assume that measure of considerate behavior extends to anyone in our group."

"Likely a safe assumption." He handed the cup to his wife, then scratched at the beard thickening at his chin. After only a few days, all the men had varying amounts of facial hair appearing. The doctor's was mostly black with a few gray spots as well, very much like salt and pepper. "Yes, but do not be gone long. There is no sense in overexerting yourself in this heat."

Hope easily agreed to that stipulation and went to inform Albert. She kept brushing her hands on her gown, but the grime of both skin and fabric meant nothing at all felt clean. Somehow, Hope needed to find a way to wash herself and her clothing. All the men had taken turns fishing and apparently used the opportunity to bathe, too. They all looked much cleaner than she felt, despite their beards.

"Hello, Irene. Your brother and I were about to take a walk. Will you be joining us?" Hope asked, hoping the question might serve as an invitation if Albert hadn't thought to extend one to his sister.

Irene crossed her arms over her chest and cast her brother a look obviously meant to convey irritation. "I think not. As dreadfully bored as I am, I have no wish to traipse about in the jungle."

"You might loan Miss Everly your shoes," Albert said, narrowing his eyes at his sister and pointing to her feet. "She has had none since we came, though I do believe Miss Everly has walked twice the amount you have."

Wearing shoes that were too large, and had been on the feet of another for several days, did not appeal to Hope at all. "Please, do not trouble yourselves over shoes. I am quite content as I am. My feet have grown accustomed to the ground, so long as it is not too rocky."

"There, you see," Irene said, her chin coming up. "Grace is perfectly adept, and you will not be gone long."

"No." Albert gave up with a weary shake of his head. "Very well. Come, Miss Everly. I found a path that I think you will enjoy." He offered Hope his arm, which she took somewhat hesitantly. Albert did not wear a coat, but his cravat was still knotted about his throat, and his hat resting on his head. How he'd had the presence of mind to keep his head covering in the midst of a storm still amused her. Had he been much help in the boat with the others, or had he kept a hand clamped to the top of his head for the whole of the row from sinking sloop to shore?

They said nothing until they were beneath the shade of the trees. Albert broke the silence first.

"I must say, Miss Everly, your reaction to our predicament has certainly impressed me. Impressed everyone, I should say. There are not many young ladies raised in society who would greet this desperate situation with such practicality and grace."

Would Irene appreciate such a subtle comparison of her reaction to Hope's? Likely not. "Thank you." What more was she to say? She could hardly offer him a similar compliment. Though not as vocal as Irene, Albert had voiced a great many complaints of his own.

"My sister is fortunate to have you by her side," he continued after a pause. "This is a nightmare for her, but your example will see her through it. You are a steadying influence upon her, Miss Everly. I cannot help but think of what may have happened had your sister joined us instead."

Hope stiffened without meaning to, and she immediately let go of his arm to brush an insect from her gown to excuse the movement. She did not take his arm up again. "I am certain Hope would have been of great help, too. She has an adventurous spirit but is as practical as I am."

"Not that I have seen." Albert moved a branch out of their path, holding it aside until she passed. "But you know her best, of course."

What did this man hope to accomplish, dragging her on a walk in which he simultaneously complimented her and insulted other women? There had to be a point to the excursion.

He cleared his throat. "I have seen you in conversation with Córdoba."

Ah, perhaps this was the crux of the invitation. "Yes, I find his knowledge of the island fascinating." And the man himself stirred her in ways she would never admit aloud to one such as Albert Carlbury.

"If he has been here a year, as he says, I find it disappointing." Albert came up beside her once more, his hands tucked behind him. "In a year's time, he has not attempted to escape. I should have built a raft already, or kept signal fires burning."

"I have heard his reasoning against both those things." They all had. Hope tilted her head back to better take in Albert's smirk. "Have you a plan of some sort, Mr. Carlbury?"

"Perhaps, though I intend to keep it to myself for the time being." His chest puffed out rather like a rooster's. "I do wonder if everything that man has told us is true. He could be no more than a deckhand from a Spanish merchant ship, you know. With the war, he would have reason enough to hide his identity from us."

As one who had spent the past few months actively seeking to deceive others, Hope saw no indication of Alejandro doing the same. She lifted one shoulder and let it fall, declining to comment.

"I certainly haven't seen any sign of gentlemanly behavior from him." Albert chuckled. "The man looks like he was raised by savages."

"I suppose a year without a barber might do that to a person," Hope said at last, bristling. "I do hope rescue will come before your appearance more closely resembles his, given how abhorrent you find beards."

"It is more than the beard." Albert flicked his hand in the air dismissively. "But I suppose you have not studied him as closely as I have. I do worry for your safety, and Irene's, when he or the sailors are about. Neither of you should be left unattended."

Hope bit her tongue and let her eyes wander into the trees, looking for something, anything, different to talk about. She caught sight of a tree bearing fruit and pointed. "Oh, look. Should we gather some of those? They look like apples."

Albert's displeasure showed plainly when he followed the line of her finger to the tree. "We haven't any baskets. And they look like crab apples. I would leave them for now. Perhaps come back when they've had a chance to ripen. If we are even here that long." As he kept walking, she had no choice but to keep pace with him.

Though Hope's sense of direction was not especially remarkable, she sensed well enough that their path had begun to loop back toward the clearing. Good. Making idle conversation with Albert had done nothing for her morale.

"We have been here for several days," Hope said, gathering her skirt in one hand to step over a particularly troublesome rock. "How much longer do you think it might take?"

"With no way to signal we are on this particular island, I cannot say." Of course Albert would bring the conversation back to his plans. "But do not fear, Miss Everly. I will not let you die an old maid upon this rock."

Hope's spine stiffened. "That is hardly something I worry over,

Mr. Carlbury." She did not turn to look at him, but hastened her step. Speaking of her marital state to this man, no matter their circumstances, remained distasteful to her.

She heard his boots against the ground, thumping at a quicker rate than her pace, and the nape of her neck sent a prickle of icy worry down the rest of her spine. Like a doe stalked in a forest, she became aware of how much larger and stronger her pursuer was than she.

I have nothing to fear from Albert.

Telling herself that fact did not erase her uneasiness. When he drew even with her and took her arm in his strong, long-fingered hand, Hope's immediate reaction was to jerk her arm away.

But he kept hold of her. Staring down at her with a puzzled frown. "Are you in a hurry to return to your boredom?"

When she spoke, her voice came out with a tremble she hoped he did not hear. "The doctor said not to be gone long."

Albert regarded her with perplexity, still holding her arm. How could he be so unaware of the discomfort he caused, touching her thus? Holding her against her will, however gentle the hold? He released her at last and it was all Hope could do not to bolt away from him again.

Though she had always found him repugnant, Hope had never been afraid of him. Of any man. But before that moment, when he threw her maidenhood into her notice, without the bounds of society to protect it, everything tilted. Albert might keep his distance when a world of rules said he must. But if they stayed too long trapped on the island, would he be as much a gentleman as Alejandro, or become more insistent in his suit?

"We had better not worry the doctor, then." Albert gestured to the path, for her to lead. Though Hope disliked having him behind her, she nodded her thanks and continued on her way, as fast as before.

When she came out into the clearing again, at nearly the same place they had entered the trees together, Hope's gaze collided almost at once with Alejandro's where he sat near the coals of the fire, weaving a basket. Even from a distance of several yards, Hope thought his eyes lit up when he saw her, only to dim again as they took in Albert coming to stand beside her.

Albert said something, but Hope did not pay enough attention to reply. She whispered her excuses and returned to her place by the doctor and Mrs. Morgan.

***

THOUGH HE WAS NOT AS INTIMATELY ACQUAINTED WITH MISS Everly as he wished, Alejandro read the expression she wore with ease. Her lips were pale, as he imagined the rest of her would be was she not sunburnt, and her eyes were round. Something had frightened her, and given the lack of a similar emotion on the face of her companion, Alejandro drew his conclusion.

When the woman sought out the married couple instead of her young friend, that further drove the idea into his head. What was the nature of the relationship between Miss Everly and Carlbury? The man acted as though he had a right to stand near her, to speak for her. The strong-willed woman continually made her own decisions, yet she never directly rebuffed him.

No one else seemed concerned with the two of them spending time together. It wasn't Alejandro's business to worry over Miss Everly's relationships with the others. Not at all. And he'd been forced into the life of a recluse for over a year. He knew nothing about the connections of the people around him, and almost nothing of people in general. At least it felt that way.

The professor tottered over, his sleeves rolled up to his elbows and wearing no shoes or stockings, though he had retained both in the wreck. The older man lowered himself with a grunt onto the grass next to Alejandro. "What are you making, sir?"

"A basket." One would think that was evident enough.

Alejandro held it toward the man for his inspection. "More mouths to feed means more food to gather and store. This will help."

"Sound thinking, to be certain." The professor huffed and scratched at his temple. "I am having a blasted time here, Córdoba. Have you seen any plants that might make a fair stand-in for tobacco?"

Alejandro studied the sallow look of the man's face, the deep circles under his eyes, and then watched the man's trembling fingers go back to his leg. "No. Not as such. Though I imagine if you take one of the doctor's herbal creations, it will help. You smoked a great deal before, *sí*?"

"*Sí*." The professor plucked at a bit of a grass and put the end of it in his mouth. "I've never been so long without a pipe. I even enjoyed a *cigarro*, once. Have you had them?"

The manner Spaniards had of rolling tobacco in leaves or paper to smoke had fascinated him as a boy. "My father said they would make me cough. They were not considered appropriate for a man of my standing." Alejandro shrugged. "But I tried one. Once. My father was right."

The professor laughed and then started coughing himself. Alejandro reached for the new cup he'd made and dipped it into the water pail, then offered it to the older man.

"Thank you," he wheezed, then threw back the entirety of the cup's contents. "Ah. Water. I cannot say I have ever liked the stuff. Give me coffee before water, rum before coffee, and bourbon above all. Though I did visit the Pacific Islands once. They had a different drink there." He hummed to himself, obviously trying to recall the name of whatever he had imbibed.

Alejandro said nothing. The professor did not seem to require any answering conversation. He remained quietly humming to himself long after Alejandro knew the topic had been passed over. He kept at his basket weaving.

"We ought to make some sort of cistern for water collection," the professor said abruptly.

Alejandro chuckled. "We say *cisterna*. The word is Latin."

"So it is." The professor beamed at him. "Our tongues borrow much from that father language, does it not? Yet yours is fully formed from it. I do so marvel at the distinct differences between cultures and languages. One can almost trace the roots backward, I would think, merely by counting the number of words associated to one another, until finding the language first spoken by man." He sighed deeply, then waved a hand. "But that is not a subject for discussion at present. The cistern. What do you think of that idea?"

"To collect rainwater?" Alejandro considered it. "More people, more water. My well can keep up, but it would be good to have more water available here instead of all down at the beach."

"I imagine the ladies would appreciate it." The professor had not wandered from the clearing for more than a few minutes at a time. He seemed as content to remain in his own thoughts as Miss Everly wanted to explore.

Alejandro's gaze traveled across the clearing to where Miss Everly leaned against the tree, her eyes closed but her mouth moving as she spoke with her companions. Was she tired? Did she need rest? They had not eaten as much as she was likely used to, even with the additional forays into the trees and fishing every day. Perhaps she only lacked energy.

It was not his concern.

"A *cisterna* we shall make." Alejandro kept twining his dry strip of bark through the slats he had formed. "It will not be difficult."

The professor went back to humming while Alejandro puzzled through a plan for a rudimentary water-collection system that would end with a basin full of clean water to drink.

Each time his eyes drifted again to where the doctor, his wife, and Miss Everly sat beneath the trees, he snatched it back to stare at his hands. Work-roughened, sun-browned, calloused hands. They had never been particularly fine. Though raised the son of a *don*, Alejandro had worked alongside his father's men as long as he could remember. He went with the *vaqueros* to hunt cattle when he was ten years old. A scar on the back of his left hand well reminded him of that event, of both the thrill of the hunt for the wild cattle, and then the horror when he watched his father's men race across a meadow to spear the largest of the beasts.

That was something he had planned to change upon his return to Río de la Plata. The Americans raised their beasts and harvested them differently, more efficiently, and used the animal less wastefully.

But he would never have the chance to implement his plans or try his hand at raising cattle in the new way.

He rose, startling the professor out of his dozing state. Alejandro gripped his half-made basket in one hand and curled the other into a fist. "*Perdón*, Señor." He did not wait for a response, but went into the trees, walking away from the people who had reminded him a world existed beyond the blue vastness surrounding his small island.

15

"This is hardly appropriate, Grace." Though she spoke her protests in a hissing whisper all the way down to the shore, Irene never actually suggested they go back to the shelter.

Hope tempered her response to soothe her friend rather than goad her. "We will be perfectly safe. And careful. We told Mrs. Morgan what we were about." In fact, Hope had tried to convince the doctor's wife to join them. She had faith in her ability to help the injured woman, now on her way to full recovery, down to the water and back. But Mrs. Morgan had insisted the two young women go and bathe themselves alone, pointing out that her husband could assist her to do the same at another time.

The relationship between the doctor and his wife continued to comfort Hope somewhat. They were thoughtful and kind toward each other, much as Hope had seen in her own parents' interactions. They reminded her of home.

"But what if something happens?" Irene asked when they stood only a few feet from the lapping waves. "What if an eel bites you, or a wave carries you away?" She sat on the sand and started unlacing her half boots.

"Then I trust you will run for help, or scream loud enough to attract attention." Hope tugged at the laces of her dress. The soiled garment had grown heavy with dirt and looked more suited to a fishmonger's wife than a gently bred young lady. Irene had to help her get all the laces undone, then she helped her friend. Next came their stays.

When they were only in their shifts, bare toes nearly in the water, Hope and Irene exchanged grins. Irene's was nervous, her eyebrows pulled together. "I haven't been sea bathing in years," she admitted quietly. "It was too cold in England."

Hope took her hand. "Only up to our knees. Come on." She tugged her friend into the water.

Irene's disposition had continued to sour up until the moment Hope suggested they wash themselves.

What was it about cleanliness that just the idea of obtaining that state once more lifted an anxious woman's spirits?

They walked in together, giggling when the water rolled over their ankles, shins, and finally their knees. Irene released Hope's hand and bent, scooping water up in her hands to rinse her bare arms. Hope did the same, scrubbing at smudges of ash from her time tending to the fire.

Soon they had walked deeper in, laughing and using the water on the back of their necks, their faces, and crouching enough that the water covered them up to their necks. The waves were gentle this time of day, barely nudging against them.

"This is heaven," Hope said loud enough to be heard, closing her eyes and pretending for a moment she was in a full tub of water back at home. Susan, her maid, would have drawn the bath for her. Hope would go first, and then Grace once the water had been warmed again with a kettle. Their bath would be scented with rose or lavender oil.

Why had Grace always let Hope go first?

"I would never call it heaven." Irene sounded more weary than disgusted. "But this is one of your best ideas, Grace."

Hearing her sister's name spoken often had ceased to fill her with guilt. Rather it gave Hope a reason to remember her family, to know her sister missed her, to know there were people in the world who loved her. "Thank you."

Irene sighed and turned to face the shore. "If only we had clean clothes to put on."

"If we find a stone large enough to act as a washboard, perhaps we could remedy that situation." Hope looked along the shore and pointed to an outcropping of rocks. "There. If we take our gowns there and scrub them against the stones, we could get a great deal of the dirt out."

"Really? You think a rock would serve?" Irene's tone was curious rather than skeptical. "Honestly, you must be the most practical woman alive. Why you are not as terrified as I am by all that we have gone through I cannot understand." She sighed deeply. "It is not a wonder my brother admires you so."

Hope winced and turned away, unwilling to discuss Albert. "We should hurry to wash the dresses. It will take time for them to dry and we do not want anyone coming to look for us before we are dressed properly."

"This is what I mean. You are intensely thoughtful." Irene rose and walked parallel to Hope back to the shore, talking the whole time. "I wish I could be more like you. But I cannot seem to form more than a thought or two before I am overwhelmed with all the horrible things about this island. I try to think on something I might do to be useful, such as gather wood for the fire. But what use would that be? We have stacks and stacks of it already, and it is not as though sticks are difficult to find here. Then I think I ought to help Mrs. Morgan pass the time, as you have, and she is napping or with her husband. There are no chores to do, there is no way for me to busy my hands. I am useless."

This admission unearthed the guilt Hope had buried. Her

thoughts regarding Irene's behavior had been less than charitable. Expecting her friend to act as though everything was an adventure rather than a miserable circumstance hadn't been fair.

"You are not useless." Hope stepped onto the sand, keeping her hem above the ground as best she could while gathering up her clothing. "We were not raised to keep house on an island. Under the circumstances, I imagine many women would behave exactly as you have."

Irene scooped up her clothing, too, and followed Hope down the beach to the rocks. "Perhaps. But not Mrs. Morgan, who is injured. I should have panicked were I in her position. And *you* have not acted afraid. Not even for a moment."

"That cannot be right." Hope tried to laugh. "I certainly have my fears."

They arrived at the rocks and Hope showed Irene how she thought they might best scrape their gowns across the rocks, right where the waves lapped at the stone to darken it and wear it smooth. They entered the water, which was considerably cooler than standing in the full sun while on the large rocks, and rubbed their dirt-streaked clothing up and down the gray stone.

"Oh—I tore a seam." Irene held up the arm of her gown to reveal a three-inch slit. "But look. It is nearly the right color again."

Hope relaxed as she worked, focusing so fully on the task that her mind did not wander away across the ocean to her family. After several minutes, both women laid their dresses upon the driest rocks, out of the reach of the water, before resuming their sea bathing.

"How long until we can wear them again?" Irene asked, closing her eyes against the sunlight.

Hope allowed her arms to float upward, though she had again sunk into the water up to her chin. "If you wish, you can put yours on right now."

Irene cracked open an eye and glared at her. "I know you are jesting."

"Not at all. Haven't you heard of the practice of dampening your gown before a ball?" Hope asked, unable to conceal a wicked grin. "Not that I have ever done so, though I did see Lady Olivia attend a private crush in such a state. My mother blushed as if Lady Olivia were *her* daughter."

"Oh, no." Irene covered her mouth to hide her own smile. "That is terrible. I can imagine poor Mrs. Everly in that position. She is such a proper gentlewoman."

Hope nodded her agreement, remembering her mother's scandalized expression. Once Mrs. Everly had expressed her feelings on the matter, saying she had rather have a daughter like Hope who raced ponies and phaetons than a daughter who would go about wearing practically transparent clothing in public.

"You are so much like her," Irene said, bringing Hope out of her remembrances.

"Do you think so?" Hope heard the wistfulness in her own voice. Was there anyone as kind and graceful, as full of goodness, as her mother? Grace, of course. But Hope had always been different. Quicker to act than to consider her words, faster to the finish line than to help others along in the race. Where her desire to move, to discover, to act, came from she could not say. Her father was not that way. No one in her family acted as she did. Did any of them even understand her?

"You are always so proper," Irene added, and Hope's heart sunk along with her body, deeper into the water. Of course Irene hadn't actually meant *Hope* was like her mother. She was speaking of Grace. "And look at how you have been so attentive to Mrs. Morgan and to me. If only you were as considerate of Albert's feelings." She sighed heavily.

"Irene." It took a great deal of control to keep the rebuke out of her voice. "I have told you, I have no interest in making a match with your brother. I do not love him."

"Oh, but why not?" Irene asked, somewhat petulant. "He is a wonderful catch. My father's heir, tall, and educated. You could only do better if you found someone with a title."

"Love," Hope said, emphasizing the word by speaking it slowly. "I said love. I am sure he has all the necessary qualifications of a suitable bachelor, but I do not love him."

Nor would she, ever. Because despite Alejandro's actions, despite his reluctance to linger near her when she would have followed him about, she could not ignore the way she felt about him. The pull had not lessened. If only those first hours together on the beach had lasted longer. If only he had felt as she did.

Irene's lips pushed out, the lower one more so than the upper. Perhaps the pout would have been sweet on a child, but it hardly suited a woman of Irene's age. "Mama says that love comes after marriage and could not possibly occur before, because it is the thing you find after you have endured hardship together. A courting couple cannot do that. But see, you and Albert are enduring hardship right now. In this cursed place."

"I think things like that—like this—would strengthen affection into love." Hope looked down into the water as a small yellow striped fish swam closer, perhaps curious as to what two strange fish hovered near its favorite rocks. "Look to the Morgans for an example. I have never seen a man so attentive to his wife, and she looks at him as though content in her pain if only because he is near."

When the other young lady's expression started to change, her eyes brightening, Hope felt sure she had made herself understood at last.

"Then your connection to my brother has grown at least a little?"

Hope paused. "That is not what I said, Irene." She stood. "Come. We had better dry along with our gowns or we will only get them wet again when we put them back on."

Irene followed her onto the rocks, the two of them sitting with their shifts spread over their knees.

"I will not give up," Irene said blithely. "I should love to have you as a sister. Albert is perfect for you."

"I do not agree." Hope kept her gaze out on the horizon, where the dark blue water met the light blue sky. "I wish rescue would come." Rescue from Albert and Irene, especially. The thought was not charitable, but she could not deny its truth.

"Imagine if it came now, when we haven't clothes to put on." Irene shaded her eyes to stare out over the waves. "I do not think I would mind at all, actually."

"Nor would I," Hope whispered, wrapping her arms about herself. Was anyone out looking for them? She had to believe so. The Carlburys would not abandon their children, and they had connections all across the Caribbean. People would search. The wreckage of their boat could not be far. If anyone came upon it, where the boat had run into the shoals, they would see the missing rowboat and know there were survivors, would they not?

"We cannot be too far from the doctor's island," Irene continued. "I think if we just made the fire that Albert suggested we would be found at once."

Perhaps. But that argument had also grown stale between them. Hope said nothing. She closed her eyes and lowered herself back to the large, flat rock's surface and spread her arms out to her side. The warmth of the stone seeped through her wet shift, and the sun falling against her skin filled her with a comforting heat.

"You are turning dreadfully brown," Irene said, ruining the moment.

It took everything she had not to sigh. Instead, Hope affected a pleasant expression. "It will be only the work of a winter indoors to undo the damage. At least I have stopped blistering."

"I am going to sit in the shade." Irene rose and walked away, but Hope did not join her. A few minutes apart might prove peaceful.

Her mind turned to the topic of love, but rather than lament

Irene's lack of understanding, she thought instead of Alejandro. Did she love him? He had not shown any true interest in her since their time alone together. It would be ridiculous to love him. She hardly knew him. Except...except every time she met his eyes she felt she knew what he was thinking. What he was feeling.

If only she could speak to him more plainly on the subject. Yet when she had asked that day watching the faraway storm, he had avoided her direct question. Ought she to try again?

Soon the only sound she heard was the quiet lap of waves against rocks, and it did not take them long to lull her into sleep.

❧ 16 ❧

Alejandro walked across the beach, carrying a turtle shell on his back and holding onto it by a natural lip on the inside of the shell. He hadn't had use for the shell six months previous, when the turtle had come upon land. He'd never seen a live sea turtle before, but the one he'd found barely qualified as such. It had been injured. Dying. Something in the water had wounded it. Alejandro finished the job as mercifully as he could, then had studied the creature with sadness and wonder.

Turtle soup wasn't an unheard-of delicacy in his parents' home, so he attempted to use the meat and make his own. The experiment hadn't gone well at all and he'd ended up only eating a little before becoming violently ill. For a whole day, Alejandro laid in his shelter and waited for death. He recovered and swore never to eat turtle again.

But the shell had stayed in the same spot, picked clean by the tiniest scavengers on the island, and was now perfect for his purpose. It would hold water quite well. Though smaller than the professor likely intended for a cistern, it would do until Alejandro came up with something else.

As he walked along the shore, Alejandro's gaze drifted to the rocks. A spot of white on the dark gray stone arrested his gaze a moment before he hastily averted his eyes. Miss Everly. What was she doing down on the beach alone? And—he did not look again. She was not appropriately dressed. He hefted the shell up further and hastened his steps, only to glimpse another snatch of white beneath the trees. The other young lady?

He turned abruptly and marched straight into the trees, going through the brush rather than all the way to one of his established paths. The women were together. That would keep them safe enough.

The first time he found Miss Everly on the beach, a vision of beauty in the semi-darkness, came immediately to mind. Six days, seven nights, previous. He had not thought of propriety, of proper dress, of anything to do with society and the relationships between men and women, until that moment when he saw her.

The way the English clung to their traditions irked him. An emergency situation called for different priorities. At least the men with coats had finally put those things aside. The island weather had necessitated that much.

He clattered through the trees, branches scraping against his shoulders and the turtle shell, cutting through the vegetation as best he could. Finally he came to his main path for fetching water, which would make the last leg of his return easier.

He met Mr. Thorne and Mr. Carlbury coming down, Thorne carrying the pail. Thorne hailed him at once.

"Córdoba, here you are. Professor Gibson said you went in search of something for your rain collection project. Is this it?" He gestured to the shell. "Do you need any help?"

Alejandro placed the shell on the ground behind him, carefully. "I will gladly accept it, Señor Thorne. *Gracias.*" He straightened and stretched his back out. "Mr. Carlbury, your sister and her friend, they are at the beach."

Carlbury folded his arms across his chest and lifted his chin.

"Passed them coming up, did you? I wondered where they got off to."

The man disappeared nearly as often as he grumbled, which made Carlbury's inattentiveness to his sister hardly a surprise to Alejandro.

Thorne walked around Alejandro, passing him the pail, and lifted the shell with a grunt. "This is much heavier than you made it look, friend."

Alejandro's lips twitched. "It is easier when you hold it on your back."

"I'll take your word for it. Carlbury, here, take the other side. We will move more quickly with the two of us carrying it."

Carlbury gave Alejandro a wide berth to come to Thorne's assistance, taking up the other side of the shell. Alejandro continued up the hill, hearing them come along behind. For a moment, he considered sending Carlbury to fetch the women, but brushed that idea aside. It was no more appropriate for that man to seek the two ladies out than it would have been for Alejandro to address them himself.

He would have a word with Doctor Morgan and advise a different course of action for the next time the ladies ventured down to the beach on their own.

Thunder cracked in the distance. Alejandro and the other men froze and turned toward the east.

Black clouds moved toward the island, lightning flashing beneath its shadows.

Alejandro took a step down the hill. "*Ve rápido.* Go. Tell the others to gather the food and water into the shelter." The trees above shook in a sudden gust of wind. "I will get the *señoritas.*" Safety superseded propriety, yet the idea of sending Albert down to fetch them left him uneasy.

Without waiting to see if the men obeyed, Alejandro ran down the path to the beach, bucket in hand. They would need what freshwater he could obtain if the storm lasted long.

But first, he had to make certain the young women rejoined the party. That storm had not been there hours ago, so it had to be moving somewhat quickly. Even if he had kept his back to the east most of the afternoon.

Alejandro left the pail at the well and sprinted up the dune, then down to the shoreline. He saw two figures in pastels coming down the beach, both lifting their hems nearly to their knees the better to run. The wind had found the beach, and the waves had started to rise.

"Señor Córdoba," Miss Everly shouted, waving at him. Her friend immediately halted and dropped her skirts, but Miss Everly took her arm and dragged her forward. When they reached each other, she shouted to be heard over nature's tumult. "What do we do to prepare for the storm?"

"Get to the shelter," he shouted, gesturing to the hill. "As fast as you can go. The others will be there."

She did not waste breath on another word, but tugged her friend forward with determination. Though the rain had not started, both women appeared damp. Hopefully they would not grow ill from that unfortunate circumstance.

When all three of them reached the well, Alejandro told them he would catch up. Before they were halfway up the hill, he was behind them again.

Mr. Carlbury appeared before them, his head down as though the branches whipping about in the sudden gale might take it off. Alejandro watched him shout at the women, but could not make out what was said. Miss Everly shook her head and then shoved her friend along. The gentleman glared at her, then Alejandro over her head, but wrapped an arm about his sister's shoulders and guided her up the path.

Miss Everly looked back once, her eyes lingering upon him, but then she gathered up her skirts and ran. Sensible woman. He kept to the best speed he could without endangering the bucket and the precious water it held.

They emerged into the clearing at the same moment the rain fell, and it pelted them heavily in the short seconds it took to cross from the trees to the shelter. The turtle shell was outside the doorway.

Alejandro stepped in only long enough to make certain everyone else was inside. The sailors were sitting nearest the door, backs against the wall of sticks and clay. Mrs. Morgan and the doctor were near the fire, Mrs. Morgan putting her arms out to welcome Miss Carlbury to sit with her. The professor and Thorne were on the other side of the fire, and Carlbury had immediately sat in the middle of the floor rather than be near anyone else. That left Miss Everly nearest the door, watching Alejandro with wide blue eyes.

"You will be safe and dry in here," he told them, pointing to the stone roof. *"Perdón."* He ducked out of the doorway and into the rain, wasting no time in taking up the turtle shell.

The professor had offered his assistance, which meant his conversation and occasional opinion, in the making of the cistern. Alejandro had managed most of the work himself, using a hollowed-out branch and the natural curvature of the stones. He'd intended to dig a hole, line it with rocks and more clay, and put the shell at the bottom to collect water. But now it would be best to catch what little rain he could with the shell.

Though the rain fell like a curtain, soaking his hair and running into his eyes, Alejandro set up the shell beneath an already steady stream of water. Then he withdrew, back to the crowded shelter.

He stepped inside again, more steps than he wished in order to avoid the rain the wind blew into the shelter. He swept the dark-ened interior with a glance, noting how everyone seemed to huddle closer to those nearest them. Even the sailors sat with their shoulders touching. Carlbury had moved next to his sister, who shivered and shook as dramatically as the trees outside.

Miss Everly still stood, her arms wrapped about herself, staring out the opening. Waiting for him? "How long will it last?" she asked, her voice a whisper in the dark.

Alejandro busied himself with the pail, carrying it from the doorway to the Morgans near the fire. "This is a season for storms. *Son huracanes.* From now until winter, storms like this may rise up at any time and last until they spend themselves."

"They destroy things," one of the sailors said. Hitchins. "When I was a child, a storm like this demolished our island. All the trees. Animals. Gone."

"What?" Miss Carlbury's shrill voice made Alejandro wince. "What about the food? The fish?"

"Calm yourself, Irene." Carlbury sounded more impatient than soothing. "I am certain we are perfectly safe."

"This island has not endured such a hardship in the time I have been here." Alejandro had no wish to hear more of her fears, but when he took in Miss Everly's calm demeanor, his tone softened further. "We will pray it passes us by without harm."

"Pray to who?" the professor asked. "God? A saint?" He nodded to the sailors. "Island deities?"

"To whoever will hear us," Mr. Thorne muttered, closing his eyes and leaning his head against the stone at the back of the shelter.

Alejandro watched as the others silently closed their eyes. Some bowed their heads, others leaned back as though settling in rather than sending pleas to heaven. Miss Carlbury started sniffling, but the doctor's wife started speaking to her in a quiet, comforting tone.

Miss Everly stepped forward until she stood next to Alejandro, she, facing the door and he, inward. "It is very dark out there," she whispered.

The shadows had grown gloomier inside, with only the firelight to beat them back. It was not many hours after noon, but the sky was as dark as if the sun had set. Alejandro settled himself onto the ground, away from the walls of the room. She carefully did the same, staying beside him, facing the opposite direction. Their shoulders nearly touched.

Before Miss Everly, the last time he sat near a woman had been at his last dinner party in Virginia, next to the daughter of his host. The girl had been no more than fifteen, round-cheeked and blushing that she sat near the guest of honor. He had danced with her older sister at a ball.

How different things were then. He'd worn fine clothing, had been clean shaven, sat with confidence in himself and his place in the world. The next day he boarded a ship to return home to his family, home to the fight for independence from Spain.

"I miss my family," Miss Everly whispered, still staring out into the rain. "My sister and I, we are the oldest children. My mother and father thought there would be no more, as we gave Mama a difficult time of things. But she had my brother, Edward, when I was nine. Then Charity and Patience after." Her voice faded away to nothing.

He watched the fire and the people around it, none of them stirring except for an occasional shudder or glance up when the thunder boomed over their heads. The first time he had sat alone through a storm, what had he felt? Fear, but not of the rain. His mother's worried eyes kept appearing in his memory, his father's pale face when they had learned of the casualties in a skirmish at the coast. Those were the things that haunted him.

"My parents had children before and after me," Alejandro said, his voice too low to carry beyond Miss Everly's ears. "But none from before survived long after birth, if they came through that alive. My father, he said he knew at once that I would live. He had never heard a child cry with my strength." Many times he had heard his father say those words, with pride and surety, even as he grew from boyhood to manhood. "Then they had my sister, who died of illness a few years ago. And my brother."

Miss Everly shivered and leaned slightly, the cloth of her sleeve brushing his. "Your father will be proud to learn how you fought to survive on this island."

Too far away from the fire to enjoy its warmth, Alejandro keenly felt the ice harden around his heart at her words. "My father will never know anything about it," he murmured, folding his arms.

From the corner of his eye, Alejandro watched her turn to stare at him. Her cheeks were pink and spotted with brown freckles, her lips dry and chapped, and the tips of her eyelashes shone gold in the light of the fire. He waited for her rebuke, for her false hope, to tell him he was wrong.

"My village is called Aldersy, and it is near the coast," she told him, her tone matter-of-fact though she remained quiet. "My friends still live there. They are as dear to me as my own family. Silas is an earl, Jacob will be the vicar by now, and Isaac is the one I told you of who returned from war to be a baronet."

Alejandro frowned and turned to stare into her eyes, the flicker of firelight reflected there. "Your friends are all men?"

She nodded and pulled her knees up, wrapping her arms around them. "We grew up together. The boys did not want to play with my sister and I at first, but I made them change their minds. I could beat them in footraces, come up with make-believe adventures better than they could, and it was my idea to form a club."

She kept talking, her voice barely audible over the sounds of the storm outside, telling him of how she had grown up as one of the five daring children of Inglewood. She had run about barefoot as often as she could, to prove to the boys she could keep up without soiling her slippers. She participated in raiding the kitchens for sweets and racing horses across the beach. Without meaning to, Alejandro relaxed as he listened, her stories of childhood so different from his, yet similar.

"I did not have many friends," he said when she grew quiet, lost in her memories. "My father, he kept me near him. I learned to be like him when I was still young. A boy. I went with him and the *vaqueros*, when it was time to take our leather to market. I walked through our fields with him to inspect the crops. I met with *los peons*, the people living on our land."

"Tenants is the English word," she told him, her lips curved slightly upward. "It sounds as though you were quite busy for a child."

His throat closed. It took him a moment to realize why. She had done all the talking. Yet he could say no more than a few words without emotion overcoming him. "*Sí*. But I never noticed. I loved being with *mi papá*."

"You will see him again, Alejandro," she whispered. Something brushed against his arm and he looked down to see her fingers, the tips barely touching his skin. "This island will not defeat you. It hasn't yet. Have some faith. Hope."

From her fingers he looked up into her gaze, her eyes certain, that smile still on her face and a glow in her cheeks. She spoke with such surety, with more faith than he had possessed in all his time living on the island. Almost, he believed her.

"Hope." He tasted the word on his tongue and his heart stirred. Whether it was to do with the idea or the way her eyes steadily stared at him, he did not know. "In my tongue, it is *esperanza*." He closed his eyes. "My mother's name." He touched the chain around his neck, finding the ring dangling at its end. He gripped it in his hand, drawing comfort from her memory.

"A beautiful name," she whispered, more awe in her voice than his words merited. "Honor her by keeping it in your heart, Alejandro." Her words sounded more like an accusation than a suggestion.

"Señor Córdoba," he reminded her of the formality between them, opening one eye to watch her as she turned again, presenting him with her profile. "Miss Everly?"

She raised her eyebrow but did not turn. "Yes?"

"How long do you think you will continue to hope?"

A secretive smile appeared, and she wrapped her arms around

her knees, leaning down until her chin rested upon them. "All my life, señor." She released a heavy sigh. "Forever."

Alejandro never had possessed such faith. If he did, he would be bolder. He might have captured her hand again, holding it tightly in his own, whispering promises to her in the darkness. "You are an inspiration, Miss Everly." She said nothing, and the storm continued to rage.

THE STORM CARRIED ON FAR LONGER THAN ANY OF THEM LIKED. Hope kept her place beside Alejandro for what seemed like years. He said nothing else, and she tried to sleep. Every flash of lightning woke her again. The wind howled outside the door, steadily, never seeming to grow weary of its noise.

Finally, Alejandro turned so his back was toward the fire, and he faced the entry as she did. "This is not the worst storm I have weathered here," he said quietly. "It will not harm the island, or you, Miss Everly."

Hope shivered and angled her head to watch him, her chin against her knees. "Can you promise that, señor?"

He shifted so he leaned back against his hands, one of his arms behind her. "I can promise that so long as I am here no harm will befall you." Why was that so reassuring to hear?

His words sunk beneath her skin, warming her from the inside out. His low, deep voice and the intensity in his eyes encouraged her to trust his word. She closed her eyes and relaxed, letting the darkness pull her under at last.

She slept until a voice spoke softly in her ear. "The storm is gone, señorita." Her cheek rested against something rough, but warm, and moving slowly up and down.

Hope opened her eyes, but there was nothing to see. Night had fallen, the fire behind her had grown too small for its light to escape the confines of the embers.

Slowly she realized that she reclined against an arm while her head rested against a most accommodating shoulder. Cheeks flaming, Hope pulled herself up and away. How had she come to rest practically in the arms of a man she barely knew? At least they were sitting upright. At least the shelter was full of people. At least—

"You should move closer to the fire," he said, invisible to her in the night. His voice was tight, as though he found it difficult to speak.

He wanted her to leave? Was he embarrassed?

"I am not cold," she whispered.

There was a pause, quiet as the night, then she heard a shuffling as he moved away. "If we were not on this island, things would be different." There was a quality to his whispers, a richness that reminded her of velvet, or the bittersweet chocolate she took with her breakfast back at home, that was familiar and enticing. Comforting.

Grace would not ask the question on the tip of Hope's tongue. Grace would swallow the question and withdraw as she was bid, respecting the social customs with which they had been raised. But Hope was not Grace. "What do you mean?"

"You are a woman with many admirable traits. Do you dance?" he asked. Beyond his voice there was nothing but the heavy breathing and soft snores of the others in the shelter, sleeping and unaware of her rapidly beating heart.

"I do," she admitted. "And I sing."

He chuckled. "I used to sing. Perhaps I would have sang a duet with you. Or asked you to dance. If we were not here."

Her insides twisted rather delightfully. "When we are saved from this place, you will have my first dance." It was bold to say such things. Bold to assume he would still want to be near her when she was no longer his only option for company.

He said nothing, though she sensed a shift in his mood.

"We will be rescued." Hope spoke with a fervency she willed him to feel. "I know it."

"Go to the fire, Miss Everly." He sounded tired. Weary of heart and soul rather than body. "Near your friend." Then she heard and sensed him moving away, standing. He walked out of the shelter, his silhouette appearing briefly against the dim light of stars and a waning moon filtering through clouds. Then he was gone.

Hope did as he asked, moving nearer the fire and where she had seen Mrs. Morgan and Irene. She leaned against the wall near them and closed her eyes, trying to sleep again.

When morning came at last, she had slept only in snatches, always waking when her head lolled to one side or the other. She had slept peacefully only when by Alejandro's side.

17

The next morning, everyone emerged from the shelter blinking in the light. Hope's eyes adjusted slowly and she had to rub at them to be sure the scene before her was real. The clearing had changed, drastically. Branches from trees, leaves and grasses, were strewn across the clearing. The ash from the fire had mostly been scattered, except for one gray clump in the center.

The sky was clear and beautiful; the ground was a mud-soaked mess.

"I must check the damage of the island." Alejandro spoke with his back to the rest of them, surveying everything before them.

"I'd be happy to help," Mr. Thorne volunteered at once.

"Aye, señor. We can divide and report," Mr. Madden announced in his deep voice. Hope nearly asked to come with them, with Alejandro and Mr. Thorne, when Irene stepped up to her side and huffed. "Look at this place. Filthy. We are lucky the shelter did not fall down around our ears." Then she saw Hope's stare and forced a smile. "Should we tidy up?"

As it was the first time Irene had offered to do any work, let alone smiled since coming to the island, Hope's wish to join the gentlemen withered away under her guilt.

What were the chances the men would let her join them, anyway?

"An excellent idea." She looked down at her bare feet in the damp earth. "It seems our bath yesterday was for nothing."

"I certainly feel better for it." Irene tucked a loose strand of her golden hair behind her ear. She then looked over her shoulder at Hope. "We ought to fix your hair."

Hope put her hands up to either side of her hair, trying to determine the damage done even though she had kept Alejandro's linen ribbon in her hair. With the movement she caught sight of him and the other men walking into the trees. Her hands fell to her side as she watched them go.

Why had she thought he would say something before disappearing? Shaking that thought loose from her head, Hope gave her attention to the task at hand.

Mrs. Morgan had sat down on a stone near the fire, which the doctor had begun trying to repair. The professor brought dry wood from inside the shelter. That left Hope, Irene, and Albert—

Where was Albert?

Hope looked about but did not see him in the clearing, but she did not think he had gone with the other men. To come and go as he pleased must be a relief to him. Every time she attempted a moment of solitude or exploration, people tended to panic.

Without anything better to do, Hope started gathering the downed branches in the clearing. If they were stacked on the stone side of the shelter, the sun would eventually dry them out enough to use them as wood.

It took the better part of an hour to set the clearing and fire to rights again. They even used a branch to sweep at the stone and dirt, clearing them of smaller twigs and debris.

Irene went about the work almost cheerfully, which ought to have been a relief. Yet Hope found herself wondering at the abrupt change in her friend. The storm had dampened everyone else's spirits.

"I think, after all of this is over, you ought to consider Albert as a suitor."

Hope nearly dropped the last of the twigs she had gathered for kindling. "Irene. We have already discussed this." Truly, the subject wore on her. Albert's snide smiles and superior way of speaking had barely abated in the face of their difficulties. She had no wish to spend the rest of her days experiencing yet more of them.

"I was thinking last night, during the storm." Irene turned her wide-eyed stare to Hope. "We have been on this island for a week. You haven't truly been chaperoned as one would expect. This is not the sort of thing people in England will understand. Your reputation might suffer. But Albert will know, as he has been with you all this time."

"Why would your brother even wish to court me?" Hope asked. It was not something she had ever understood. She did not come with a great fortune. Her dowry was three thousand pounds, which was a healthy sum, but not exactly life changing for the Carlbury family. Though they had lived in the same neighborhood, the Carlburys were undoubtedly wealthier than the Everlys.

Irene dusted her hands off, then examined her fingernails. "Oh, how dirty we are. It will take a month of scrubbing to feel clean again." She shivered and folded her arms before her. "Albert has always admired you. I believe he finds your practical nature appealing, especially since he has considered going into politics."

Hope vaguely recalled Albert speaking with Grace on the subject of their county's representation in the House of Commons. Very vaguely. When the Carlburys came to spend time with her family, Hope did her best to be on the opposite side of the room from Albert. She had no patience for him and did not want to risk offending the whole family by telling the eldest son what she thought of him directly to his face a second time. As often happened, Grace saved Hope by sacrificing a bit of her own happiness.

How could someone misinterpret such blatant disinterest? "My practical nature?"

Had Albert mistaken Grace's patient and polite conversation as genuine interest? Even if he had, Hope had hardly given him reason to continue on in such a manner. The number of times he had attempted conversation with her, she had forced herself to smile and remark inanely upon whatever subject he chose.

Hope shook that thought free. They had wandered back to Mrs. Morgan's side. The doctor picked up the pail as they approached.

"I am off to fetch water," he said. "Will you ladies be all right in my absence?"

Hope glanced to where the professor had taken up his customary place beneath the shade of the trees. He seemed to treat the entire of their ordeal as nothing more than an extended holiday. At least he never complained.

"We will be fine, darling," Mrs. Morgan answered, her smile warm and tender. Hope's heart ached to see their obvious affection for one another. She hadn't given much thought to courtship and marriage at home. Most men would not wish for their wives to have adventures, and she had no wish to settle until she'd seen at least a little more of the world than what England had to offer.

Seeing the doctor and his wife share in a hardship, still able to smile at and care for one another, set Hope's mind down another path. A path that led to a certain half-naked gentleman with a Spanish tongue and soulful eyes that made her wish—wish for things he said could not be.

Would Alejandro be the sort of man to take his wife with him into the world, once he escaped from the island? Yes. Somehow, she could not imagine him leaving someone he loved behind.

Hope sat on a stump someone had moved near the fire. She

watched the doctor disappear and kept her eyes fastened to the trees as she thought.

Her friends, for all that she adored them, were not men who longed for adventure. Silas was steady and responsible, a perfect earl and member of Lords. Jacob longed to live a life of compassion and caring for others—surely, he must soon see what a help Grace would be to him. Then Isaac, a man of courage and honor, was less suited to her than nearly any gentleman of her acquaintance. They were too alike. Too apt to charge into a fray without thought. He would settle eventually, too, to care for his estate.

Men like Albert Carlbury were far worse options. Staid, pompous, and set on the idea that they would dictate to their wives for the rest of forever.

"Mrs. Morgan." Irene's voice cut through her thoughts. Her friend had settled on the opposite side of the fire circle. "Grace and I have a difference of opinion on a matter. You see, my brother has expressed an interest in courting my dear friend, yet she rebuffs him. Even though he would make a good match."

Mrs. Morgan's dark eyebrows raised, and she glanced from Irene to Hope. "Miss Everly doesn't believe him to be right for her, I would assume."

"I do not." Though this topic would mortify Grace, Hope stuck her chin out and braced herself to speak her mind.

"But you would be the perfect politician's wife," Irene interjected strongly. "You are always calm amidst calamity, your manners are above reproach, and only look at how you have managed this horrid island. Besides those obvious points, you must also consider your reputation."

Hope's head snapped back. "My reputation? It is perfectly intact. Mrs. Morgan is here, you are here—"

"Yes, but the longer we are on this horrid rock the less protected you are." Irene folded her hands in her lap and turned again to Mrs. Morgan. "I am right, am I not?"

Mrs. Morgan hesitated a moment, but her eyes pinched at the

corners when she offered Hope a half-shrug. "I am afraid Miss Carlbury might be correct. Despite my presence, being away from civilization for so long, our story will make a sensation in society. I cannot see how you will avoid the rumors. Miss Carlbury has only one advantage over you, my dear, and that is that she is here with her brother. You have no relation to protect you."

A startled laugh escaped Hope in a breath. "You cannot believe that. We are surrounded by gentlemen, and there are three of us. My reputation must be safe. Should anyone question it—"

"Of course we would defend you," Irene said with a dismissive wave of her hand. "But no one can stop rumors once they are started. You would do best to tell Albert you will entertain his suit after we are rescued."

Hope's insides went cold, then hot, until she felt her sun-pinked cheeks burning. She did her best to remain calm. Grace would never shout, after all, or stomp her foot as Hope wished to do. With a tremulous hold on her outrage, she met Mrs. Morgan's gaze. "Do you think I am ruined if I do not enter into such an understanding with Mr. Carlbury?"

Since their introduction, Hope had viewed Mrs. Morgan as an ally of sorts. The doctor's wife was not much older than Hope, and she seemed to share her husband's spirit of excitement in discovering the world around them. Hope had, if she were honest with herself, looked up to the woman as the type of person she wished to grow into.

"I am afraid that will be the case, Miss Everly." Mrs. Morgan's agreement with Irene pierced Hope's heart. "I wish it were not so, but when news of what has happened gets to London, to your family...." Her voice trailed away to nothing.

Hope jolted to her feet, startling the other two women enough that they both jerked back somewhat to stare at her. "I am collecting more food."

Mrs. Morgan reached out a hand. "I really do not think that is necessary—"

"Grace, come now—"

Hope would not give heed to her sister's name. Not this time. Not when her insides trembled and buzzed as though she were a thunderhead ready to unleash another storm over the land. The previous evening's weather did not rage as she did. But nature had been given leave to vent its feelings upon whoever it wished. She did not have that luxury.

Instead, she scooped up one of the baskets Alejandro had left inside the door of the shelter, then she brushed past Irene.

"Really, you should not go alone, and I have no intention of straying where more of those dreadful spiders lurk."

"Then do not come," Hope said, her mouth snapping sharply over each consonant. Basket on her hip, she kept walking without a backward glance. If the men could wander about unsupervised, and Albert himself could disappear without a word to anyone, she could leave to do something useful.

Her head buzzed as though filled with angry bees, and the only way to quiet them seemed to involve walking briskly. She barely paid attention to where she went. Her eyes stayed on the ground to avoid roots and thorns, but her mind turned completely inward.

Irene and Mrs. Morgan were wrong. Hope's reputation was safe. She would be an object of curiosity, people would ask for her story, but before long no one would remember she had been the woman trapped on an island with ten other people. Only spiteful old cats, gossips who no longer held power or sway, would speculate over whether Hope might have behaved in a less than ladylike manner while waiting for someone to save her.

The sun climbed overhead before Hope slowed, her body weary and sweat breaking out across her forehead. She stopped and looked up through the canopy of leaves, glaring at the sun marking yet another day without rescue.

She dropped her basket on the ground and took two steps

back, until her hands found a tree, then she slid to the ground and covered her eyes with her hands.

Hope had never feared weeping. Crying could not show weakness if one remained strong *after* one's emotions were spent. She went about spending them, letting the tears fall down her cheeks and her lungs heave great sobs of fear, frustration, and desperation.

Help would come. It must. But she had never had patience. And if help came too late, marrying Albert was out of the question. No matter what. She detested him. All she wanted to do was go home and tell her family she loved them. Tell Grace how glad she was it had been she and not her sister trapped on the island. Promise her father and mother to mind her emotions better.

But would she give up on seeing the world?

Never.

Hope's tears slowed to a trickle and she sniffled, missing her handkerchief for the first time since waking on that beach to find Alejandro kneeling at her side. How did one clean up after tears without a handkerchief?

Alejandro. If only he presented himself as an option to her. Not that she wished to force any gentleman to wed her for the sake of her reputation. She had seen the pain such a thing caused her friend Esther, even though she and Silas were perfectly suited to one another. No. She would never want that from him.

What she wanted from Alejandro was deeper. She wanted a chance at love. Instinctively, she knew he would be a match for her in every way, if only he felt as she did.

She wiped at her cheeks and eyes with her hands, sniffled more, then took in her surroundings. With the sun directly overhead, her sense of direction was a bit off. If she waited a little while, it would sink, and then she could easily find her way back to the clearing. In the meantime, perhaps she could put her basket to use.

Hope inspected the tree she sat beneath and saw nothing edible growing within its branches. But another tree, full of small green fruits that looked like crab apples, captured her attention. So what if the fruit was a little bitter? It would be better than returning empty-handed. She walked toward the tree, eyeing the fruit and branches swaying in the breeze. It seemed as though none of the fruit had been bothered by birds or lizards, or insects.

When Hope extended her hand, wrapping her fingers around one of the green apple-like fruits, she did not expect to hear a sudden rush of footsteps. She turned, ready to scream if some unseen predator came toward her—but it was Alejandro. Coming through the trees. He did not shout, or stop, and ran directly into her, wrapped an arm about her waist and twisted with her, pulling her back against the same tree she had leaned against moments before.

He held her to him, tight against his chest, the basket crushed between them.

"*¿Qué estás haciendo?*" he gasped out. "*¿Comiste la manzana?*" He pushed her away abruptly, though he kept a firm hold on her shoulders. He searched her face, his wide eyes full of fear. He gave her a single shake. "Did you eat the apple?"

Fresh from a loss of temper and shedding of tears, Hope's befuddled mind did not know whether to give way to tears a second time or start shouting at him for frightening her.

"I didn't," she whispered, still stunned.

Though he had held her close, it had not felt like an embrace. But now, his eyes closed in relief and the hands on her shoulders gentled. He leaned down, resting his forehead against hers. "*Gracias a Dios.*"

Was it his heart she heard pounding or her own? She could not be sure. Then he withdrew, but pressed a kiss against the top of her forehead as he did. A flood of warmth, this time of the pleasant variety, started at the top of her head and filled her to the tips of her bare toes.

"Señor?" she squeaked.

He did not release her, instead wrapping one arm firmly around her shoulders. She dropped the basket in favor of leaning into him, her aching heart drinking in his presence and the surprising affection he offered. Had anyone embraced her since she left England and her family? Irene was not an overly demonstrative friend, and all her touches lately had been demanding comfort from Hope rather than offering it in equal parts.

Alejandro's breathing finally slowed, after perhaps a minute of just standing there, his arm forming a half-circle around her. "That fruit. We call it *manzanita de la muerte*. Little apple of death."

His words sank into her mind, and his actions at last made sense. He had been afraid she'd eaten a poisoned apple. She closed her eyes and exhaled. "I am sorry. I did not know."

He shook his head, which she felt more than saw, and at last released her. "Are you hurt at all? If it drips sap on your skin, it burns and blisters. Sometimes, even water dripping from its leaves carries poison." He held her hands and inspected her bare arms, then turned them over to check the insides of her wrists.

The concern, honest and open, brought the tears back to her eyes at last. "I am not harmed. I promise." She swallowed back as much of her emotion as she could. He would not welcome her affection. "Thank you for stopping me."

Alejandro lifted his head, his gaze meeting hers, his deep brown eyes pulling her in. She leaned toward him, biting her lip before asking, "How did you come to be here?"

His eyes narrowed abruptly and his body stiffened. He leaned back against the tree, dropping his hands from where they had held her wrists.

Oh dear. Hope braced for something unpleasant.

"How did you come to be here?"

Nothing about his former life had prepared Alejandro for the situation in which he found himself. When he returned to the others with Thorne, ready to make his report that their food resources had diminished but not dangerously, the women had been upset.

"Grace ran into the trees," Miss Carlbury said, hurrying to him and Thorne. "She left upset. I am not certain how long she has been gone—"

"A quarter of an hour," Mrs. Morgan had interjected with a wince. "She was distressed when she left. I am concerned she might come to harm if she isn't careful."

"And the professor wouldn't go after her." Miss Carlbury pointed accusingly at where the older man sat with his back against a tree.

The professor folded his arms and shouted across the small clearing. "A futile exercise, since I do not know this island well nor how to track someone through a forest."

Thorne and Alejandro had exchanged a glance. "Go ahead," Thorne said, nodding to the trees. "You will find her faster than I could."

Alejandro picked up her trail quickly enough. Broken twigs, light indents in the still damp, soft ground, led him directly to the woman crouched by a tree and sobbing. Perhaps he ought to have gone to her. Held her while she cried. But it was easier, safer, to wait until she had spent her emotions. Each sob had broken his heart, but he forced himself to remain still. They barely knew each other. She was not his responsibility. Not really. She was not his to comfort.

He had lowered his head to pray for her, mouthing the words silently in his native tongue, his hand holding tightly to his mother's ring dangling from the chain around his neck. What would his mother think of him, sitting so near a woman in pain and doing nothing about it?

When he'd looked up at last, realizing he hadn't heard her crying for several moments, it was to see Miss Everly reaching for a manchineel fruit. His fear choked him, and he moved rather than cry out.

What a fool he was. Refusing to comfort her while she cried, but holding her tightly the moment he feared she had come to real harm.

"Miss Everly," he said at last, seeing she still stared at him. "You cannot keep disappearing like this."

Her blue eyes flashed, like lightning upon the sea. "People are fond of telling me what I can and cannot do of late."

Though not certain what she meant, he took in a deep breath and tried to order his thoughts. He rubbed the bridge of his nose. "Your friends worried for you."

"Yet they sent you, even after all their warnings," she muttered, crossing her arms and directing her glare to the dirt between them.

"Warnings?" Did he even wish to know what she meant?

The woman released a deep sigh and dug the toes of one small foot into the ground. "It is of no matter, Señor Córdoba." She bent and lifted her basket, tucking it against her hip. She avoided looking at him, her jaw tight with determination. "Is there some-place nearby I might gather food?"

Alejandro stared at the top of her head for a beat of silence, then pointed. "There are vines this way. They grow something that reminds me of *almendras*."

She followed the line of his finger and her shoulders fell. "I do not know that word."

"A nut." He considered her profile as he spoke. "I think it is close to the English word."

"*Almendras*," she muttered, then her eyebrows lifted. "Almonds."

"*Sí*. Almonds." Alejandro started walking and she fell into step beside him.

Miss Everly said nothing for several steps, paying more atten-tion to where her steps fell than to him. Her expression remained thoughtful, less hostile than before. "I am sorry you were sent to find me. Again."

Why did that make him smile? Why did her voice, soft and gentle in the quiet surrounding them, remind him of music? Perhaps because her words stirred his heart as the beautiful ballads of the *vaqueros* had, long ago. There was a depth to her, something he did not yet understand, secrets hidden just behind her eyes. Though she spoke of her home, her family, her friends, there always seemed to be words unsaid, thoughts unfinished. He had thought it safest to leave her alone, but—but she had been in pain. And sitting still while her heart ached had wounded him.

"I will always come looking for you, *señorita*," he said quietly.

"Miss Everly," she corrected, the corner of her mouth twitching upward.

"You may call me Alejandro," he replied without thinking.

The woman cast him a glance and her steps slowed to a stop. "You would not let me call you that before. Why be so familiar now? The others would think it inappropriate. Especially since I do not even allow Irene's brother the use of my Christian name."

Alejandro felt heat creep up the back of his neck. His beard would hide any evidence of a blush, thankfully. "Yet I have heard him use it." He still did not understand that relationship. The way Carlbury watched over her, as though she belonged to him. There was no understanding, perhaps, but the Englishman expected one.

Her eyes narrowed. "It is presumptuous of him and means nothing."

"Would using my Christian name mean something?" Alejandro asked, then bit his tongue. A year on an island and he had lost his ability to converse with a beautiful woman without appearing a fool. He knew what it would mean. The skeptical raise of her eyebrows prompted him to try to dismiss his own words. "There is no one here to disapprove of you, Miss Everly. No ladies or lords. No king or queen. This island is outside of civilization. It is foolish to cling to all the conventions of a world you may never see again."

Her lips parted and her cheeks paled. "What would you have me do? Forget all my manners? Forget that when we are saved from this place there will be consequences to my behavior?"

"I would have you use my name," he said, stepping closer. Even before the tragedy of his ship sinking, who had ever called him by name? He had made friends in the former English colonies, but people called him *Córdoba*. The few times his name had fallen from her lips had soothed his aching loneliness. "I am not asking for you to break with all traditions, Miss Everly."

Her chin tipped up, she did not flinch away from him but her eyes dared him, challenged him, as her next words challenged him. "Which do you recommend I discard, *Alejandro?*"

All that would keep you from my arms. The words came from his heart and nearly rose to his wayward tongue. Alejandro pulled them back, fought another moment against the pull he felt every time he stood near her. They did not know each other. Not well enough. Not for what he considered doing with her standing this close.

But why did he fight his attraction to her? Had she not said she felt the same force drawing them together? But he had rebuffed her. Perhaps things had changed, and he had crushed a bud of something beautiful before allowing it to bloom.

Instead of speaking from his heart, he drew from a different place, a different emotion. "You discard the conventions of staying near your chaperones and protectors, Miss Everly. You apologize for disappearing, yet I have the feeling this will not be the last time you do so."

"You said you would always come looking," she retorted with a toss of her head, the lightning in her eyes flashing again. Had he angered her? "Where are the nuts, *Alejandro?*"

"You mock me with my name?" he asked. "Perhaps I should leave you to your own devices if you take what I have given and throw it back in such a manner." No anger or temper colored his words, yet he saw her nostrils flare and her cheeks flush. He gentled his next words. "Your friends worried after you. They said you were upset."

"I had good reason." She bit her bottom lip, staring at him as though debating what to say next. Finally, her eyes lowering in a vulnerable manner, she said, "Perhaps I have been too emotional of late."

"One excuses such behavior in times such as this," Alejandro said, his arms folded tight across his chest. "You have been through a great deal." The silence stretched between them, the only sound the birds calling to one another in the trees, the occasional chirp of a tiny frog hidden somewhere nearby.

At last she sucked in a deep breath and raised her head, her shoulders going back as though she prepared to face battle. With him? "It would be easier if you would tell me the truth. Alejandro." This time his name was soft, a caress. "Please answer me. Did I imagine—am I still imagining—something between us that is not there?" She clutched the basket to her, her expression turning sad before he even had the chance to speak.

What could he say? He could not tell her that he dreamed of her each night, thought of her all day long, wished they had met long ago in a place he could do something about his feelings rather than keep them in check.

"What is the point of speaking of it?" he asked, lowering his arms and reaching for the basket, taking it from her gently. "I will not have this conversation. I cannot. You must understand."

Her bottom lip trembled, but she nodded tightly before she started walking again. He kept pace with her.

"You cannot keep disappearing. It is selfish, Grace." He spoke her name without permission, and she whirled on him with such fury in her eyes he drew back a step.

"Miss Everly," she snapped at him. "I have not given you permission to call me otherwise. As to my selfishness, I think I have earned it. At least a few moments of worrying over myself. I have done everything I could to be helpful. I have stayed put when

I had rather be out walking the beaches and exploring our beautiful prison. I have even forced myself to remain patient and understanding with Irene though I wished to shake sense into her." She snatched the basket from his hands, and it crackled when she tightened her grip around it. "I have put up with Mr. Carlbury, too, even though I find him to be the worst sort of bore. He is an arrogant lout, and I cannot abide his company." She gestured with one hand to their surroundings, her voice's pitch raising. "Selfish? Perhaps I am. That's what my father said before I—"

She broke her words off abruptly. Turned pale. "Before I left."

At last he saw the woman he glimpsed beneath the exterior of peace, the mask of calm, that she had worn nearly every moment since they met. The hints of fire had built into a flame. This was who she was, he sensed. A woman of energy, passion, and the ability to speak her mind.

"Do you feel better now?" he asked, crossing his arms over his chest.

A rather cross frown turned her lips downward. "No." Then her glare fixed on him. "And stop smiling that way. It is not amusing in the slightest."

Was he smiling? Alejandro shrugged. "Do you know what is interesting about your complaints, Miss Everly?" She did not answer him, but turned away. "Not a word you have said is against the island. But the people forcing their expectations upon you."

She squeezed her eyes shut. "My sister would not have said even that much."

"I have heard about your sister. That she is bold where you are quiet. That she acts without thinking while you consider matters carefully, always." He studied the line of her nose, the sweep of her hair piled up and twisted tightly. He preferred it down, dancing in an ocean breeze. Never mind how impractical such might be.

Her lips pressed together, the sounds of chirping birds and humming insects the only noise for several long moments while she appeared to gather her words. "Hope Everly is all the things you say."

"Yet you think she would be silent in the face of what you have endured?" He did not understand that. Not at all. Except. Something, in the back of his mind, tried to come forward in his thoughts. "Though you do not say it, I know you must be afraid. Everyone here is afraid."

"You aren't."

Alejandro lowered his arms to his sides again. "I have made my peace with this place. If rescue comes, I will thank God. If it does not, I will die here, as I would anywhere else." He started walking again, holding a branch out of her way when she followed behind. They came to the vines crawling up the trees and into shrubs full of thorns. Dark green pods hung from the plant. He plucked one and held it out to drop in her basket.

She allowed it, then plucked her own pods. "The others will worry, as you told me," she said quietly, as though chastened.

"Then they worry. They have done little else." He dropped several more pods into her basket. "When we return, they will tell you how wrong you were to leave them. As they did before. Both times."

She grimaced and yanked a pod off with more force than necessary, thrusting it into her basket. "You are certainly right."

Alejandro softened his tone. "It is because they care for you."

The response she gave was whisper-quiet. "They do not even know me."

What she meant, he did not know. But her movements, strong and confident, perturbed, continued to make quick work of the vines. When they had gathered most of what they could see, Alejandro suggested they return. She said nothing but fell in behind him on the path back to the clearing.

Why did he get the feeling she was right, and not one of her companions truly understood who she was?

❧ 18 ❧

Alejandro watched Miss Everly. At their return, Miss Carlbury refrained from lecturing her friend, but the doctor wasted no time or energy in telling her how foolish it was to disappear, how childish. She'd taken the lecture with a stiff back, whispered apologies, and went into the shelter.

"I cannot help her if she will not help herself," the doctor muttered to his wife and Alejandro.

Mrs. Morgan looped her arm through her husband's and slanted a look at Alejandro. "What state was she in when you found her, Señor Córdoba?"

Although he had no wish to reveal private matters, Alejandro had regarded Mrs. Morgan with respect from their first meeting. Perhaps she would have better luck soothing Miss Everly's troubled spirit than he had, as the two women seemed to have a positive regard for one another.

"She was crying," he admitted. "As though the world itself is against her. She has remained strong throughout this ordeal in a way one would not expect of a young woman who has been protected her whole life." Perhaps if he pointed out more of Miss

Everly's stronger qualities, the others might hold her in higher regard.

Mrs. Morgan's arm tightened around her husband's and the two exchanged a look of concern. "Will you speak in private with us a moment, Señor Córdoba?" the doctor asked, seemingly at his wife's behest.

Confused, Alejandro agreed, and the three of them withdrew from the fireside, to a part of the clearing where no one sat or worked. The doctor helped his wife sit on a fallen log, then tucked his hands behind his back. "I am informed by my wife that Mr. Carlbury wishes to pay court to Miss Everly, with the intention of marrying her."

Alejandro might have laughed at the idea if the couple before him did not appear perfectly serious about the matter. "Miss Everly informed *me* she does not care for the gentleman." That was putting it mildly. She seemed more likely to shove Mr. Carlbury off a cliff than to entertain his suit. Something that had immediately made him feel lighter, though he had no right to react in such a way. "I would say he might find it difficult to persuade her."

"Would you find it difficult to court Miss Everly?" Mrs. Morgan asked without warning.

What were these people after? Why ask such an impossible, personal question? He narrowed his eyes at Mrs. Morgan, pressing his lips together tightly a moment. "The question—it is irrelevant. There is no courtship on an island because there can be no marriage."

The doctor groaned and lowered himself to sit next to his wife. "You see? He is a practical man. Irrelevant." The doctor pinched the bridge of his nose. "Señor Córdoba, the question may be entirely relevant, whether we are rescued or not. Turn your practical mind to this. If rescue comes, and Miss Everly has been trapped upon an island full of men without the benefit of a relative to vouch for her virtue, will Society welcome her with open arms or regard her with suspicion?"

Oh. Alejandro had given no thought to such a thing. Which only proved how much he had forgotten of the civilized world in such a short time. "You worry for her reputation. I see." He glanced toward the shelter. How could anyone question that fiery woman's virtue? If they did within his presence, he would settle with anyone who dared—

"You see," Mrs. Morgan said with a brightness in her tone. "Miss Everly is in a difficult position, though she has no wish to see the truth of it. Her friend has attempted to speak to her of it several times, and I have as well, but Miss Everly refuses to acknowledge her difficulty."

Doctor Morgan picked up where his wife left off. "That was what upset her today. At least in part. I do not think she will ever agree to Mr. Carlbury's suit, but her honor might be protected by another. By you."

"Me?" Alejandro asked, feigning surprise but failing rather miserably at it.

"Her eyes follow you whenever you are near," Mrs. Morgan said softly. "And do not think it has escaped my notice how often you have watched her, too." The woman's smile was not precisely triumphant, but she was certainly pleased with herself. "If rescue comes, you could protect her from Society's cruelty."

He shook his head. "I could not. Doctor, Mrs. Morgan, I may be a poor man. My family may have lost everything in the fighting. They might not even be alive. A woman such as Miss Everly does not deserve such uncertainty. It would not be honorable."

"But you do like her," the doctor said, ignoring everything else Alejandro said. "And your name could protect her."

Alejandro narrowed his eyes at the older gentleman. "She should not require my protection. Her family would support her. And we are not discussing an important point. Rescue may never come at all."

"In which case," the doctor said with a deep frown etched into his face, "she is still an attractive young lady, surrounded by men who will become lonely and less apt to conform to the rules of civilization the longer they are away from it. You have proven yourself an exceptional man, Señor Córdoba. At present, I have agreed to act as a sort of guardian for Miss Everly. But I believe you would do a better job looking after her."

What the man suggested, implied, made heat rush into Alejandro's cheeks. He averted his eyes a moment, trying to form an argument, a denial, anything to end the conversation decisively. But Doctor Morgan had a sensible argument, and a far too realistic view of the situation that would unravel if rescue did not come.

The promises he had made Miss Everly came back to him, one by one. Promises to keep her safe, to look after her, to always find her. He had as good as declared himself her protector, and by extension the man who would stand between her and anyone who would do her harm. He did not regret those promises. He meant each of them.

He loved her, after all.

Swiftly he buried the confession deep, hiding the emotion as best he could from himself, as he had done all along. It was impossible.

"The honorable thing," Mrs. Morgan said quietly, using his own word against him, "would be to do what is best for Miss Everly, in any situation. Perhaps that is what you should consider, señor." She stood and her hand briefly brushed across her midsection in a curious manner. "At least think on it, please." She walked away, not waiting for her husband to follow.

The doctor watched his wife, then stood and extended a hand to Alejandro. "Please do as my wife asks. She likes Miss Everly a great deal. Neither of us wish to see her hurt."

"I will keep what you have said in mind." Alejandro shook the doctor's hand, sealing his agreement.

When night came, and the fire was built, Miss Everly finally emerged from the shelter to partake in the evening meal. She sat on a rock, back bent and expression dejected, avoiding the eyes of everyone. Alejandro was on the opposite side of the fire, twirling fibrous bark into a long strand of braided rope.

The sailors were laughing, speaking of their efforts to build a shelter. No one else spoke much. The professor was carrying on a quiet debate with Thorne.

Then Miss Everly, barely picking at her food, raised her head enough to address the sailors. "I heard you singing today. It was most cheerful. Might you sing for us now?"

Madden and the other two laughed. "We bellow like frogs, miss. No one wants to hear us more than they already have."

"I notice you did not ask me," Mr. Thorne said chipperly. "Everyone must have heard me singing yesterday."

"Which is why she did not ask you," the professor pointed out. Thorne laughed good-naturedly, as did the others around the fire.

There was a brief moment of silence, then Mrs. Morgan spoke from her place leaning against her husband's shoulder. "Come now, there must be more musical talent among us. I cannot claim to have great command over my voice, but I know my husband whistles most excellently."

"Bird calls," the doctor protested. "And we hear enough of those all day long." A loud night bird twittered at that moment from outside the clearing, giving everyone reason to laugh once again.

"Then what are we to do for entertainment?" Mrs. Morgan asked, dramatically disappointed. "I should so love a song. Something to lift our spirits. Even a nursery rhyme, or poetry recitation."

Alejandro's eyes drifted back to Miss Everly, whose head had lowered again as soon as Madden denied her request for a song. If anyone's spirits needed cheering, it was hers. He cleared his throat. "I might try, señora."

Miss Everly's head came up, her eyebrows high and her lips parted in surprise. He did not hear much of what the others said, though his offer inspired more mirth. But Miss Everly's expression, and Mrs. Morgan's encouragement, had him coming to his feet.

If there was one thing he had learned well from the monks who educated him, it was how to sing in a manner that would lift the souls of others. He had sung as a boy for the church, as a young man for the *vaqueros*, and for himself alone living on the island.

Tonight, he would sing for Miss Everly.

He chose a ballad, in his native tongue, which spoke of love. What else could he sing beneath the stars with the woman who had unknowingly captured his heart sitting and watching, listening, to each word?

He tried not to look at Miss Everly as he sang, though the words and gesture were meant for her. Declaring himself in such a way would do neither of them any good. So he kept his eyes closed, or looked to the fire, his heart aching.

Were the Morgans right? Was the honorable thing to acknowledge his feelings rather than hide them? If rescue never came, what was the honorable thing to do? Leaving Miss Everly in a state of frustration, of hurt, because he would not even discuss his feelings with her—was that honorable?

When he finished the song, Alejandro opened his eyes, his gaze landing on Miss Everly. She stared up at him, her eyes swimming with tears. Then someone started clapping, as though he had performed for the whole of the company rather than one woman, and then everyone else did, too. Everyone except Miss Everly.

She ducked her head as a tear fell from her eyes.

What was he to do?

Alejandro made a slight bow and retook his seat. The professor offered to recite a poem, "to continue the evening's entertainment." Alejandro had no wish to be entertained. He rose and left the fire, going into the night, to the beach. He needed time alone to think.

HOPE RESTED NEXT TO MRS. MORGAN, BENEATH A TREE, WHILE THE sun climbed higher in the sky. She had nothing with which to busy herself at the moment, and keeping Mrs. Morgan company was far easier than attempting to converse with Irene. Thankfully, Albert had invited his sister on a walk, and Irene had joined him. That gave Hope some peace at last.

The situation on the island had not worsened, exactly. But the mask Hope wore had cracked, making it difficult to hide her true feelings. The night of the storm, when she had realized how much she and Alejandro seemed to understand one another with few words spoken between them, had left its mark in more ways than one. His song had widened that crack in her mask.

How could he sing of love and not wish to speak to her, not wish to recognize, what her heart told her with such clarity?

Perhaps it was her own fault, lying about her identity. Perhaps he sensed the falsehood. Yet, to give way to him, to expose that secret merely because he had held her comfortably in his arms those few moments in the trees would be imprudent. Wishing he might take her in his arms again only more so.

If he would not declare his thoughts, his feelings, then speaking her own might prove nothing more than her undoing. Yet she was tired, so very tired, of living a lie.

The day after Alejandro sang, the sailors continued their work of constructing another shelter, using the rocks as one wall while building two more to form a triangular building. They sang again as they worked, in a language Hope did not understand. She sat beneath the shade, watching them, hugging her knees to her chest. Their deep voices filled the air, the songs not exactly cheerful.

Mrs. Morgan sat next to Hope, waving a large leaf the doctor had found her as though it were a fan. "They are songs about freedom," the woman said.

Hope's contentment in the moment dissipated. "Freedom?"

"I have heard the songs before. During festivals. Slaves and free men mingle together on certain days. Overseers dislike it, but at night, when there is no work to do, the only other option is to lock the slaves in their homes. So no one fights it. Perhaps that is why they did not wish to share the songs with us last night. They are not meant for us." Mrs. Morgan shifted and put a hand over her abdomen. Not her ribs.

Turning swiftly away from the telling sight, Hope stretched her legs out in front of her and studied a new tear in her skirt. "I cannot imagine what life is like for a slave. I have seen them working in the fields. The sailors here have deep scars on their arms and backs. It is so wrong."

"Very wrong. Evil, I should say. To think any man could subjugate another in such a way." Mrs. Morgan's words held a sorrowful tone. "They wait for freedom. Their songs, all of them, are about losing the right to go where they wish, their homelands, and dreaming to be free again one day."

Hope watched the sailors use long strips of braided bark to lash together sticks. "They do not think we are leaving the island, do they?"

"Apparently not." Mrs. Morgan pushed herself to her feet. "Would you walk down to the beach with me? I would like to feel the cool air on my face and walk in the water." Mrs. Morgan had removed her stockings and walked barefoot, like Hope.

"Please." Hope rose and brushed off the dirt and grass from her dress. Alejandro's shirt was tattered at the sleeves, his breeches at the knees. How long before her clothing was as ragged as his?

Irene and Albert had disappeared shortly after sunrise. They had invited Hope to come, but she had declined the invitation to go anywhere with them. Most likely, given Irene's conversation from the day before, they would only embark upon a joint effort to pressure her into accepting Albert's suit.

Living with a ruined reputation would be preferable to marrying into the Carlbury family.

Doctor Morgan, the professor, and Alejandro had left for the beach a short time previous. Alejandro had mentioned that the storm had left more bounty scattered across the beaches, and all seemed interested in looking for anything of use to them. The sun neared its zenith, which meant the men might return soon to get out of the heat of the day.

"Why do the men get to go where they please?" Hope asked as they walked down the hill. "They did not ask us if they could go. They did not tell us when they would return."

"Because a man is capable of defending himself from danger." Mrs. Morgan's matter-of-fact answer did nothing to make Hope's attitude better. "If you wandered off alone and fell in a ditch, could you pull yourself out? If confronted by a wild animal, could you fight it off?"

"There is nothing on this island more dangerous than we are." Hope hadn't seen anything bigger than birds. Not yet. Alejandro had told them nothing but small spiders and certain lizards would harm them. There were no snakes, no rats, not even any large birds of prey.

The warm sand turned hot the further up the dune they walked, then down the other side. Mrs. Morgan led the way to the lapping waves, holding her skirts up to reveal most of her shins.

Water pushed against their legs, each wave rolling up the sand and then withdrawing again, almost politely. The water was calm today, as far as Hope could see. She shaded her eyes and examined the horizon, looking for anything to indicate they were not alone in the world. Where was rescue? Why had no one come for them?

A coil of hair fell out of the restrictive knot she had attempted to keep her hair out of her face. "Botheration." Hope brushed the hair out of her eyes. "It is only a matter of time before the whole of it falls to my shoulders again."

Mrs. Morgan touched her hair, braided and coiled about her head like a crown. It did not shine with the luster it had when they first met, but at least she kept it out of her way with some success. "Would you like my help?" the married woman asked.

"Please, do not trouble yourself. Even my maid could never

quite get everything to remain in place." Hope found the linen strip Alejandro had given her. It had begun to fray, with many tiny strings loose from the main cut of fabric. She pulled the strip out of her hair and shook her head. Her hair tumbled down, thick and waving in the damp air.

"I ought to plait it and leave it at that," she said.

"Oh, look." Mrs. Morgan stared down the shore. Her eyes brightened. "It is the doctor and the others."

Hope glanced over her shoulder. Her eyes found Alejandro first, walking as he always did, confident in each step he took. Her heart flitted upward in her breast, most inconveniently causing her lungs to constrict. She put her hand to her chest, willing the offending organ to go back to its proper place.

He may not wish to discuss it, but that did not stop Hope from feeling something whenever he was near. It was not at all fair, that she finally came upon a gentleman who made her heart soar and ache, a man she knew she could love if given the chance, in a place where nothing could be done about those feelings.

Mrs. Morgan came out of the water. Hope followed, somewhat reluctantly. They met the gentlemen walking along the beach and the doctor fell back to walk with his wife, while Hope took up his place between the younger two men. She glanced over her shoulder once, after a few steps, to see the doctor had taken his wife in his arms, holding her in an embrace.

She faced forward again, catching her skirts in both hands. An overly cheerful voice broke in on her thoughts. "What have you busied yourself with today, Miss Everly?"

Hope glanced from Alejandro's unsmiling face on one side to Mr. Thorne's grin on the other. "Not a great deal, Mr. Thorne. It is not my visiting day, or my at home day."

He chuckled. "No? Have you a ball to attend this evening? Or will it be the theater?"

"An opera." The game made her smile. "I love music."

"Do you?" Mr. Thorne's eyebrows raised upward, and he darted a glance at Alejandro. "I am afraid everyone now knows I cannot carry a tune. But thankfully we have Córdoba. Have you a taste for the opera, sir?"

"I have never seen one." Alejandro made the admission flatly. "In Buenos Aires, we had *El Teatro Coliseo.* But my father did not attend many plays, and fewer still with the war. My family's land is several miles to the west of the city. We made most of our own entertainment."

Her heart softened as she recalled the many parlor recitals Grace and she had taken part in. "I have only been to the opera once," she admitted. "My parents rarely travel to London. They much prefer the quiet of the country."

Mr. Thorne made a sound of disapproval. "A quiet country life is all well and good, but I should not like to stay still for long."

"What of your betrothed?" Hope asked, her desire to change the subject getting the better of her manners. "Does she enjoy the city or the country?"

The smile faded from his eyes and Mr. Thorne shrugged. "I do not really know. I have only met her once." He cleared his throat and nodded to the trees. "I think I will gather some of those bending saplings the storm uprooted. I am certain they will weave together nicely for the new shelter. Excuse me." He stepped away, but Alejandro kept walking, so Hope did, too.

They said nothing to each other at first. Then Hope dared move closer to him. Not close enough to touch his hand as they walked. Not quite. Just enough to attempt a more companionable stroll.

"If we were in London," she said aloud when he remained quiet, "you would offer me your arm. We would walk down a path in the park together, perhaps."

"Why would we be in London?" He did not sound as though he were interested in the flight of fancy the way Mr. Thorne had been. Yet she persevered. Anything to make conversation, to take her mind off their present situation. Anything to spend a few moments nearer him.

"I imagine it is the only place we might have met, were it not for the island. Perhaps you would visit there as part of a political delegation. I would have persuaded my family to spend some time in Town during the Season. We would meet at a party or by chance have a mutual acquaintance." She studied him from the corner of her eye, trying to imagine what a fine figure he must have made in a coat, cravat, and clean shaven.

Alejandro's steps slowed, his tone changing to one of curiosity. "What would you have made of me there, I wonder?"

"I likely would have found you intriguing. A diplomat from South America. You are rather exotic, you know." She did not bat her eyes or speak flirtatiously. But she grinned at him and tried, with all her might, to pretend he was the same to her as Isaac, Silas, or Jacob. They always teased one another. It was part of their friendship. But those three men did not make her stomach flip or her heart stutter the way Alejandro did when he cast her a sideways glance.

It was hopeless, really.

Alejandro stopped walking completely. "I would have found you stunning." His hands balled into fists as he turned to face her, and all desire to see him as no more than a friend fled. Her heart beat a staccato rhythm. This time she did not bid it stay in place. Alejandro's gaze had arrested her, fully capturing her attention with the sincerity in their depths. "Witty. Beautiful. Charming." He stepped closer. She had to lift her chin to maintain eye contact. He did not tower over her, but his greater height was comfortable, almost reassuring.

"Are you a flirt when you are in Society, Señor Córdoba?" she asked, her voice coming out strong enough that she almost sounded unconcerned. But her blush, if he saw it, would give her away.

His smile flashed through his beard at her. "Perhaps. I used to practice so that when I met the right woman I would know precisely how to woo her. But a year is a long time. I am likely out of practice. That might make it difficult to win a lady's hand. What do you think? Will any woman find my suit worthwhile?"

Never had Hope participated in such a frank conversation of the games men and women played with one another. Was Alejandro serious? He couldn't be. Given what he said, how strongly he felt that rescue would not come.

Hope turned from him and started walking again, up the dune that would lead to the well and the path back to the shelter. "You will meet her, señor. I have faith in that."

He quickened his steps to catch up to her. "Miss Everly?"

She nearly stumbled going up the sand, but caught herself in time to avoid falling face first into the dune. "Yes, señor?"

"Would you care to walk with me in the park?" he asked.

They had reached the top of the sandy hill, allowing her to stop and look at him without fear of losing her balance. The wind from the ocean pushed her hair out of her way as she regarded him with confusion. His deep brown eyes, like chocolate with not more than a splash of milk to cool the heat within, pulled her perilously closer.

"There are no parks here, señor."

"Along the beach?" he countered, leaning nearer to her.

Her heart shuddered, and her eyes briefly fell to his lips. How easy would it be to kiss him? No one was near enough to see. Society would never know, never judge her. But— "To what end? You have made it clear you will not discuss certain things with me, as there is no reason to entertain the idea of a rescue, there is no reason to hope for more."

He bent closer, as though he had heard her thoughts and was as tempted by a kiss as she was. "Then I must have faith in rescue once more," he murmured, voice growing softer. He raised a hand to brush back her hair, tucking it behind her ear. "I must pray again for rescue, and I will watch for it every day. Because you did not imagine the connection between us. I felt it, too. I still do. My heart has not ceased to reach for yours."

Hope's heart soared, and she lifted her head, her lips parting in surprise.

Alejandro closed the remaining distance between them slowly, though without hesitation. He gave her plenty of time to turn her head, to step backward. Instead, Hope rose on her toes and put her palms against his chest to lean into him as his lips pressed against hers.

Thunder curled upward from her chest and lightning hummed between them. His kiss was not tentative and testing. It was as he was; he kissed with confidence and a surety that made her brave and bold, too. Her hands left his chest and crept to the back of his neck and head, holding him to her while his arms wrapped around her waist and shoulders.

The kiss was like nothing she'd ever experienced. Everything inside her fizzled and sang.

His beard tickled but did not give reason enough to stop the kiss.

Hope knew what she had not dared allow herself to think on before. This man was her other half. His steadiness and confidence, his courage and strength, was a match for her. She felt it in her soul.

They parted and his forehead rested against hers before he stepped back, taking in a deep breath. "Hope," he whispered.

Her thoughts stopped as abruptly as a carriage slamming into a brick wall. Her heart froze. He couldn't know. But shouldn't he? If he was all she wanted him to be—but how—?

"We must have hope," he said firmly, and disappointment mingled with her relief. Yet to have him say her name, his beautiful voice drawing out the word like a caress, made her heart ache. "I cannot behave dishonorably, *mi hermosa*. Rescue must come." Then he ran a hand through his hair. "And so many other things after."

"Rescue," she repeated, staring up at him. "Do you think—"

"Grace!" Irene shouted from the hillside, and Hope grimaced. Alejandro immediately chuckled. Horrid man. Beautiful, horrid, wonderful man.

Turning, Hope called back to her friend. "Irene?"

She wasn't alone. Albert was at her side, but he appeared to be looking at Alejandro. Not Hope. And the frown he wore made her wonder what he made of the situation and how much he may have seen.

"Go," Alejandro murmured. "See to your friend. We will speak more later."

She cast a look over her shoulder at him. "It is about time you agreed to that," she said, smiling. Then she gave her attention to Irene, leaving Alejandro behind, though she carried their glorious kiss in her heart.

❧ 19 ❧

Alejandro leaned back against a tree, watching the fire and those gathered around it. Mr. Thorne roasted fish over a spit that Professor Gibson had put together. The sailors had caught several small fish between the coral and beach on the north side of the island, and with the nuts and fruits cooked, the islanders were practically feasting.

His mind too preoccupied to notice whether or not he was hungry, Alejandro allowed his eyes to linger on the object of his thoughts. Miss Everly. She sat between Mr. and Miss Carlbury, listening to her friend speak and wearing a smile on her lips that did not quite reach her eyes.

How did a woman with such fire in her heart abide the friendship of the Carlburys? How, day after day, did she patiently endure Mr. Carlbury's arrogance and Miss Carlbury's complaints? He could not imagine they were much different out in the world away from the island. Hardship tended to make people act more themselves, not less.

Miss Everly accepted a fish wrapped in a large leaf from Mr. Thorne, then stood from her place at the fire. She walked around the ring of people and came to where he sat in the dark. His eyes flicked from her oncoming form to the people she had left. As he suspected, Miss Carlbury watched her with confusion and the brother glared directly at Alejandro.

He kept his expression flat, though he did not know how much Carlbury discerned through the flickering shadows. If the Englishman gave Alejandro reason enough, Alejandro had little doubt he could put Carlbury in his place. Dissentions in a group this small, stuck together for who knew how much longer, had the potential to prove dangerous. But the Morgans were right. Alejandro could defend himself and Miss Everly well enough.

But this gave him yet another reason to avoid kissing Miss Everly again, though the temptation stirred to test if a second kiss might be as good or better than the first.

The beautiful woman came to his side, sitting on the ground next to him. "Are you not eating, Alejandro?" she asked, her voice low and sweet in the darkness. She proffered the fish and nuts on the large leaf. "I brought some dinner to you." He caught the glint in her eye, the slight smile turning up her lips.

"Thank you." He accepted the offering, his hands sliding beneath hers to take the makeshift plate without spilling the food. The back of her hands slid across his palms as she withdrew them, tucking her hands tightly into her lap while he tucked into the food. He ate with more care than usual, aware that she watched him from the corner of her eye.

Incredible, how swiftly a woman's attention changed his behavior as well as his outlook on the future. Rescue must come, for her sake.

"Tell me more about your home," she said, her words a gentle command he did not hesitate to obey.

"*Mi padre*, he is a gentleman, as you would say. He owns land. So much land, overrun by wild cattle everywhere; and there are fields of corn and tobacco. We have vineyards, too." He took care to clean his fingers in the grasses, then lifted his mother's ring to where it gleamed in the firelight. "This ring, *mi mama* bought it when I was born. She gave it to me when I set sail, to take it with me to remember her. All the women wear this stone, and she wanted to remind people where her first son had been born."

Before he tucked the ring away, Miss Everly leaned closer and lifted it from his palm. She examined the ring closely for the first time, and he held his breath. She was so near, he might easily brush her cheek with his lips. Instead, he traced the line of her profile with his eyes, committing each detail to memory.

"It is beautiful. The stone, it looks like amber."

"The women in my country, they wear these stones and almost no other jewel." He touched her hand with one finger, tracing across her knuckles. She shivered and released the ring. "My mother, she would like you."

Her eyes flashed at him through the shadows. "Do you think so? I cannot say many mothers have liked me, to my memory. Most think I am a poor influence on their children."

His brows lowered. "I cannot see how that could be." She conducted herself with grace, especially in company.

Abruptly, Miss Everly turned away from him. She laughed, but the sound was choked, nervous perhaps. Alejandro considered her for a long moment, that hidden part of her nearly peeking out intrigued him.

He gave his attention back to the food in his hand. "Tell me about you. Why did you come to the Caribbean? There is more to it than the invitation you received." He ate slowly, giving her ample time to think through her answer. He watched her eyes, noting the expression she wore when she phrased her answers carefully. Somehow, he would discover her secret.

"The Carlburys offered, and how could I turn down an experience such as this? No other time in my life would I have the means to visit distant lands in so safe a manner." Each word she spoke with precision, with exactness.

"But it was to be the other sister who came. Your sister Hope."

He saw Miss Everly's throat constrict as she nodded and squeezed her eyes shut.

"That is right."

"Do you miss her?"

She nodded tightly and wrapped her arms about herself. "Nearly every moment. She is my dearest friend as well as my sister. We have never been apart this long."

His heart fell. "I do not suppose you will be eager to separate yourself from her again when rescue comes." His dreams of courtship were foolish, as he had told the Morgans. Miss Everly and he barely knew one another. Miss Everly was an English-woman, from a world far different from his own. From a privileged life in an established country. His family practically lived on the edge of a wilderness, if they still held his father's land.

"I will be glad to be near her again," the lovely woman said, closing her eyes. "But neither of us expect to be near the other all our lives. We are not ignorant of the fact that our paths will part. They already have."

"I admit, I do not know what such a bond would be like." Alejandro crumpled up the leaf and tossed it aside. "I am much older than my brother. By twelve years. I am my parents' heir. And here I am. On an accursed island."

"At least you have company now," she countered, a smile back on her face as she nudged him with her shoulder.

Despite his bleak thoughts from a moment before, Alejandro found it easy to return her cheerful expression, warmth spreading from the place their shoulders touched throughout the rest of his body. How fortunate, to have one of the people who landed upon his beaches be someone who completely enchanted him. The peace that came when he stopped fighting against the pull they both felt had nearly overwhelmed him.

"Miss Everly." He turned his attention back to the fire. "Your company would be welcome no matter where I found myself."

A shape crossed between them and the firelight, and both

looked up to see Miss Carlbury standing over them. "Grace, I think we had better turn in."

There was no reason for doing so. Why keep to traditional hours when they had nothing that called for their attention in the morning? He did not give voice to his thoughts. If Miss Everly wished to stay, she would stay.

With a more gentle expression, a lesser smile, upon her face she answered her friend in a quiet tone. "I will be there in a moment, Irene."

Her friend hesitated, clearly surprised. "Do not be long." With that last command given, she turned on her heel. Alejandro watched as she cast a look back to where her brother sat, then disappeared into the darkness of the shelter.

"Why do they think they can tell you what to do?" The question had tugged at his mind since the first time Miss Everly had clearly refused Carlbury's command to leave the conversation to the gentlemen. It had been the only time he'd seen her go against their expectations of her behavior.

"Perhaps they feel responsible," she said softly, avoiding his eyes. "I would not be here had they not invited me."

"There is more to it than that." Alejandro leaned so their shoulders brushed again, which brought her gaze up to his. "*Mi hermosa*, if you need anything, any help, any comfort I can give, you have but to ask."

She ducked her head, her lips pressing together to hide how pleased she was by his offer. "Thank you, Alejandro. I will remember that. For tonight, I had better go to bed."

He leaped to his feet before she moved, in order to offer her his hand and assistance to her feet. She put her hand in his and beamed at him, nearly lighting the night with the pleased glow of her eyes. "I hope you sleep well, Miss Everly. *Duerme bien y dulces sueños.*"

"Sleep well," she translated, eyebrows drawing together. "And...?"

"Sweet dreams." He bowed over her hand in as courtly a manner as ever he'd bowed. She curtsied. "Thank you, Señor Córdoba." Then she left him, looking back once before fading into the shadows.

Heaven help him, but his heart went with her. Weeks and months of meeting other women in his travels, of escorting them to balls and theaters and church, sitting in their parlors, had not prepared him for what he felt now. His heart burned, his every thought full of Miss Everly's beautiful blue eyes and bright laughter. How were they to dwell on the same island together if help did not come soon?

A hand landed on his shoulder heavily.

Alejandro's jaw tightened, and he curled both hands into fists. He kept his voice cheerful, however, when he spoke. "If you wish me to remove your hand myself, it will not go well for you, *amigo.*"

The hand disappeared, and Alejandro took a swift step forward, turning at the same time to face the tall Englishman who had crept up behind him. Others still sat around the fire, but none gave heed to them.

Carlbury raised both hands to show he meant no offense. "I am only come to tell you, Córdoba. Miss Everly is a sweet woman. She is not for you."

Bold words. "I have made no attempt to claim her." Not yet. Alejandro tipped his chin up, taking the man's measure.

"That isn't what it looks like," the arrogant man countered, a grimace twisting the features of his unremarkable face.

Carlbury obviously thought himself capable of winning in a fight, but his posture clearly marked him as one unused to so much as throwing a punch. Whereas Alejandro had grown up scuffling with the sons of the *vaqueros*, and then the *vaqueros* themselves, to pass the time and settle disagreements during long nights of the cattle hunt. In Northern America, he had learned to wrestle, and he'd worked every day to survive living on the island.

He almost wished Carlbury would try something. Anything.

"I cannot help what it looks like to *you*, señor." Alejandro adjusted his stance ever so slightly. "Miss Everly is a lady, and I have treated her as such." After all, she had returned his kiss rather than spurned it, so there was nothing dishonorable in *that*. "Should she express dislike for my company, I will not burden her with my conversation. You ought to consider acting in a similar manner."

That made the other man jerk his chin upward. "Are you suggesting I am not—that I do not respect the lady's wishes?"

"Not at all. I am saying you ought to ask if she wants your company rather than impose it upon her. *Perdón*. I have work to do elsewhere." If he didn't leave, he might say more that he would regret. There was no need to bring Miss Everly's name into a disagreement simply because he disliked another man who admired her.

Without giving Carlbury time to respond, Alejandro ducked into the trees and went for the beach. Sleeping near the surf would do a great deal to ease his heart and mind, listening to the waves come in with the tide. Perhaps he would check the makeshift signal flag, too. Make certain it still beckoned ships to come closer. He needed to get the woman he loved off the island.

❧ 20 ❦

"What is the word for weave?" Hope asked, carefully focused on her net weaving. Alejandro had given her a section of the sail that had torn off in the wind, making their signal flag yet smaller, and shown her how to braid it to create a rope to use as a snare.

"*Tejer*. It is the same for knitting." He was using a flat, sharp-edged rock to whittle the ends of long sticks, to create another fishing spear. "And rope is *cuerda*."

"Like cord." She grinned. "Teach me words such as that one. Give me the easy words."

"*Las palabras fáciles*."

Hope did not bother to hide her exasperation, scooping up a handful of grass and tossing it at him. "None of that was comprehensible."

"I said what you told me to say." He raised his dark eyebrows at her and leaned slightly nearer. "*The easy words*."

She covered her mouth to muffle her unladylike snigger. "You are a rascal, Señor Córdoba." She attempted to give him a withering look, though the way he looked at her sent her tingling from her fingertips to her toes. "You know what I meant."

"Easy words." He narrowed his eyes at her and pressed his lips tightly together a moment. "I will teach you as I have seen children taught. Here." He tapped his nose. "*La nariz*. The nose."

"*La nariz*," she repeated, pleased to finally get somewhere. "That is close to the French word. I can remember that. What are the eyes?"

"*Los ojos*," he answered simply, as a gleam appeared in his.

Hope huffed and glared at him. "That is not at all like the French word. *Los o-hos*."

"*Ojos*," he corrected. "You have *bonitos ojos azules*." The way he said that phrase, staring intensely at her, made heat rush into her cheeks. Obviously the man flirted with her and thought to get away with it by speaking in his native tongue.

"One thing at a time," she said, purposefully looking away from him. "The ears?"

"*Las orejas*."

An English equivalent that helped her remember that word came to mind. "Like orator."

"If you say so, *hermosa*." He lowered the fishing spear and lifted another branch, ready to transform it into a hunting weapon, too. "Mouth. *La boca*."

"*La boca*." She glanced at the doctor and his wife beneath the trees, catching another glimpse of Mrs. Morgan with her hands across her abdomen. Hope watched the two Morgans speak with one another, their voices not carrying to where she and Alejandro sat on the other side of the clearing. Their expressions were strained while they spoke, though they leaned near one another. Their troubles unified them rather than parted them, growing their affection rather than straining it.

"*Sí*. Now. *Bésame*." Alejandro's deep voice instructed clearly, his words warming her. She repeated him without thought.

"*Bésame*." She started when he took her hand and placed a kiss upon her knuckles, the heat from her cheeks spreading quickly throughout the rest of her. "Alejandro," she whispered, though she did not remove her hand from his.

"*Bésame* means 'kiss me.'" He gave her an unrepentant grin, then sprang to his feet with both spears in one hand. "You must excuse me now, *mi hermosa*. I join the fishermen today. Though I had much rather sit with you."

"You are a brazen flirt, Señor Córdoba." She bit her bottom lip when he bowed. Perhaps some distance between them would be a good thing, given how easily she blushed in his presence. "Enjoy your fishing."

"*Gracias.*" He went on his way, his step lighter than she had seen it thus far.

The task in her hands, though not strictly necessary, captured her attention again. At home, she detested sewing and embroidery, while Grace excelled at both. Hope could create lovely things when she set her mind to it, but it took her three times as long to finish a project as it did Grace. Hope simply had no patience to sit at what felt like idle work. But this, creating an item that might prove useful to survival, felt entirely different.

Her mind wandered to her sister as Hope hummed to herself, to how Grace kept busy with Hope away. Likely she went about her life as always, making visits to their neighbors and the poor, listening to the problems of others and offering well-thought-out solutions, proving a calming influence everywhere she went.

Grace would have been a better friend to Irene in the aftermath of the shipwreck. The patience Grace possessed, the ability to bite her tongue, to soothe others before worrying over herself, would have been invaluable to their little group. Instead, it fell to Hope to fill the place meant for her sister.

Thus far, Hope had proven less apt than Grace at soothing ruffled feelings and feathers alike.

Movement in the brush alerted Hope to the return of members of their party, and she stopped humming when she saw Irene and

Albert coming through. They both wore large, satisfied smiles. Hope raised her eyebrows. What had they been doing all morning?

Albert's stare met hers, and his smile faded slightly. Irene looked from her brother to Hope, then tugged him forward.

"Oh, Grace. You simply must come with us on a walk. We have had such a diverting morning." She gave up on tugging her brother closer when Albert took no more than a step out from the growth, still under the shadows of the trees. "Albert has found such a lovely place. Do come."

Hope's hands stilled and she lowered them to her lap. "But you have only now returned. Surely you have no wish to turn back." Irene's sudden cheerful behavior ought to have been a relief. Instead, Hope found herself suspicious. Hardly the mark of a good friend.

"We are only hungry," Albert said, finally coming closer. He regarded Hope with something like curiosity. "After we eat and drink, we are on our way again."

"Do say you will accompany us," Irene said over her shoulder before disappearing into the shelter, where baskets of dried berries and nuts were kept.

Hope stared after her friend, then glanced up at Albert where he stood close to her, towering over her. "What have you found to cheer her so greatly?" she asked, her voice too low to carry to Irene.

Albert lowered himself to the ground, almost hesitantly. He took up a stick and poked at the embers of the fire. "You will have to come and see for yourself if you wish to find out." His gaze darted away from her when she tried to meet his eyes again. To find him undemanding surprised her nearly as much as Irene's sudden agreeableness.

When Irene emerged with the basket of food and shared it out between the three of them, guilt smote at Hope for her suspicions. Fate had dealt them a hard blow, marooning them on the island.

She could not be angry that Irene reacted differently than Hope. To regard Irene's change in attitude with such apprehension did not seem like something Grace would do.

"If you two truly wish it," Hope said at last, as she examined the dried berries in her hands, "I should be happy to accompany you on a walk."

"Marvelous." Irene popped several nuts in her mouth and shared a superior sort of smirk with her brother. "See? Though Grace is not as fond of exploration as her sister, she will certainly appreciate something other than sitting about here all day."

Hope winced at the comparison. As much as she wished to reveal her true self to Alejandro, to give him a name to call her other than the formal Miss Everly, it would be wrong to disclose the truth to him while those that knew her better still had no thought that she had taken Grace's place. This walk, as reluctant as she was to venture anywhere with Albert, would prove a perfect opportunity to tell the truth at last.

They began their ramble through the trees after both Carlburys pronounced themselves refreshed for the journey. Hope had managed to tie her hair up and back again, presenting at least some semblance of respectability, and she trailed along behind Albert and ahead of Irene.

"I am surprised you wished to enter the trees again, after the incident with the spider," Hope said after they had walked for a short time.

Irene made a sound of disgust. "Horrid creature. We saw another on the path this morning. Albert took care of it."

Somehow, Hope doubted that meant he hurried the spider out of the way. Most likely the poor creature had met the bottom of Albert's boot in an unexpected manner. Hope wasn't one to enjoy the creeping creatures of the world, but she did let them alone if they did nothing to bother her.

She fell quiet and before long the brother and sister were

having a conversation about the weather. Though something about it felt unnatural.

"Do you think it will rain?" Irene asked.

Albert answered as haughtily as ever. "If I thought it was going to rain, I would not have arranged things as I did. That last storm blew over and everything is finally dried out. We will be fine."

"It does not seem as though such things are so easily predicted out in the middle of the sea." Irene's response, though somewhat petulant, gave Hope leave to relax. They were themselves after all.

"I know what I am doing." Albert held a branch out of the way for both women to pass, then took up the walk again next to Hope. "We are going nearly to the opposite end of the island. We will break from the trees here and walk along the beach, if you like. To save your feet."

She looked down as she walked and sighed. "Nothing will save my poor feet now, I am afraid. They are as tough as a bloodhound's paws."

Irene made a sound of distress. "You poor darling. I have nearly worn my shoes through, but at least they have offered some protection."

Though Hope did not mind going about barefoot most of the time, as it had reminded her of the childhood she left behind, Hope did not deny that the sand would prove easier for her. They veered out of the steep tree-lined path and emerged onto the beach somewhat above where the little boat had been wrecked.

The sailors had not allowed anyone to pull apart the board of the vessel, though it was no longer sea-worthy. Perhaps they yet held hope in repairing the split and cracked boards well enough to row away from the island.

She couldn't guess how it might be done.

For a time, they walked in silence. The surf's dull roar made it difficult to exchange conversation without shouting, and a breeze came up from the other end of the island. If they ever stopped, Hope had determined to reveal her identity to them both. It might cause some embarrassment, given the number of times Irene had spoken of Hope's attributes in a less than kind way. But the truth would most likely alleviate Albert's concern at her continually ignoring his advances.

They turned into the land again, where a hill sloped upward. How long had they walked? A quarter of an hour, at least, bringing them to the northeastern edge of the island.

"You have done some exploring," Hope said, nearly panting in the upward climb. "What is it you have found?"

The wind shifted, coming from ahead of them, whisking a curl out of Hope's eyes. She lifted her head to enjoy the sensation, only to stop in her steps so abruptly Irene bumped into her shoulder.

"Grace, are you—?"

"Something is burning," Hope whispered, unable to keep the horror from her voice.

"Oh." Irene laughed. "Come. It is safe." She took Hope's arm and tugged her forward. Albert had gone ahead several yards and did not even realize they had stopped. "Albert has been so clever about it. You will see. I do not know why we ever trusted that horrid Spaniard with anything. He obviously knows nothing of being rescued or he would not have been stuck here for so long. Perhaps he wants to stay. Some people are not right in the head, and this life might appeal to him. But I am quite finished with it." Irene chattered on, her hand on Hope's arm.

Hope had to know what they had done. She kept moving up the hill, the scent of fire growing stronger with each step.

They emerged on a flatter area, where only a few yards from the trees a strange fire burned. It looked like something out of a druid's tale, with logs stacked upon one another to form a large box. The logs were stacked up taller than Hope's waist, with fire burning inside, a plume of white smoke rising up.

"We have been collecting dry leaves and twigs, and a few green branches, too, to help with the smoke," Irene said with obvious pride. Hope turned, shocked, to regard the absolute glee on her friend's face.

"This isn't safe," Hope said, pointing up to the branches hanging nearly over the fire. "What if those trees should catch?"

Albert snorted. "They are far enough away. And after the rain, I doubt much would light even if they caught an ember or two."

Hope wrapped her arms about her waist. What would Grace do? How would she diffuse the situation? Grace was forever stopping arguments and solving disputes— But Grace wasn't here.

"This is the most idiotic thing I have ever seen," she said, her voice steady and firm as she glared from Irene to Albert. "The sun has dried out what the rain did, and fire does not care if the earth is wet when it leaps from tree to tree. Put it out, Mr. Carlbury. Consult the others before taking such risks."

Albert's eyes grew dark as he stepped toward her. "Miss Everly, you have no say in the matter. I have considered our options and built this signal fire with absolute confidence in my abilities. Look." He pointed upward where a plume of smoke rose nearly thirty feet. "A passing ship will see this."

The white smoke made her cringe. "Will they? This is not the highest point of the island. The smoke is white, which hardly stands out against the blue of the sky or the clouds on the horizon. And while it seems large to us, ships will be miles off. How will they see it?"

"Acting as though you know things is not the same as actual intelligence," Albert said, the last word nearly a hiss. "Do not be foolish, Grace. This will work, and then everyone will thank me. We will be off this island without the assistance of the Spaniard."

Hope turned from him to Irene and tried to take her friend's hand. "Irene, you must come with me. It isn't safe—"

Irene snatched her hand back. "Staying on this hateful rock is not safe. Albert is right. We must get off the island and go home. I miss my mama and papa."

They would not listen to her. All thoughts of confessing her identity fled, and she did the same. Hope ran down the hill to the beach, though she realized belatedly that Alejandro would be fishing to the north rather than the south. She cut back into the trees, making her own path despite the brambles that tore at her dress and the roots scraping against her feet.

Lifting her skirts higher than anyone would ever think decent, she ran through the trees, her lungs burning from the inhaled smoke and her exertion.

How could the Carlburys so selfishly put people at risk, consulting no one with their plan? Alejandro had explained everything to the group, time and again, about the possibility of rescue and the conservation of their resources. The superiority of the Carlburys had proved more destructive than stupidity.

A crash in the brush ahead of Hope almost made her pause, but Alejandro had promised her there was nothing on the island larger than she. It had to be someone—

Alejandro himself appeared, pushing around a tree, without a shirt once more. Had he removed it for fishing? She did not have time to wonder, or to blush.

"Fire," she said, pointing in the direction she had come from, up the northern rise of the island. "Albert built a fire." Alejandro's hands came upon her shoulders, steadying her as he stared into her eyes.

"Is it under control?" he asked. "I smelt it—then I saw—"

"He says it is safe, but I did not feel it so." Hope took hold of his wrists. "He will not put it out. You will need help."

His expression darkened, eyebrows drawing down and the line of his jaw tightening. "No. I will not." Then he started up the hill, and she followed. He knew the island better than she ever wished to and soon had them on a path less painful for her to follow. He did not wait for her, but ran ahead. Hope kept going, her skirts snagging on every branch that reached for her.

She was going up the rise, hands before her to grab onto branches, when she heard the screams.

BEFORE ALEJANDRO MADE IT TO THE TOP OF THE RISE, HIS HEART sunk. The smoke rose into the sky, but he saw fire burning in the branches before him. How fast it would spread, he could not tell. All he knew was that he must save a man and his sister from their own arrogant mistake. He shoved himself up the hillside faster, sweat already running down his back when he passed beneath the first tree with a branch ablaze.

"Carlbury!" He shouted the man's name through the sound of fire crackling and branches snapping ahead of him.

"Here!" the shout came back. Alejandro turned and stepped toward the sound as Miss Everly came to his side. She gasped, then started coughing.

"Go back," Alejandro yelled, taking her shoulders in a firm group. "Go back, *mi hermosa*. Tell everyone—gather our food and supplies. Take it to the beach. The fire may spread."

She covered one of his hands with hers, meeting his gaze squarely, her eyes unafraid. "What about you?"

"I will meet you at the place I found you," he promised. "Go." Then he released her and took a step back.

"Alejandro," she shouted, her voice cracking. The depths of her blue eyes conveyed an emotion for him she had not named. Not yet. And not in that moment. But she lunged forward as fierce as a lioness and pressed her lips to his. Alejandro returned the kiss, unable to savor the moment as he would wish. But at least he had the answer to one question about this unexpectedly wonderful woman—the second kiss was better than the first.

She broke away, turning at the same time, and fled without looking back. She would do as he asked and left her kiss as a talisman of protection. He touched the other token he wore, his mother's ring, before charging further into the now smoke-filled trees.

After calling again, he found his way to a soot-streaked Carlbury. He stumbled about, frantic, his eyes streaming. He pointed through the trees, upward. "Irene—I cannot reach her. She is on the other side. The rocks."

The picture clearly formed in Alejandro's mind. "You built the fire on the flat land near the cliffs. She fled that way and fell."

"Yes." Albert grabbed Alejandro's shoulder, nearly his neck. "We must go. We must save her. My sister." His voice broke.

"You cannot help her," Alejandro yelled, knocking Albert's hand off of him. "Go to the beach. I will bring your sister to you." Albert's face transformed from frantic into a fierce snarl, but Alejandro shoved him down the mountain. "Do not make a second fatal mistake today, for it will cost your sister's life." Not waiting to see if the man did as instructed, Alejandro skirted the fire, heading east to where the slope cut off abruptly, creating a steep drop-off almost straight down into the sea below.

Alejandro came to the rock's edge and climbed over, then down. With luck, Irene had landed on a shelf of rock just beneath the cliff. He shuffled sideways along a ledge no wider than the palm of his hand, gripping the rock as tightly as he could. After a few yards, the ledge widened. When he looked up, white plumes of smoke wafted overhead. He cursed Carlbury for a hundred types of fool.

A shriek interrupted his mental rant. "Help! Albert!"

"Miss Carlbury." Alejandro put as much force into his shout as possible, shuffling sideways until he rounded a rock onto the ledge. There she stood, back pressed against the stones, her face streaked with dirt and tears.

She stared at him, shocked, and then a relieved sob burst out of her chest. "Help me. Please."

Alejandro took a steadying breath. "You must do exactly as I say."

✣ 21 ✣

With baskets of provisions in their arms, everyone at the shelter followed Hope without question when she told them Alejandro said they must flee to the beach. It did not take long for the smell of smoke to reach them, or for their steps to turn to a run. They came out on the beach and everyone stopped, looking northward into the sky.

"We are supposed to meet them further up the beach." She pointed and they followed. Each moment that passed increased the tension in her muscles, the ache in her heart. The air grew heavier with the smell of burning greenery. The birds were shrieking, with high-pitched notes far different than their usual songs. Other animals fled to the sand, lizards scampering along the shore. The fire hadn't spread everywhere, but there was more smoke than before.

The sailors appeared, panting and demanding an explanation for the smoke.

Then Albert emerged from the trees, throwing a fretful glance over his shoulder as he came. Hope ignored the frantic conversations taking place behind her and ran to Albert. "Where is Señor Córdoba? Where is Irene?"

He stopped walking and stared at her. "It happened too quickly. The logs collapsed and rolled."

She dared grab one of his arms and gave it a hard shake. He lacked the muscle, the strength, she had felt in Alejandro. "Where are they, Albert?"

He pulled away from her. "They will come." Then he stomped down the sand to the water. She watched him, confusion and fear dancing in her heart. Albert walked directly into the water, up to his knees, then fell into them.

Mrs. Morgan was praying, but everyone else had gone still and silent. Hope swung her eyes from Albert to Mrs. Morgan, whose words asking for safety and mercy somehow lifted over the waves without sounding like shouts. Then Hope watched the tree line, counting each second with care. How long did they wait before attempting a rescue? Before giving up on one?

The smoke above the island whirled and drifted away, disappearing in an unseen wind, white and gray as clouds. But she could see the flames licking the tops of trees where they had come from.

"How swiftly does fire move through woods?" Hope asked.

"Depends." Hope jumped when the professor answered her. He stood just behind her. "They move uphill faster than down. They eat up more when the wind is with them." His eyes held fascination as he watched. "The wind is blowing against this one, taking the smoke away. It is at the top of a hill."

Hope shook her head, horrified at how calmly he explained the facts when two of their own were still missing. "We must go and save them," she said, half-pleading.

The professor's gaze flicked briefly to hers before returning to his study. "I think not. The wind shifts. The fire changes direction. None of us know the island as Córdoba does. He will come, or we will do without him."

The very idea made her stomach turn and lurch, the scent of charring trees nearly choked her. "But—"

"Look." He pointed past her shoulder, and Hope did not hesitate to obey.

Alejandro, arm around Irene's waist, stumbled out of the trees and onto the beach. Hope shouted.

"Alejandro. Irene."

The two of them stumbled closer, Irene limping. Silent tears streamed down her face. Her hair had turned gray from dirt and smoke. Before Hope took a step, Albert ran past her to his sister. Alejandro released Irene, allowing Albert to lift her up in an embrace. Alejandro kept walking, hardly a pause in his step, and his rich brown eyes gazed at Hope with an intensity that made her worried stomach untie itself long enough to turn a cheerful somersault.

He practically marched to her. There was nothing gentle in his approach. It was precise. Measured. His handsome face, smeared with soot, was calm though he'd set his jaw.

Hope instinctively opened her arms when he was only two steps away, ready to receive him.

In the space of a single heartbeat, she went from standing on her own two feet to being held in his arms, lifted from the sand, pulled tightly against him. His bare chest was coated in dirt, she felt scratches where her arms wrapped around the back of his neck, and he smelled of smoke and sweat.

Three things settled in Hope's mind and heart, facts as clear to her as the knowledge that the sun must rise every day in the east. With Alejandro, she was safe. She was loved. She was *home.*

"Miss Everly," the doctor said, appearing at Hope's side. He cleared his throat and Alejandro slowly, reluctantly, lowered her back to her feet and stepped away. The doctor cast Hope a look of disapproval before fixing his stern glare on Alejandro. "How bad is it, Córdoba?"

"We cannot know until the fire burns itself out," Alejandro

stated, his voice rasping as though his throat pained him. "Was the food saved?"

"Yes." The doctor waved that question away impatiently. "But we may not be safe here."

"Safer than anywhere further inland." Alejandro turned and looked up at the smoke.

Doctor Morgan groaned and rubbed at his eyes. "This is a disaster greater than anything I could anticipate."

Hope stared incredulously at the doctor. Would he say nothing of Alejandro's heroics? Of Albert's stupidity?

"None of this would have happened if Albert had listened to Señor Córdoba," she said, her temper flaring dangerously. She had nearly lost a friend. Nearly lost the man she loved before even getting a chance to tell him how she felt, to even tell him her true name.

"Grace." Irene's ragged voice brought attention to where she stood, leaning into her tall brother. "He was trying to help. At least he did something to get us off this—"

"Help?" Hope interrupted, ire rising by the second. "He was told repeatedly why his idea was ludicrous and juvenile. But Albert Carlbury thinks he can do whatever he wants by virtue of his privilege, no matter that he is an imbecile. He nearly killed his own sister."

Albert Carlbury did not even have the decency to appear ashamed. Rather, he stared at Hope as though she had been the one to put their lives at risk.

With a calming gesture, the doctor attempted to soothe her. "Miss Everly, this is hardly the time—"

Scoffing, Hope stepped away from the gentle hand the doctor had put on her shoulder. "Have we more pressing matters to attend to, Doctor Morgan? For I am fairly certain that our food, our shelter, and all reasons to keep hands busy are currently in danger of going up in flames." She pointed violently to the spreading fire.

Mrs. Morgan appeared at her husband's side. "Miss Everly, dear, you are over-excited."

"Hysterical," muttered Albert.

Alejandro's fists clenched, and he turned his attention in that man's direction. "The only person on this island to have given in to hysterics, sir, is your sister. Miss Everly has never once been less than courageous and practical."

Albert's head snapped up, a sneer curled his lips, but before he voiced a word, Hope was snarling at him. "If you should dare to say a single word against the man who has kept us alive, I swear that if he does not trounce you, then I shall!"

All eyes went to her, rounded in shock, and the only sound Hope heard was the crash of waves behind them.

Releasing a soft whine, Irene sniffled. "Grace, this is unseemly."

That was the last drop needed to turn Hope's well of fear, impatience, and irritation into a roiling stream of anger.

"I am not Grace!" Her shout carried over the sand and, far away, she thought thunder rumbled in reply. She turned away from her friend, no longer caring about her secret, but needing to see Alejandro. Meeting his gaze, Hope stared up into his eyes and spoke the truth firmly. "I am *Hope* Everly, and I am tired of pretending to be someone I am not."

Alejandro's black eyebrows furrowed and his eyes narrowed.

"You *lied* to us?" Irene cried out, her voice pitched at an uncomfortable octave to hear.

Albert actually swore, and that was when Hope reluctantly tore her gaze from Alejandro's perplexed stare to look at both Carlburys.

"I am sorry for the lie," she said, "but more that it was necessary than anything. I cannot regret everything that has happened. I wanted to travel, to come with you to the Caribbean, and that was only possible as Grace. Not as myself. Grace had no wish to come."

Irene's fists were balled up tightly, and she glared at Hope as though she hated her. "Then we ought not have been burdened with either of you. You horrid, reckless, dishonest—"

Her brother closed his hand around her arm and looked down his nose at Hope. "Enough. You waste your breath. I always knew you were irresponsible and brash, Miss Everly, but I never thought you to be such an unprincipled creature. It is reprehensible."

Hope gaped at him, though more than once she had worried over such accusations. She bit her tongue, something that Grace would likely recommend in the present circumstances. *Oh, Grace.*

Mrs. Morgan had taken hold of her husband and looked from one angry person to another, her eyes wide. The doctor appeared perplexed. Mr. Thorne had wandered over at some point in the conversation, and he stared at Hope with a crooked sort of smile. Alejandro, standing at her back, had said nothing about her false-hoods. Not yet.

Releasing her brother, Irene turned away and walked to the wet sand. Hope went to follow, guilt taking her two steps before Albert grabbed her arm roughly and pushed her back. He had never particularly liked Hope. Not since the day she told him, after less than a week's acquaintance, she found him distasteful, arrogant, and pompous. He'd deserved every word of it after giving insult to a tenant child in the gardens. But Irene had never been quite like her brother. She had been sweet to both Grace and Hope.

Albert proved his old grievance with her ability to deliver a scathing set-down with no more than the hardness in his eyes, but poisonous words escaped his lips, too. "Stay away from my sister, treacherous slattern." There was a collective intake of breath.

"See here—" That was the doctor, but his words cut off when Alejandro stepped between Hope and Albert, necessitating Albert release her.

"*Eres un maldito tonto,* Carlbury," Alejandro spat, the Spanish having the unmistakable sound of insult. "The only treacherous one here is you." Alejandro pointed emphatically at the island behind them. "Our survival depends on everything that you set on fire."

Though his nostrils flared, Albert's words were cool and calm. "They will see the smoke. We will be rescued." Then he turned and marched away, head held as high as ever, to where his sister stood with her arms wrapped tightly about herself. As she stared at the two people on the island who knew her, knew her family, with their backs turned to her, Hope's body chilled despite the sun beating down upon her.

"Will—will the smoke be visible to those at sea?" Mrs. Morgan asked her husband quietly.

It was Alejandro who answered, his tone as angry as before. "We can barely see it, and we are on the island with it." He swore in Spanish, the words flowing from his tongue with a searing heat that rivaled the fire itself. Hope kept her back to him, afraid of what it would feel like, of whether his eyes would be cold or angry, when he turned his attention back to her and her lies.

Mr. Thorne surprised her by coming to stand on her other side, so he and Alejandro flanked her. "Miss Everly. Are you well?"

She bit her bottom lip and shook her head. "As well as any of us, Mr. Thorne."

He tucked his arms behind his back and nodded thoughtfully. "A wise answer. And you really are not who they thought you were—you are the sister left behind?" Wincing, prepared for another reprimand, she started to nod. The man barked a laugh, startling her. "I should have done the same, were I to have a twin."

Hope gave him her full attention, staring at him with open confusion. "You would?"

"If the choice was adventure or sit at home." His unabashed grin was so warm and kind that she nearly returned it.

Mrs. Morgan did not possess his same level of humor or understanding. "You have been pretending to be someone you are not for a very long time." She shook her head. "Though I confess, not knowing your sister, it is difficult to understand the lengths to which you went to deceive everyone."

"Why?"

It was the first word Alejandro had uttered directly to her since the revelation, and it made guilt squirm within her stomach. She pulled in a breath, hoping to take a little courage with it, and turned to face him.

"It seemed better to keep the lie alive. At first, I pretended to be Grace just to board the ship. I planned to tell Irene everything, and then her family. Turn it into a joke, perhaps. But Irene said things that made me realize she would not welcome Hope as she would Grace. So I stayed Grace a little longer. Then once we were here—" She broke off and shrugged, crossing one arm about herself. "It seemed unwise to say anything when circumstances were already less than ideal."

He shook his head and stepped closer, closer than anyone not a family member truly had the right to be. He bent, his forehead nearly touching hers. "I know why you lied to *them, mi hermosa.* But why did you lie to me?"

All the excuses she had used over the last several days were too weak to stand on their own legs. She barely knew him, yet her soul knew his. She did not think it mattered, but no one mattered more, no lie mattered more, than he did. It wouldn't be right to tell him the truth while the Carlburys believed a lie, yet she had known they would not support her falsehood in any way long before they set foot upon the island. If rescue came, she and Alejandro would go their separate ways. Except in her heart her path had melted away and become his.

He waited for her answer, watched her eyes as she thought through what words to give him. Nothing would soothe the hurt in his eyes.

"I am sorry," she whispered. "I did not understand what it would mean to keep this from you."

"Hope." Her name on his lips spoken without warmth but

ample astonishment did not warm her heart. "That is why you said you must hope all your life."

"You said hope was dead on this island," she answered softly.

He grasped his mother's ring hanging on the chain around his neck, holding it tightly in his fist.

"Esperanza," Hope said the word aloud. The word for hope, his mother's name, and as she said it his eyes flashed with an emotion she could not name. Then he was gone, walking away at a fast clip to the side of the island not yet on fire, his steps in the sand disappearing amid the lapping waves.

So much water, yet no way to use it to quench the fire. The cruelty of that observation nearly made her angry again.

"Miss Everly." The doctor. Of course. They had been standing there the whole time, watching the uncomfortable exchange and each excruciating detail likely causing greater speculation on their part. "I think it best you come with us. We cannot sit near the trees, but we should move closer to the surf, and take some food. The stress of the day cannot be good for any of us."

Mrs. Morgan's arm went around Hope's shoulders. Hope looked into the woman's friendly, compassionate expression. "Come with me, dear. Tell me your story."

Wearily, Hope nodded and followed the woman to the outcropping of rocks where she and Irene had washed their clothing. It was a safe distance from the trees. The trees she could not bring herself to turn toward, to see them engulfed in flames, to see how far the fire had spread, and watch as all hope of surviving vanished because of one foolish man's vanity.

❧ 22 ❧

The day of the fire, thunder had rumbled for some time before the storm clouds appeared. Two hours passed with the fire licking away at the trees, only slowing at damp patches and when the wind pushed it away from the greenery. After the rain, Alejandro, Hitchens, Madden, Smith, the doctor, and Thorne scouted the edges of the charred and smoldering remains of trees and vegetation.

Their discovery had been grim. The doctor delivered the news to those who waited on the edge of the beach. Bedraggled, soaked through from the rain and waves, no one had said another word for a long time.

Here, two days later, Alejandro braved the ash and embers to walk further into the trees. He tested each spot on the ground carefully, his bare feet warning him when patches of ground were too hot for him. He found small creatures that had succumbed to smoke or been too injured by fire to flee. His stomach rolled, but he forced away the sick feeling. What little food he'd managed to eat had to stay put. The rations would not last long.

He came out of the trees to the shelter, where everyone sat doing nothing. Everyone except Hope.

How strange, to know her name at last. It made sense now, why she would not allow him to call her by her Christian name. She had not wanted the man falling in love with her to write the wrong name within his heart. At least, that's what Alejandro told himself.

He and Hope had barely spoken past what was necessary. She remained silent. Kept her head down. The truth ought to have set her free, but it appeared to be a greater burden if the slope of her shoulders and the deep purple crescents beneath her eyes told him anything.

Alejandro did not ask if anyone knew where she had gone. He walked around the rocks and up to the top of the island. The rocks here formed the back of the shelter, and stretched upward, stacked upon one another, as though attempting to reach the sky. Wedged deeply in those rocks was the broken mast he had pulled ashore, along with the sail, and Hope.

She sat on a rock at the same level as his head. Arms wrapped around her legs and chin resting on her knees, Hope's eyelashes did not even flicker when he climbed up beside her.

He had seen her keeping vigil the day before.

For a long time, he said nothing. He sat beside her, watching her from the corner of his eye though he pretended to watch the horizon. She hadn't eaten very much. He had watched her return part of her portion of dried berries, nuts, and roots back into the baskets each day. Her cheeks already appeared less full than before, and they had hardly been round when he first met her. Beneath the tan, there was little color to her skin.

Alejandro's thoughts turned dark too quickly. He needed to distract himself. Distract her. The specter of death hung over the island, but that did not mean they had to let it have power over their hearts.

"The first thing I want to do when we are rescued," Alejandro said abruptly, "is eat fresh-baked bread. I have missed it."

She let out a sigh and turned her head, laying her cheek on her knee in order to stare up at him. "The first thing? Perhaps you ought to consider a haircut as the second." Her gaze flicked from his face to his shoulders, then his beard. He still had no shirt. He had removed it the day of the fire while fishing, and when he'd gone back to that side of the island had seen no trace of it.

"What of the beard?" he asked, pleased to at least have her speaking of something frivolous. He stroked the long whiskers, thick and almost curling, growing from his cheeks and chin. "Are you fond of it?"

Her eyes warmed somewhat, but she blinked and the worry returned. "I am fond of the man beneath the beard, though he may no longer be fond of me."

Alejandro grimaced and mimicked the way she sat, pulling his knees up close to his chest and wrapping his arms loosely around them. "I am fond of you, Hope. More than fond." He whispered the last sentence, giving her the opportunity to speak of it or ignore it.

Tears shimmered in her eyes, and she wiped them away with the back of her hand. "You do not even know me. You know who I was pretending to be."

The nonsense of her words nearly made him laugh. He tempered his response to no more than a smile. "You think I know your sister Grace? I have never met her. I know nothing of her but what others have said. I have come to know you, Hope. And admire your strength. Your courage."

She scoffed and turned away. The bun she wore was loose enough that a great deal of her hair had already come free, laying limply down her back in straggling waves.

"It is true," he said quietly. "No one can pretend the things I have seen in you. Patience and compassion for your friend, though she sorely tried the rest of us. Kindness and understanding to Mrs. Morgan in her delicate condition." Hope turned at that and raised her eyebrows at him. "I have eyes," he said, leaning toward her enough to nudge her shoulder with his.

"You are not supposed to notice a woman's *condition.*" Her lips twitched upward. "It is not polite."

"When have you known me to worry overly much about what is polite?" he asked, allowing himself to smirk before turning back to the matter at hand. "I have admired your courage from the beginning. That is something you cannot pretend belongs to your sister."

Hope considered him carefully, a thousand thoughts behind her eyes, the depths of which he could only guess at. "Grace is courageous, in her own way. A quiet way."

Chuckling, he nudged her again, relishing the momentary connection between them. He had missed her. "You are not quiet, Hope. You never have been."

The observation made her grimace. "Then how did they not know?" she asked plaintively. "How did Irene not guess—?"

"She is not as good a friend as you are." He had seen that truth time and again. Irene enjoyed possessing a friend, not being one herself. The woman was no more than a spoiled child, thinking always of her own comfort and wants, never anyone else's needs.

Hope's eyebrows furrowed and her frown returned, deeper this time. "Are you angry that I deceived you?" she asked. "I do not blame you if you are."

"I did not understand it. But anger—it is too strong a word. As I said. I never knew Grace. Only you. What does it matter what name you used? I believe it was one of your Englishmen who said something about a rose, by any other name, smelling as sweet."

Her cheeks pinked, giving him a blissful moment of triumph. Her heart had not closed to him. She had not pretended her feelings. He knew, but it was good to see that indicated by something she could not hide.

"Thank you," she said quietly. "But if that is truly how you feel, why have you avoided me?"

A large bird flew overhead, coming in from the sea. It circled the two of them, then went toward the trees, only to veer away before landing. He had seen this happen enough times to despair over it. The animals would not return to the island, those that had the power to, until the stench of smoke and death had faded away. That was another source of nourishment gone.

"I needed to think." Alejandro closed his eyes, as much to gather his courage as his words. "You and I, we have something between us. Something I have not felt before. With anyone." She did not deny it, and when he opened his eyes again to look at her, he saw the slightest of smiles upon her lovely face. His heart dipped painfully. "But it cannot be, as much as I wish it could."

She blanched. "What?"

"What we feel, even if we ever leave this island, nothing can come of it." Alejandro swallowed away the tightness in his throat, watching the joy fade from her eyes. "I do not know if anything or anyone even waits for me out in the world. My parents may be dead. My country may yet fall to Spain's rule. Our holdings could be gone. I must find a way to journey back home and discover all that has passed while I have been away. I cannot think of myself, and I cannot think of you."

Hope's eyes had stayed wide, full of pain, but she did not cry out. She did not rail against him. "You said before," she whispered. "You said you wished to know me better. You practically asked to court me."

"I was dreaming," he admitted, his heart splitting slowly in two. "You will go home to England. We know you must. The Carlbury family, they no longer welcome you. I cannot go across an ocean to be with you. Not when my duty is to my country, my family."

Finally, she wiped at her eyes with the heel of her hand. "It is not because I lied?" Though a petite woman, Hope had never looked or sounded smaller than she did in that moment. Alejandro could not allow her to remain uncomforted. He moved closer, wrapping one arm around her shoulders and pressing a kiss to her temple.

"No, *mi hermosa*. You kept your name from me, but never your heart." She leaned into his chest, despite his lack of proper attire, and he had to smile at her boldness. If only he could keep her forever at his side. "It is because I must go, because I am not free."

"Won't you be? Someday?" she asked quietly.

"Free enough to cross an ocean?" He sighed deeply and tugged at his hair with one hand, then pushed it all back from his face. "I do not know. But even if I could—Hope, my country is not stable. It may be a very long time before it is safe, before I know what my future holds. I cannot ask a woman, any woman, to join me in that way. To be part of a life filled with war."

She did not move from her place, the warmth of her cheek on his skin made each word harder to speak. He had promised himself to do this, to tell her the truth of all matters.

"My whole life has been lived during war," she told him. "Napoleon—he took friends from me, from everyone I know."

"And you have said the war with the French is over. You will never need live that way again." He said it firmly, leaving no room for argument. "I will not keep your heart captive, waiting for a day that may never come."

For a long time, she said nothing. Hope did not shrink from him, or plead, or anything. Though he felt her swallow several times, as though trying to keep back words or tears. Finally, she nodded against him.

"I wish I could come with you." She spoke as though they were already off the island, already on their way back into the world. They could yet be on the island together for many years. If they survived that long. He did not point that out to her.

"But your duty is to your family." Alejandro gave her one more gentle squeeze before guiding her back from him. "Hope. *Mi esperanza*. Will you take this?" He touched the ring on the chain. The one thing he had kept to remind himself, every day, of who he was and that someone in the world thought of him. Perhaps it would give her a measure of comfort, as it had him. "Please?"

Hope immediately leaned away from him, her eyes widening in shock. "It is yours. Your mother's."

He pulled the chain over his head, then dropped it over hers, despite her protest. "And now it is yours. I think it fitting. From Esperanza to Hope. Women I will always keep with me in my heart."

She touched the ring and her smile, though faint, reappeared. "I am honored. Thank you, Alejandro."

"Thank you, Hope Everly. You brought back my faith in rescue. My hope." He forced a smile, but his composure began to slip. Pain flowed from his broken heart through the rest of him, making his soul ache. He needed to leave. Take a long walk. Perhaps douse himself in the ocean or walk on hot coals. Whichever sensation distracted him from the gaping wound in his chest.

"Thank you for keeping me safe." She did not make eye contact, she kept her gaze on the ring in her palm. "And for everything else."

Alejandro slid down the rock, murmuring his farewell. They might be dead of starvation in a few weeks. Or disease. Or injury. He might bury her in the sand, or she mourn his loss. There was no telling what would happen next. But they had said their goodbyes.

He had not gone far at all when he heard a plaintive sob break from her, but he did not turn around. It was best this way.

Best to do the honorable thing.

23

Everything tasted like ash.

Tears spent, Hope tried to get down more of the dried berries. Her stomach clenched and tried to reject the food but she determinedly swallowed again. Mrs. Morgan had a worse time of things. She had barely eaten anything and the doctor could no longer find the herbs to make her tea. He had boiled what they had left into a sort of broth that was gone already.

Though they had not been in the best of circumstances before, there had been no chance of them starving to death. Now, however, they couldn't get through a day without hunger pains.

The men had dug another well. The first had been contaminated with floating ash and the small animals trying to flee the fire. The new well still had bits of ash drift into it when the wind was strong enough.

At least they had the water.

Irene sniffled loudly enough that Hope dared look at her friend. Were they still friends? She had stayed away for days, waiting for the anger the Carlburys exhibited toward her to die down. They were the only people who still held her falsehood against her. Albert glared every time their gazes met and Irene turned away with her nose in the air.

How had she ever been friends with someone who behaved in such a way? Why had she never noticed before how snobbish Irene acted? She took up the rest of her meager rations and carried them across the little clearing to Irene. "Would you like my food?" she asked, though her mostly empty stomach did not thank her for it. "I do not need so much. I am the smallest one here."

Irene looked from the meager offering of berries and edible leaves in Hope's hand back to the ground. "I have sufficient for my needs, thank you."

Hope withdrew the food and went to offer it next to Mrs. Morgan.

"Pretending to be generous and noble now does not negate your prior behavior," Albert snarled from the other side of his sister. Hope had tried to ignore him. Apparently, he could not stand to lose the opportunity to deride her.

The others around the fire, eating their meager breakfast, stilled. Perhaps they all thought as she did. Albert had destroyed their ability to survive. His hypocrisy added yet another facet to his character that made her grateful she had never once considered him a possible suitor.

Grace would tell Hope to bite her tongue. To pretend she had not heard. To make peace.

Hope was not Grace, and she was tired. Hungry. Impatient. And hurting. She turned on her heel, glaring down at the man on the ground. "My prior behavior? Whatever do you mean, Mr. Carlbury? Could you mean all the times I soothed your sister's fears and nerves while you went sneaking about the island to build a bonfire? Or perhaps you mean my efforts to gather food and water, while you disappeared nearly every chance you could when the rest of the group was at work? Are those the reprehensible deeds you charge me with?" She tossed her head and scoffed at him. "However will I make restitution?"

Albert sprang to his feet. "At least I attempted something to save us from living like savages," he snarled. "Better to die with some semblance of decorum than live no better than animals."

Standing her ground with fists balled up, Hope barely registered Mr. Thorne and Alejandro coming slowly to their feet. Her focus was on the man before her. "You are not the man to decide if we live or die."

Perhaps something inside Albert broke. He threw his head back and laughed. "Of course you would not mind a life outside of society's bounds. We all saw that well enough as soon as you started throwing yourself at that—" he thrust a finger in Alejandro's direction "—lout. Your pretended virtue does not erase your wanton—"

He didn't get another word out. A fist flew past her shoulder, followed by an arm and well-muscled shoulder, as Alejandro defended her honor with his bare hands. His knuckles connected with Albert's jaw, and the tall man stumbled back. Irene squeaked and scrambled out of the way. Thorne started forward and the sailors came to their feet much more warily. As Albert had expressed his view of their inferiority several times, Hope had no doubt whose side they were on.

Recovering from the blow, Albert squared his shoulders and assumed a boxer's stance. "Try again, Córdoba. Make it a fair fight, if you even know how."

Alejandro barked a laugh, the angriest, snarliest laugh she had ever heard. Yet his hand reached behind him, finding her shoulder, touching her gently. Urging her to step away. She moved several steps back, watching, more interested than afraid.

"I have wanted to knock you down since I met you, *cerdo egoísto*. My manners are all that have saved you." He got into a fighting stance that appeared far more threatening than Albert's high-held fists. Alejandro stood with hands open and body crouched, like a jaguar preparing to spring.

Albert's nostrils flared. "You cannot even fight like a gentleman."

"I will let you take the first swing." Alejandro came closer and lifted his chin, presenting a target. Hope held her breath. What was he doing?

Without so much as a pause, Albert lunged forward, using momentum from his step through his shoulder and propelling his arm toward Alejandro's face.

With an ease Hope did not believe, Alejandro snatched the taller man's wrist out of the air, twisted it, then lifted a knee into Albert's abdomen. Another twist, and Albert flew forward, stumbling but somehow remaining on his feet. He whirled around, his face redder than a boiled lobster's.

"You cannot do that!"

One of the sailors clapped his hands. "It is like the slaves' dance." The other two sailors nodded and clapped as well, as though Alejandro's technique was not at all unusual. Hope stared at them, then at Alejandro.

"Where I am from," Alejandro said, "there are many who fight like this. It is far superior to anything you English might come up with." Albert charged again before Alejandro finished speaking, but Alejandro deftly stepped into a thrust with the heel of his hand that caught Albert on the chin. Alejandro hooked Albert's knee with one foot and sent the arrogant man down to the dirt.

Alejandro leaned over a groaning Albert. "You will never give insult to Miss Everly again. Swear it."

"I swear," Albert hissed.

Alejandro walked away. He did not even look back at Hope. Madden, the tallest sailor, patted his shoulder as Alejandro passed.

Hope turned away from everyone, not wanting to see what the reaction was to the fight, though she kept her head held high as she walked to her usual place to watch the horizon, praying for rescue. The walk was easier this time. While she wished no harm on any creature, Albert's insinuations had filled her with enough anger that she had been ready to challenge him to a duel herself.

She climbed up the rocks and settled herself in her usual place, heedless of the sun upon her mostly bare arms. She took down her hair and studied the scrap of linen. Why bother with it now? She tied the linen around her wrist, using her teeth to tighten the knot. Then she pulled the chain from beneath her gown and wrapped her hand around the ring Alejandro had given her.

Earnestly, she prayed for rescue. Prayed for Alejandro's mother to see him again. For her mother, father, brother, sisters, to welcome her home. Then she opened her eyes, wrapped her arms around her legs, and waited.

Hours passed, and she only shifted positions when she began to ache. Then she stood for a time, staring out to sea. Alejandro came, but he did not speak. He only put food on the rock near her, smiled wanly, then settled on the ground below where she kept watch.

She nibbled at the offering, out of politeness more than anything.

"Rescue will come."

Hope blinked and looked down at Alejandro, finding him still staring out to sea.

"I had stopped believing, before I met you. An angel on the beach." He glanced up at her, a smile on his face. Yet again, she wondered what he would look like clean shaven and with a cravat tucked at his neck. Would his hair still appear curly if it were shorter?

"I truly hope you are right," she said, heaviness settling over her shoulders. She turned back to the water, staring, and then—

Hope came to her feet and pointed. "Alejandro. Is that—?"

"A ship," he said. Then he was scrambling over the rocks toward the sail. He grabbed an end of it and pulled, helping it open wider and catch the wind. Hope hurried to help him, taking the corner and pulling it out further. The wind whipped at them both, but filled the white cloth. It would stand out against the black rocks of the island, billowing and waving.

They watched, though tears blurred Hope's vision, and after a time she realized the ship was coming closer. Toward the island. To them.

Signal flags. A cannon firing. And—a British flag.

With the cannon shot, others came to the lookout position. Hope did not take her eyes off the ship, even though she heard the others screaming, crying, praying, shouting for joy.

They were saved.

Her arms aching, she turned to Alejandro, the one who had waited longest for rescue. He wasn't looking at the ship at all. His dark gaze rested upon her, sadness and joy mingling in his eyes. She forced a smile and the wind caught the tears falling from her eyes.

Hours later, Hope stood at the rail of the English trading ship. A ship that had not known to look for them but had been blown off course by the same storm that finally put out their fire days before. Someone had given Hope a blanket which she held around her shoulders.

Mrs. Morgan stood beside her. Irene and her brother had retreated below. Alejandro had withdrawn to speak with the captain, as had the doctor and Mr. Thorne.

"I have certainly had my fill of adventure," Mrs. Morgan murmured, covering one of Hope's hands with her own.

Though Hope did not answer, she knew in her heart that she did not feel quite the same. What was life without adventure? True, she had come closer to calamity than ever before while living on that island, but she had no wish to spend the rest of her life by a hearth in a sleepy village, either.

"You will stay with us, I think, when we return to St. Kitt's," Mrs. Morgan continued.

Hope turned to her, startled. "With you?"

"I cannot see the Carlburys forgiving you anytime soon." Mrs. Morgan smiled, despite the seriousness of her words. "Even if their parents are more reasonable than the children, there are other things to consider. You had best stay with us until you decide what to do."

Hope already knew her course. "I am going home."

Mrs. Morgan's eyebrows raised, and she glanced toward the stern of the ship, where the captain stood with the other men. "You will not wed Señor Córdoba?"

The tattered remains of her heart twisted. "I will not. He has his duty to return to, and my parents will expect me to come back to them, I think, after all that has happened." Though Mrs. Morgan appeared dubious, she said nothing and put her other hand over her abdomen. "Thank you for letting me stay with you until things are sorted out for my journey," Hope added.

Watching the island recede, Hope wondered at what had happened to her while there. She could never hate the island. Not when she had met Alejandro on its shores, and fallen in love with him. If he had asked her to wait for him, she would have. Had he asked her to join him on the journey to his homeland, she would have. But he did not ask. He gave her all the reasons it could not be.

Though Hope had often done as she wished in the past, she had never attempted to dictate to another how they ought to feel or behave. She would not start now, with the man she loved.

Hope wiped away a tear, not caring that Mrs. Morgan saw.

❧ 24 ❧

In a gown of green, a wide straw bonnet, and delicate shoes, Hope sat beneath a willow tree. The tree did not seem to mind the heat and humid air, but Hope kept the fan in her hands moving rapidly in an effort to cool herself. Mrs. Morgan's maid had done up Hope's hair in a variety of twists and tucks that nearly kept it in place, but the back of her neck still itched where one too many pins pulled at her skin.

Going about with her hair loose and no shoes covering her feet had undoubtedly been the freest and coolest she had felt since her original arrival on St. Kitt's shores.

The hand that did not work the fan grasped Alejandro's ring on its chain. He was coming today. Doctor Morgan had told them at breakfast. And Hope had excused herself to the outside as quickly as possible.

Alejandro had not visited even once before. She had not even caught a glimpse of him since they were rescued and returned to the safety of St. Kitt's. The Carlburys had swooped up their children in their arms; Mrs. Carlbury had embraced Hope, too. But the Morgans had been right about the true lack of welcome.

The doctor and Mr. Carlbury had worked together to secure her passage and the companionship of a married woman returning to England. She would leave tomorrow for home.

Was that why Alejandro finally decided to pay her a call? Because he knew she would be gone? Perhaps he had not missed her the last week as she had missed him.

"How did I guess you would not be inside?"

Hope's fan stilled. She swallowed and raised her head to see beyond the brim of her bonnet. Even in boots, Alejandro walked with the silence of a cat. The boots she saw first, polished, though worn. Then trousers, neatly pressed and tucked into the tops of the boots. Coat-sleeve tips, strong brown hands peeking out of them. She swallowed.

Lifting her chin all the way, she found his eyes as deep, warm, and gentle as ever. The rest of him, she realized with a blush, was just as handsome. He had kept a close-cropped beard, but the strong line of his jaw was easily visible now. His cheekbones were defined just above the beard. His hair had been trimmed shorter than most would allow was fashionable, yet it suited him.

He bowed. "Might I introduce myself? I am Alejandro Felipe de Córdoba y Verduzco, of La Plata." When he raised up from the bow, she finally remembered her manners and stood from her chair.

"I am most pleased to meet you, Señor Córdoba." Her voice trembled, which would not do. She sank into a curtsy. "I am Miss Hope Everly, of Aldersy in Suffolk."

Only the smallest of smiles touched his lips. "Hope. *Es un honor conocerte.*" He stood still, staring at her, and she made no effort to speak, either. As near as they were, as much as she had tried to put him from her mind, it took all of her control to stay out of his arms. If he held out even a hand to her, she would wrap him in her embrace.

"I came to say goodbye."

Hope's heart trembled. "Why?"

His expression fell from one of warmth to a pained frown. *"Mi hermosa,* we discussed this. We cannot—there is too much uncertainty in my life."

She laughed, a helpless sound. "More uncertainty than whether you will be trapped on an island your whole life?"

His lips twitched, but he shrugged. She noticed how loose his cravat was about his neck, how casually tied, as though he had done it himself. The clothes he wore, she realized, were not of the finest quality. They did not fit his frame. How had he come by them?

"Hope." He gestured to the garden behind them. Small. Simple by English standards. But a little green with trees to stroll beneath. "Will you walk with me?"

She nodded and came to take his arm, finding it felt so natural to slip her hand through the crook of his elbow. Everything inside her ached anew the moment they touched.

When he spoke, he began hesitantly. "On the island, I was not thinking clearly. Though you gave me reason to pray, to have faith, that we would be rescued, I did not think much beyond that event. Here we are, safe now, and I must face the realities of my situation. I have learned much about what happened in my homeland, but no one can tell me of my family. Spain has marched on my people, my people have fought back. Lands have been taken and redistributed. People have fled inland, or back to Europe." His tone grew more earnest, more firm, with each word.

"I could go with you to find out what happened," she whispered, already knowing his answer. She'd known since they spoke on the island that he would never allow it.

Alejandro stopped their walk in order to turn to her, placing both his hands on her shoulders. His dark eyebrows were drawn down, his mouth set in a firm line. Oh, how she wished to kiss him once more. "My honor requires that I not take a wife until I know if I can provide a stable future. I do not know how long it will take."

"I will wait for you," she promised, as she should have on the island.

But he sadly shook his head. "For how long? I must return to my father's home, and I cannot simply leave when I see what has happened. I have been away for too long. My family likely will not let me on a boat right away. My country is at war. I do not know how long it will take. We could not even write to each other without waiting months and months for responses." Alejandro's right hand came up to cup her cheek, and she leaned into it.

"How could I ever wish for a man other than you?" she asked, voice soft. "There can be no other, Alejandro."

He bent beneath the brim of her bonnet, touching his forehead to hers. Why not kiss her? Why not make promises of love and a future together?

"You are breaking my heart," he whispered. "There is no easy answer. No easy way. I cannot ask you to wait. I will not expect it of you. We barely know each other. With time apart, you might realize your feelings for me are nothing, magnified only by the desperate place we were in."

Hope pulled back and stared at him in shock. "Is that how you feel?" Why else would he assume her emotions and heart were so fickle?

"No." His shoulders dropped, and he reached a hand up to his beard, then to the back of his head. "I feel tired. I must find a way back to my family. I cannot even afford passage on a ship without working, or offering to work for my passage. Do you see, Hope? I cannot take you home with me. I haven't the means to transport myself. These clothes—they are cast-offs from Thorne and one of his friends on the island. I have nothing. *Nothing.*"

"You have me," she whispered, heart aching. "But it sounds as though you do not want me."

He growled and wrapped his arm about her waist, pulling her close. "I love you, impossible woman. *Mi bella inglesa. Quiero besarte. Abrazarte. Cada día. Por el resto de nuestras vidas. Pero, no.*" He scoffed at himself and stepped away, releasing her on the last word. "The world is too uncertain a place. Go home to your family. Plan a new adventure. I will think of you every day for the rest of my life. In time, perhaps these feelings will weaken."

Hope stripped off the necklace, the ring still upon it. "If that is how you feel, you had better take your mother's ring with you." She kept her tone even, her words neither cold nor warm. The pain in his eyes was enough to tell her the truth of his feelings, had his words not done the trick. He could not see a future for them. "I can do the honorable thing, too."

He caught the ring in his hand and she released the chain. "Hope—"

Eyes stinging, she forced a smile. "Miss Everly. Goodbye, Señor Córdoba. May God go with you and keep you safe."

Alejandro's smile was as broken as her own. "*Y a tí también,* Miss Everly." She rushed away before he could bow again, running for the kitchen door that would let her back into the Morgans' house. She ran up to her room, which overlooked the street, and sat in the window. Watching. Waiting for her last sight of him.

No man's head had ever hung so low, she thought, as his when he stepped back into the street. He did not look up. And he took her heart away with him.

ALEJANDRO WENT TO THE DOCKS THE DAY HER SHIP DEPARTED. HE avoided seeing her. Stayed behind carts and carriages as the Morgans bid her goodbye. The Carlburys had not even come to bid her farewell. An older woman waited on the deck of the ship and greeted Hope with a smile. It seemed she would be looked after.

He stayed until the boat was guided from the harbor. Stayed until it faded from view on the horizon. In his borrowed clothes, Alejandro did not even look fully like a gentleman amid all those working, conducting business, and no one gave him a second glance.

A new boat had come into the harbor while he stood there, its ropes tied off on the deck near him. When he finally turned to leave, his last sight of Hope's ship long since passed, he saw the people disembarking. Mostly men stepped off the boat, never sparing him a glance, and he gave them just as little attention.

Until someone grabbed his shoulder. "Señor Alejandro?"

He turned, his heart choking him. "Señor Flores!" The older gentleman, one of his father's friends, appeared nearly the same as the last time Alejandro had seen him, years ago. Perhaps a little grayer at the temples. But—

When Señor Flores embraced him, Alejandro returned the gesture whole-heartedly. Then the older gentleman kissed him on both cheeks, murmuring praises to heaven the whole time. He spoke in Castilian, the lilting language music to Alejandro's ears.

"We thought you dead. Your parents. Your brother! They would not give up. They said you would come home someday. But the news of the wreck finally reached us. *Hijo*, they will be filled with joy."

"My parents—they are still in good health?" Alejandro stood back from the man and watched for any sign of hesitation. But Señor Flores merrily struck Alejandro on the shoulder. "The best of health. I have only just seen them. Well. Two months ago, they were in good health."

"You are come from Buenos Aires?"

"No, from Spain. Madrid." Señor Flores clapped his hand to his forehead. "Ah, you will not know anything about that. Come. Let us find some place to sit, and I will tell you everything."

Madrid? Alejandro's head started to spin and he turned, looking out to sea. Europe. His family was in Europe, and Hope would soon be nearer to them than he.

"Alejandro? Are you—are you well?"

Shaking free from his melancholy thoughts, Alejandro gestured to the shore. "Come, Señor Flores. I have a friend who is letting me stay at his home. We may have refreshment and speak there."

It did not take long to walk to Thorne's rented rooms. Alejandro told his story as they went, of the wreck, being left alone on an island, and finally how a sloop full of English citizens had washed ashore. They had passed St. George's Anglican church by the time he finished. Señor Flores listened raptly and asked few questions, except to clarify a point.

Thorne came out of the larger house just as they reached it.

"Córdoba, you have returned. I wondered if you had changed your mind and were on your way to England." Thorne's smile was one of understanding, perhaps an empathetic bitterness.

"I was tempted," Alejandro admitted. "More than once. But look, the saints have rewarded me for staying firm. I have met with an old friend. Señor Flores, might I introduce Mr. Thorne, one of those Englishmen who lived on my island after a storm."

The men exchanged greetings and Thorne took his leave, pleading a prior engagement. Alejandro took Señor Flores into the house and the sitting room of Thorne's flat. The windows were open to allow in a cooling breeze, and Thorne's manservant offered to bring them lemonade.

Once they had settled, Señor Flores fixed Alejandro with a piercing gaze, his lips pursed in concentration. "That man. He said you were tempted to go to England. Why?"

Alejandro's heart smote him all the harder. He could not speak of it. Not yet. A simple comment to Thorne, who understood, was one thing. But revealing his heart to another while still in the midst of pain would only cause him further damage. He brushed aside the question. "Bidding farewell to someone from the island is all. Will you tell me of my parents? Why are they in Spain?"

"The Spanish royalists have taken captives and refuse to nego-tiate with the people fighting for our new republic," Flores told him. "And the Royalists are aiding the armies at the expense of the commoners. Your father went to Spain as an ambassador of the new government. The Spanish court refuses to recognize our efforts as anything other than a rebellion and will not yield prisoners or even acknowledge your father. Though they have not arrested him for treason, and that is something." The older gentleman rubbed at his temples but kept his posture as stiff and proud as he always had. "Your father seeks to build sympathy to our cause in the common man. If Spanish citizens resent the war, if popular opinion turns in our favor, that could be another means of ending the conflict. Wars are expensive, after all."

"So is losing a colony." Alejandro tapped his fingers against the armrest. "How fair things at home?"

"It is war." Señor Flores shrugged and his expression changed into a dark frown. "Though we have had some promising moments. You will have heard something of our general, José Francisco de San Martín. He had just come to fight with us from Spain a few years ago. He has given us great hope, for he has had success in driving the Spanish armies back."

"That is good news. People need a hero to rally behind." Alejandro reflexively reached up to grasp his mother's ring, but his hand closed over his cravat instead. The ring now rested beneath his proper clothing. With a wince for the wrinkles he'd likely just added to the neckcloth, he lowered his hand again to the armrest. "Thank you for all the information. I am relieved to hear my parents and brother are well."

"Quite well. You will join them in Madrid now, yes?"

Alejandro stood and paced away from the chairs to the window, looking out over a quiet courtyard. "That would be the best place for me to go. I am not sure when it would be possible."

"Leave with the first ship bound in that direction." Señor Flores said it as though he could think of no impediments to such a plan.

"I have nothing, Señor. I have been on an island for over a year. Even my clothes are not my own."

"Ridiculous. You are the son of one of my oldest friends. I will purchase your passage myself, first thing tomorrow if possible."

Señor Flores waved a hand somewhat carelessly. "I would hope you would do the same for any son of mine. I know your father would."

Alejandro shook his head. "The cost is too dear, Señor. I can manage."

"No doubt you would, in time, but your dear mother has lived without word of you too long already." He thumped the chair and stood abruptly enough that it pushed back several inches. "You are going to Spain, and you will repay me by praying for me as often as you come upon a cathedral. Agreed?"

Moved, Alejandro's answer was hoarse with his emotion. "Sí, Señor Flores. And even when there is no cathedral. Thank you."

"Good. That is settled. Come. Show me where I can buy you dinner."

Heart lighter, Alejandro agreed, and they were out into the cool evening air. He looked again in the direction of the harbor, thinking of Hope. Would she forget him? Would he forget her?

As the distance stretched between them, and time, perhaps her feelings would fade. There would be no point in going to England, following behind her like a lovesick dog.

At least, that is what he kept telling himself.

❧ 25 ❧

The Silver Birch Society gathered at the vicarage to hear Hope's story. Though the house was smaller than any of the others belonging to members of the group, it was comfortable. Grace had done an admirable job of making the space her own, and had filled the main room with beauty. Esther's painting of the old boat, their former clubhouse amid the silver birches, hung above the mantel.

Esther and Silas themselves sat next to each other in comfortable armchairs, Esther resting one hand upon her slightly rounded abdomen.

Sir Isaac had settled in an overstuffed chair near the window, his chin resting on his fist as he stared outside, though Hope knew he listened as raptly as the others.

Jacob and Grace occupied the small sofa, holding hands tightly, as perfectly in love as Hope had known they would become. And she sat near their hearth, on a padded footstool, trying to tell the story as brightly as possible.

She avoided using Alejandro's name as much as possible. Glossed over how often she had been alone in his company. If she could hide her feelings from her dearest friends, perhaps she could stop the ache in her heart every time she thought on him.

The eight weeks since she had sailed from Basseterre and St. Kitt's, the weeks on the ocean, the last several spent at home, had not cured her of her love for him. Hope did not know how anything ever would.

They had tea while she spoke. They ate sandwiches while she described the *manzanita de la muerte* and Albert's attempts at courtship.

By the time she told the story in its entirety, the sky had grown dark. Late October. Of course it was dark earlier and earlier each evening. What a change from the long days on the island.

"I am grateful for your rescue," Grace whispered. "To think how near we came to losing you forever."

Hope exchanged a gentle smile with her twin sister, their love passing from one to the other with ease. "I never gave up hope that I would be here again among you."

"But where is the man now?" Isaac asked from his place near the window. Hope and everyone else turned to look at him, while he only stared out the glass into the darkness.

"What man?" Esther asked. "Carlbury? If he ever comes back to this county, we ought to banish him."

"Earls cannot banish people, love," Silas told her with a crooked smile.

"Not Carlbury," Isaac clarified, finally swinging his gaze around to those inside the room. "The man she fell in love with. The marooned South American." He raised his eyebrows when no one said a word, though Hope lowered her eyes and found her hands clenched tightly in her lap.

"Hope?" Grace moved to kneel in front of Hope, peering up at her with a curious stare. "Is Isaac correct? Did you fall in love?"

Denying her heart ought to have been easy. Such a thing might well help her on her way to recovery. Instead, Hope's bottom lip trembled and her eyes grew damp, quite without her permission. Grace's expression fell. "Oh, darling. What happened?"

"He had to return home," Hope answered. "It was the right thing for him to do. The honorable thing."

Isaac snorted. "Honor? Honor was my excuse to go to war, but I doubt I would ever use it if I were in love."

"Oh, do be quiet, Isaac," Esther said, glaring at her brother. "You have never been in love. What do you know of Hope's gentleman? Hope. What happened? Will he come here when he settles things at home?"

Hope shook her head slowly. "I do not know."

Isaac made another sound of displeasure, but when Esther turned another glare on him, Jacob spoke. "I am with Isaac on this topic. If he loves Hope, he will come for her."

"And if he never comes?" Grace asked, glaring at him. "Patience is only a virtue for so long."

That started a debate between them that nearly made Hope smile. Jacob and Grace were well-matched, indeed. Esther and Silas appeared happy, too. Happier than she had ever seen either of them.

She stood and wandered to the window, standing near Isaac. "You would like him," she said quietly, allowing the conversation behind her to continue. When it ended, Grace would see everyone off except Hope. That was when she could allow herself to fall apart. With Grace and Grace alone. But Isaac's astute observation of all the things she did not say had surprised her.

"Perhaps," Isaac said with a noncommittal shrug. "I like lots of people."

"Have you ever been in love?" Hope asked him, her voice softer still.

"No." He leaned back in his chair and stared up at her, puzzlement in his eyes. "I am not certain I ever intend to try for it. Love, as wonderful as it sounds, also tends to make fools out of people.

Like your Señor Córdoba. Like our friends." His crooked smile softened his criticism.

"You jest," Hope accused. "I can tell. You want a love match as much as the rest of us do."

Isaac sighed and leaned his head back against the chair. "What will you do?"

"Stay busy. Join my sister on her charitable visits. Learn to be a better person."

Pushing himself out from his chair, Isaac put his arm around her shoulders in a brotherly fashion. "You are the best of people, but I suppose one can always improve." Then he gave her a kiss on the cheek. "I will take my leave, so the earl and countess will take the hint and go home. Then you and Grace can have a proper coze."

"Thank you." Hope needed the time with her sister. She needed someone to understand the words she could not say, the things her heart barely understood.

They were up late, long after Jacob retired to bed, curled up together on the guest bed prepared for Hope. Their parents had understood, after Hope stayed with them a few days in her own room, she needed to be nearer Grace. Perhaps they had sensed her broken heart and believed time with Grace would heal Hope.

Every day and night for a fortnight, the two were in each other's company. Grace shared her story of hiding the truth, of how quickly Jacob knew which twin had stayed at home, and of all that happened leading to Jacob's declaration of love. They laughed and cried over their misadventures. Hope's tan and freckles had begun to fade on her voyage. The matron she was with insisted she wear her bonnets and carry her parasols to undo the sun's damage. The good food Grace provided filled Hope back to her normal proportions.

As time passed, Hope examined her heart again and again, waiting for the day when she would find it whole and healed. But she dreamed of Alejandro every night. Sometimes, he was as he had been on the island, with long hair and a beard, barefoot, and incongruous in her family's parlor or music room. Other times, she dreamed she walked along the beach with him, both of them in finery fit for a ball. Every morning she woke with fresh longing to see him again.

If she crossed the ocean twice, could she do so again? Would she find someone to take her all the way to his homeland? How would she even find him?

Her love never lessened. Hope missed Alejandro every moment of every day, no matter how busy she kept herself.

She helped her mother, sat and read to her father, played with her younger brother and sisters, and visited with Grace as often as she could manage. When her family had their fill of her, she took baskets to the poor, visited all their friends, and took long rides and walks so that she might sleep at night, exhausted, rather than lay awake wishing she had known how to keep Alejandro with her.

She had been home six weeks when she woke one morning to feel a chill in the air. November was near giving way to December and winter. She shivered in her bed and thought with longing of a warm sandy beach and a blue cloudless sky. And Alejandro, holding her hand as they watched the sun rise.

It was pure fantasy. The island had been a prison, as he said. Alejandro had never held her hand as dawn crept across the sea to the island. But that made the joy no less real to her as she let her mind linger upon the scene in her heart.

ALDERSY, SUFFOLK, WAS NOT SO HARD TO FIND. THANKFULLY, despite what had passed between Alejandro and Albert Carlbury, the senior Carlburys had happily given him adequate instruction for finding Everly Refuge. For finding Hope.

The horse he had hired carried him up the drive, snorting

occasionally as though put out with both the weather and his rider. Alejandro's time out of a saddle had made the trip from London difficult. A boat around the whole blasted frozen country would have been better, but his funds were running low. He needed every coin he had left, thanks to Señor Flores's generosity, if he were to accomplish his goal.

If Hope would have him.

Querido Dios, ayúdala a perdonarme, he prayed again and again. *Let her forgive me.* It took time to find passage to England, and time to sail across a stormy sea, and time to travel across the country. At last, the day had come. He would see Hope again.

Alejandro came all the way to the door, the only sound in the chill air his horse's hooves on the ground. The house was quiet, though it was near noon.

The door opened while he yet tied his horse to a ring, and he turned with a polite smile in place to address a servant.

A woman stood in the doorway, her deep brown hair piled atop her head and her bright blue eyes wide with surprise. She said nothing, only stood frozen, as though shocked to see him there.

Alejandro took one step to her, his confession of love already upon his tongue, but he stopped and stared instead. Something was not right. Something was decidedly wrong. His heart told him in very hard terms that this was not the woman he loved.

"Grace." The name shot from him like an accusation, and when her jaw dropped open in shock he hurried to bow. "*Perdóname.* I did not mean to be rude. I am—"

"Alejandro," she supplied, her eyes somehow growing wider. "Merciful heavens." She put a hand to her heart and hurried out of the house to him, both hands extended in welcome. "Oh, you have come. I am so glad. I told her, we all told her, you ought to come if you loved her." Her eyes filled with tears, and she started dragging him to the door. "Hurry. You must come inside at once."

Alejandro allowed her to lead him, perplexed as he was by her greeting. "You knew I would come?"

"Not precisely. But we prayed you would." She tugged him inside and shut the door behind them. "Father is in his study. This way."

He gently extracted his hand from hers. "I had rather see Hope."

She huffed at him, much as her sister had done a time or two, and narrowed her eyes. "Of course you would, but if you are going to propose, you need Father's blessing first."

His heart raced. "I meant to see if she even wished—"

"She does." Grace, who had been described to him as rather meek, stood her ground on the issue. "There is no time to waste. Now that you are here, we must act with all speed. You will stay until the banns are read, I hope, before you take her from us."

"I—I think so." Alejandro followed her again, somewhat dazed. But one thing at least had become clear. If Hope's sister had such faith in him, in their eventual union, Hope had not given up her feelings for him. Not yet.

❧ 26 ❧

Winter did strange things to the North Sea. In winter, there were frequent gales and storms, causing the waves to crash almost violently against the shore. As Hope walked along the beach near Inglewood, she found the sea reflected more of her feelings that day. The water was calm, though in motion, like her. She had come to visit Esther and Silas, and listened as the two of them discussed ridiculous baby names in a playful manner.

Though she rejoiced in their obvious happiness, she could not sit with them long. She had asked their leave to take a walk.

"Since when did you ever need my permission to walk on our beach?" Silas had asked, perplexed. "I feel it is as much yours as mine, or Jacob's, or Isaac's. Grace has her own beach now, near the vicarage, but she is welcome, too."

They let her walk alone. Though some might consider it unseemly, Hope did not care. She had been stranded on a desert island. Little else in the world could frighten her, whether it was man, beast, or Society's gossipy old cats.

With her cloak warm around her shoulders, she pushed the

hood back and faced the water. Wind tugged at her clothing and her hair. With one scandalous thought, Hope reached up and pulled several pins from her hair. The result would not be pretty, but she could put the hood back up on her ride home and no one would ever know.

No one would ever see her with her hair down, as it had been upon the island, a mass of waves all tangled by the briny wind. Closing her eyes, she allowed herself to dream again. She saw no harm in dreaming anymore. Her heart had fixed itself on Alejandro, and someday she would go to him. Hope would find a way.

"*Mi ángel*. I find you on a beach once more." The words wrapped her in warmth and her heart performed a strange flight in her chest. Hope's eyes flew open, and she held her breath. "Do you need me to save you from the waves this time?"

Hope turned slowly, afraid she had imagined his voice, afraid she would find the beach empty. Had she slipped too far into her dreams?

Alejandro stood before her, dressed in respectable clothing complete with a cravat and a forest green overcoat that made his chocolate brown eyes stand out. He was completely clean shaven now, and his hair just long enough to curl above his ears as she had thought it might. None of her dreams had prepared her for this moment. She had thought it too far in the future to plan for seeing him again.

His gentle smile faltered somewhat. "Hope?"

A laugh mixed with a sob broke free at last, and she set herself to running the ten steps to him. Alejandro opened his arms, a grin wider than any she had ever seen on his face, and he scooped her up against him, gathering her as close as possible. She buried her face in his coat and held him as tight as she could.

"Oh, Alejandro. You came for me. You *came*."

"I told you. I will always find you." Staring deeply into her eyes, he added softly, "Forgive me for letting you go. I did not see any other way. I regretted it before you were even gone."

"I forgive you," she whispered. "With my whole heart. Alejandro. What changed?"

"I have learned my parents are well. They are alive, in Spain with my brother, and I am not destitute. Well. I will not be, once they know I am alive."

He kissed her forehead, but she had much more in mind. Hope lifted her face to his and wrapped her hands behind his neck. She stood on her toes and pulled him down to meet her lips with his.

His hands held her waist, pulling her tight against him, and he returned her kiss ardently. Their lips collided almost desperately at first, but then their kisses turned more deliberate and gentle. She tangled her fingers in his thick hair and his hands moved up to hold her face. He leaned back enough to examine her again, his eyes flitting across her face.

His lips were swollen from their kisses. His eyes dark and burning. His cheeks had filled out, he no longer looked lean and starved, but she saw the same man from the island. Fierce. Determined. Passionate.

"I love you," she whispered. "*Te amo.*"

His eyebrows pulled together, and he bent to brush his lips across hers, a soft acceptance of her declaration. "I did not teach you that, my love."

"No." She smiled against his lips. "It was easy enough to learn for myself."

"Marry me?" he asked quietly. "And I will teach you every word I know." He kissed her again—a deep, full kiss.

"I will."

"I must travel," he warned, pulling back suddenly. His hands locked together at the small of her back. "To my family in Spain. Then someday, back to my country. There is war there. I cannot promise you a peaceful life."

Hope laid a finger upon his lips, stopping his words. "I want adventure, Alejandro. With you. I will follow you to Spain, to

Buenos Aires, anywhere you go. Your people will be mine. I belong with you."

He swept her up in another kiss, one hand tangling in her loose hair. They stayed upon the beach for quite some time, sometimes speaking with words, more often with gentle touches of the hands and lips. Hope had not felt truly at peace, or at home, until she stood in his arms.

Never again would she part from him. Their love would be the greatest adventure she could ever know.

THE DAY BEFORE THE WEDDING, ALEJANDRO HELD HOPE'S HAND while driving her phaeton and ponies. "Your animals have a complete disdain for traveling as slowly as they should," Alejandro told her. His soon-to-be-wife laughed.

"They are used to moving a great deal faster, it is true." She wrapped her arms around his and leaned into his shoulder, not caring if anyone who passed saw them.

Alejandro cast her a suspicious glance, one eyebrow raised. "Are there to be more races in your future, *mi amor?*"

"Would you object?" she asked, though Alejandro suspected she already knew the answer well enough.

"As long as I am there to watch you win, I have no objections." His heart full, Alejandro reveled in her sigh of contentment. Watching her with her family and friends the past three weeks, Alejandro had come to know all those she loved and loved them himself. She introduced him to everyone they met with pride, and everyone told him how fortunate he was to wed Hope Everly.

"You will never have a dull moment," one matron had remarked, making it sound rather like a warning.

"I can think of nothing more wonderful," he had responded with complete honesty. Hope had rewarded him handsomely for speaking that truth. Everyone seemed to approve of him, which was a relief. He still could not quite believe he had found her, that she loved him, that she would give up all that was familiar to her to follow him halfway across the world.

Hope bounced in her seat as they entered the gates of the Inglewood property. "That way." She pointed to a stand of trees. "That is where we must go."

"In this weather?" he asked, surprised. Alejandro directed the ponies as she instructed. "The countess will not be there?"

"Esther most certainly will. You stop worrying over her. She is with child, that does not make her an invalid." Hope sniffed and narrowed her eyes at him. "You had better not intend to coddle me so when I carry our children."

The very thought sent a thrill of fear and excitement through him, the emotions inseparable. "I refuse to reveal my plans for that occasion at the present time." Hope would never allow coddling, but the way she wrinkled her nose and glared at him made it too much fun to tease her. Of course, he also found such expressions incredibly distracting as they made him wish to kiss her until she smiled again.

There had been a great deal of kissing. At least until Hope's father entered the parlor one evening and caught them at it. He had given both of them a lecture on appropriate behavior the likes of which Alejandro would never forget. But Hope had kept biting her lip as though amused. The next day, she told him she would miss her father's lectures on decorum, but all she could think on was how the last one he had given her had ended with her pretending to be Grace, bound for the Caribbean.

Alejandro had very nearly kissed her again, out of sheer gratitude. But he honored her father's wishes and tried for patience.

He leaped out of the cart and then extended his hand to help her down. She wore a cloak and her hands were tucked in a muff. Hope guided them through the trees, until they broke through to a clearing where a rowboat rested near the trees, the wood painted a bright white with blue words painted across its hull.

"The Silver Birch Society," he read, his eyebrows drawn down. "Ah. Your club."

The others already stood, except for the Countess of Inglewood. She sat inside the boat, a sketchbook in her lap and her pencil at work.

"Here they are at last," Sir Isaac said loudly, bringing everyone's attention to Alejandro and Hope.

The friends met him with smiles and good cheer, though each had made certain to tell him, in private, how he had better take care of Hope or their society would come after him, showing no mercy. Everyone should have such loyal friends, really.

"Welcome." The Earl of Inglewood waved Alejandro forward, and Hope stayed on his arm. "It seems oddly fitting now that our club was formed around this boat, found by Hope many years ago, abandoned and in need of repair."

Alejandro regarded the woman he loved with adoration. "Hope certainly makes the most out of damaged boats."

She blushed and nudged him with her shoulder. "Please, Alejandro, do not curse me so. Finding an old rowboat has nothing to do with being wrecked on a sloop."

"As long as you stay clear of any more unworthy sea vessels, we shall all be happy," Grace said with mock solemnity. She had informed Alejandro, upon their second meeting, that Hope had never entertained callers who could not tell the two of them apart. Alejandro did not see how anyone found it difficult to do so. Hope's eyes burned with passion and adventure, even when she had polite conversation. Whereas Grace's eyes held a gentler warmth, reminding him of banked coals in a hearth.

The earl brought them to order again. "We are here today to induct our newest member into the Society. Though there were only five of us as children, it is only right that the club should grow to include the people we love most. Today, Señor Córdoba joins our ranks. Hope has agreed to marry him, and that is the highest recommendation one might receive."

"Hear, hear," the baronet and the vicar shouted.

"I second the movement to add him to the club," Grace said, beaming at her sister.

"I did not call for seconds yet," Inglewood said, glowering at her. "You are out of order, Grace."

She waved a hand at him. "Oh, stop. It is freezing out here, and I happen to know your cook has made fresh gingerbread."

The countess stood abruptly, startling her husband into holding a hand out to balance her. "I carry the motion. Now we vote." She cast her husband an apologetic smile. "I do adore the gingerbread."

Everyone laughed, and Alejandro looked about with honest admiration for the people gathered around them. "It is an honor to be considered," he said.

"All in favor?" The earl asked.

Five "ayes" filled the air. Then Hope threaded the fingers of her gloved hand through his.

"Congratulations, Señor. You are part of the Society." The earl bowed to him.

"And now we shall adjourn for refreshment," his countess stated with a lofty tilt to her head. "Before our noses freeze and fall off."

Alejandro and Hope returned for the ponies, to take them where they might be warm and cared for while the Society visited together.

"Are you sure I can take you from them?" Alejandro asked as he helped her step up into the phaeton. "They adore you."

"They know I will always be part of the Society," Hope stated softly. "No matter where I am. My friends want my happiness, and they know I shall never have it fully without you. There are dozens of men who might ask for my hand. Perhaps some I might even come to care for. But I cannot imagine a life without you. There is as much adventure in your soul as there is in mine."

Alejandro lifted her hand to his lips and pressed a kiss across her gloved fingers. "That is how I feel about you, my love. I will bring you back here as often as possible. Your family, your friends, they will see you many times in the future. I promise."

He produced his mother's ring from his pocket. "I believe this belongs to you, my dear. I ought to wait until tomorrow, give it to you with the wedding ring, but I cannot go another moment without knowing it is on your finger."

Hope's cheeks turned rosy. Her eyes teared up as she removed her glove and held her hand out to make it easier for him to slip the ring upon her finger. As he had suspected, it fit perfectly. His parents would see that as sign enough that she belonged in the family as her friends had made certain he belonged to theirs.

The journey across the ocean was a small price to pay when he had Hope's heart and hand as his own.

EPILOGUE
TEN YEARS LATER

Hope rested one hand over her stomach where her third baby stirred, as though upset he missed all the fun of his older brothers. She knew, somehow, she carried another son. Which was perfectly fine with her. The first two had come out so handsome and vivacious, their charming brown eyes always searching out mischief, that she knew another would make her family absolutely perfect.

Silas and Esther were beneath the trees, Esther holding Grace's youngest babe in her arms while Silas appeared to nap. Their two children were in the Silver Birch Society rowboat, pretending they were pirates. Alejandro and their sons were rival pirates, using a log for their own vessel and hurling insults at the earl's children.

Grace sat on the blanket next to Hope, her two elder daughters with them, pretending to be above such raucous play. Even though they kept peeping with interest at the louder children. Jacob had not joined them yet, as he had business to attend to with one of his parishioners.

"When did you say Isaac will join us?" Hope asked, watching one of her little lads tumble off the log. Her three-year-old son wailed as though he'd fallen out of an oak, but Alejandro made a show of jumping off their ship and into the imagined sea to save him. The boy started to giggle, though he pointed toward Hope rather than the log.

"Tomorrow," Grace answered, leaning forward to correct the hold of her daughter's needle and thread. "With his wife and their little brood."

Hope directed her attention to her husband and son. Alejandro placed little Diego on the ground in front of her. "Tell your mama."

"Me caí del bote."

Alejandro chuckled and ruffled the boy's hair, his lips turning up in a fond smile. "In English, Diego."

"I fell," the boy said, pointing backward. "Out. Of *el bote.*"

Hope barely managed to keep a straight face, nodding in as serious a manner as possible. *"Qué lástima, mi hijo.* What a shame. Are you going to be brave and try again?"

"If you kiss me," he said in perfect English.

Grace laughed aloud. "Oh, he will be a dangerous gentleman someday with that sort of charm."

"Inherited directly from his father," Hope stated, then she turned adoring eyes on her son. "Yes, come here." She kissed his little round cheek. "Go now." The boy grinned and skipped away, all his hurts forgotten.

Alejandro collapsed beside her, leaning back against the tree. "I think I would rather be marooned on your island for a time, my Hope. If you do not mind."

She leaned down and kissed him, her heart full and happy. "My dear Alejandro, I could think of no place better for you."

If you enjoyed this novel, make certain you read the others in the series, *Rescuing Lord Inglewood* and *Discovering Grace*. If you have already enjoyed those love stories, perhaps you would like to order your copy of the next book in the series, *Engaging Sir Isaac.*

Readers can connect with Sally in a variety of places. The best place to say hello is Sally's Sweet Romance Fans on Facebook. You can also sign up for Sally's email list.

AUTHOR NOTES

Dear Reader,

The events which take place in this book are fictional, but I put in a great deal of time researching every detail of this book. While no such island as the one on which my characters are stranded exists, and I cannot be certain which seabirds and plants coexist together happily on small bits of land in the Caribbean, I did my best to be true to the area and the knowledge that would have been available to my 19th Century cast.

On several occasions, I have wished to devote more time and energy to the question of the slave trade during this era. Sadly, I feel I cannot do that aspect of history the justice it deserves in my novels. I highly recommend a curious reader search out books and articles devoted to the study of slavery in the Caribbean. In this regard, I have hinted at the struggle only, though my heart has often ached with the details my personal studies have uncovered. Thankfully, there were many who fought against this grave evil, and in 1834 all slavery ended in the British Caribbean.

Thank you for reading my novel. I hope you enjoy many more.

-Sally Britton

ACKNOWLEDGMENTS

As always, I must thank the other authors in my life who have encouraged me, listened to me bemoan the difficulties of writing, and set me straight when I wandered into tangents and unhelpful attitudes. These women are incredible and you should read all their books! Joanna Barker, Arlem Hawks, Shaela Kay, Heidi Kimball, and Megan Walker.

I also want to thank my family, because they are absolutely patient, supportive, kind, and understanding. My children proudly tell everyone they know that their mother is an author, which is a humbling thing to learn when at a parent-teacher conference. My husband manages to slip my profession into many conversations as well, and he has proven time and again to be my most enthusiastic fan.

I greatly appreciate the ladies who do the difficult work with me at the end of each book, my editor Jenny Proctor, proofreaders Carri Flores and Molly Rice, and my team of ARC readers.

A big thank you also goes to the members of Sally's Sweet Romance Fans on Facebook. They're always kind and encouraging. They make this writing thing an absolute joy!

ALSO BY SALLY BRITTON

ABOUT THE AUTHOR

Sally Britton lives in the desert with her husband and four children. She started writing her first story on her mother's electric typewriter, when she was fourteen years old. Reading her way through Jane Austen, Louisa May Alcott, and Lucy Maud Montgomery, Sally decided to write about the elegant, complex world of centuries past.

Sally graduated from Brigham Young University in 2007 with a bachelor's in English, her emphasis on British literature. She met and married her husband not long after and they've been building their happily ever after since that day.

Vincent Van Gogh is attributed with the quote, "What is done in love is done well." Sally has taken that as her motto, for herself and her characters, writing stories where love is a choice.

All of Sally's published works are available on Amazon.com and you can connect with Sally and sign up for her newsletter on her website, AuthorSallyBritton.com.